Pragma

BECA LEWIS

Published by:
Perception Publishing
http://perceptionpublishing.com

This book is a work of fiction. All characters in this book are fictional. However, as a writer, I have, of course, made some of the book's characters composites of people I have met or known.

ISBN-13: 978-0-9885520-4-3
ISBN-0-9885520-4-3

Table of Contents

One

It lay on the side table by the door all by itself. The light from the window reflected off the gold bands around the edge. Sarah Morgan could have wondered how an envelope ended up inside, on a table, when she was the only one home. But she didn't.

Instead, she turned to look out into the forest that lined their property and smiled. It was possible that a light blinked in return.

She made a cup of coffee, enjoyed the sound of the heated water as it rushed through the Sumatra coffee pod and released the dark, smoky smell that always brought comfort.

With cup in hand, she stepped outside and waited. She knew what was in the envelope. It could only mean one thing, and she wanted the moment of anticipation to last as long as possible.

Clouds floated, birds sang, flowers nodded before blooming. It was spring in Idaho. Still, even in late May, little mounds of snow rested in the dips and crevices, waiting for more warmth. In town, massive piles of snow sat by the lake waiting to melt as spring moved into summer.

Almost a year had passed since she and her husband, Leif,

had last seen Evan Anders and Ava Evans. The coincidence that Ava's last name was so much like Evan's first name was not lost on Sarah. Everyone had seen the connection between them on that last day when they had all been together.

In that very living room, she mused as she glanced back into the house. Although a designer at heart, Sarah hadn't changed anything since that day. It was still too full of memories.

That day, Tom and Mira's grandfather Earl Wieland had shown them what they all had begun to realize. They had been expected. They were a Circle. Just one of many, but a Circle, a Karass, and their circle members had finally made their way together to that day.

Earl showed them their history, but not their future—only a hint of what was to come. Sarah and Leif were asked to give up their beloved home on the lake and move to the house on the mountain. Gifted to them by Earl, and as they discovered, a meeting place for circles.

Craig Lester had returned home to his wife, Jo Ann, to open a healing center. Mira had joined Tom, her newly found twin brother, in his work. And Ava and Evan had—well, that was the question the envelope on the table was going to begin to answer.

Finishing her coffee, rinsing the cup, and putting it in the dishwasher extended the pleasure of anticipation, but it was time.

The envelope was a thick vellum. Of course, it needed to be; it had important words inside. Addressed to Sarah and Leif Morgan, it had a return address in Pennsylvania. *One question answered,* Sarah thought.

With the malachite-handled letter opener, a treasured gift from years before when Sarah was more visible in the world, she slit open the envelope and slowly lifted out a card that glowed with the beauty of the words.

Ava Evans and Evan Anders invited Sarah and Leif Morgan to their wedding.

Could there by any more joy than this? Sarah wondered as she sank to the floor by the table, holding the treasure of those words to her heart. They had not squandered the love that they saw that day; they had nourished it and were ready to live it and share it.

Could there be a greater joy?

****

I should be happy. No, joy should be filling my heart, Ava thought. Her wedding to the love of her life was only a few months away. They had sent the invitations. All their friends, new and old, would be there.

It was something she had dreamed about her whole life. She and Suzanne Laudry, her guardian and friend since her mother had passed away, had often talked about the moment she would realize that she was cherished.

Suzanne and her husband, Jerry, shared that kind of love. Even when Jerry passed into the next event of his life, they still knew each other. They still loved. They proved that love transcends time and space.

"Stand in love," that's what Suzanne used to tell her. Jerry and Suzanne lived the love that the Greeks called *Pragma,* the love that lasts through time; a true mature love.

She had doubted the possibility for herself. Too many non-cherished moments had passed in her life. Too many promises broken. Too many abandonments. Even the love of Suzanne and Suzanne's father, Earl, had not healed Ava's heart. She loved them, but the door to love without limits had never opened for her.

But, they had promised her, so she kept the dream alive, buried behind mounds of self-doubt. Still, Ava trusted enough to leave her heart open a crack.

And then the moment arrived. The gathering of the newest circle at Earl's home, almost a year ago.

Of course, she was aware of Evan. She and Suzanne and Earl had expected him, along with the rest of their circle on that day. Earl had promised her that there was more to the meeting than she thought, and she had been content to wait because she trusted Earl and his daughter to guide her to her destiny.

But she was still stunned into silence when she looked across the room and saw Evan. She knew him. He knew her. Promises made to each other in the past rose up within and reminded her that he was the one she had expected. And there he was, waiting.

They were building a life together. Evan never doubted her. He let her know she was cherished. Her heart had opened more, and she expected that over time it would continue to open as she learned to trust. Evan already trusted. Trusted her. As hard as that was for her to imagine, it was true.

Yes, joy should be filling her heart. She was marrying her soul mate. She was trusted, loved, and cherished. What more could she want?

But joy wasn't what she was feeling at all.

Instead, she was terrified. The letter she had just opened lay on the floor, daring her to look at it again. Perhaps she had read it wrong? No, because the picture that accompanied it said it all.

Her past, the one that no one—not even her mom—knew about had come to the present. The past that was long buried, and long forgotten by her, was apparently still out there. Someone remembered it. And now, they threatened to destroy everything.

Two

Evan's heart was racing—not just from the wild run through the mountains of central Pennsylvania, but with anticipation.

I once thought only brides try to get in shape for weddings, he thought. Bracing his hands on his knees to control his breathing, Evan thought back over the past year. Since the meeting at Earl's house, so many things had changed, but all for the better.

Since he was no longer seen to be the villain who stole from Tom's group, but the one who helped bring their Karass together, the pressure had eased from his heart. Sarah helped. She listened and understood that his intentions were good. She was the first to know he belonged there.

Perhaps the methods he used were not the best, he reflected. But he meant well. Evan wanted to make his parents proud of him. He had needed to make them proud of him. Every day, he missed them. But he believed that they watched over him, although it was strange that he hadn't seen them yet. They didn't appear to be in the Forest Circle that gathered around Sarah and Leif's house in the woods.

That probably meant they were in a different circle doing good things elsewhere, he figured. All the more reason for him to do good in this world.

All that had been put aside the moment that Ava walked into the living room at Earl's house. It felt as if his heart had stopped beating. Her long brown hair was clipped back to reveal the face he had often seen in his dreams. Piercing blue eyes met his brown ones, and life changed forever.

It was easy. Ava knew him, too. All that guff about romance and love being hard had not been part of their experience.

Sarah and Leif had suggested that it would be wise for Evan and Ava to find a new home. It was easy for Ava to move. She had lived at Earl's house on a temporary basis, so she was ready to go. It took a few weeks to get things ready on his end. He put his home in Sandpoint, Idaho, up for rent, and he and Ava began traveling around the country looking for where they felt called to live.

It gave them time to get to know each other's lives and personalities. He knew she liked french fries and coleslaw at the restaurants they stopped at along the way. She discovered that he had a penchant for time alone in the woods. For six months, it was just them. They checked in with Leif and Sarah, of course, but were told to put finding their way together as their priority.

Mira had decided to join her twin brother, Tom. It didn't take long before she became the heart of Tom's group the Good Old Boys, otherwise known as G.O.B. Craig was busy building his healing center, Sarah and Leif were listening and planning. That meant Evan and Ava had the gift of time alone.

It was when they drove into Pennsylvania that they heard the word "home." The rolling hills and the valleys dotted with farms called them. They had traveled the country, discovered amazing treasures, camped in forests and deserts, breathed in the ocean air, and rested in tents pitched in fields. They were ready to make a home.

They pitched their tent in a local campground and began house hunting. Evan was grateful once again for the money his parents had left him, and his gift of increasing his returns on investments because they could pay whatever was necessary to have the home of their dreams.

They wanted to find a place that would be a sanctuary for them and their Circle when they came to visit. Eventually, they found an old farm house with a barn, a bunkhouse, and forty acres of open land and forest and purchased it in the name of a trust they set up, with their own names buried deep within.

The danger that they had been facing was not gone. Members of the Circle had merely side-stepped it for a while by remaining quiet and hopefully undetected. Evan and Ava hoped that they would appear not to be worth watching, just two young people in love.

Still, they needed to be careful. Ava and Evan knew that wouldn't prevent them from being found, but it was a start.

Once they moved in, Evan proposed. He waited for the perfect moment. Out on the swing under the elm tree. Birds sang nearby, squirrels called from the trees, and flowers bloomed in their newly planted garden beds. The hawks that had taken up residence in a big tree were calling to each other.

It was a simple proposal. Nothing fancy. Just, shall we be one? Shall we stand in love together?

Ava's "yes" made his heart sing. They would declare to everyone their intent to work together and raise a family.

They had sent out the invitations to the wedding that would take place in August. It was a new beginning. It was a declaration that love is always present.

He was ready. Ava was ready. The wedding was only a few months away.

What could go wrong?

Three

Who would think of looking here? That was the beauty of it, Grant Hinkey thought as he glanced around the room at his colleagues. A back room in a Panera's in rural bum-cluck Ohio. Just a bunch of old white men gossiping in the dark, watching a big-screen TV with talking heads.

Sure it was a fish bowl. All the walls were glass. Everyone could see them watching their show. Harmless. Old white men whiling the day away together, enjoying their retirement.

Wrong. So wrong. Those clueless people would never know what was going on because they were too busy and self-involved to notice.

Nice, sweet, kind people who've done a few wrong things in their lives. Perhaps they shoplifted when they were young for fun. Drove too fast. Drank too much. Maybe they get angry over stupid little things. They probably go to church, talk about God, and discuss politics as if what they think matters.

Clueless. Powerless. Because right there, hidden in plain sight, were some old white men who planned how to keep them all stupid and contained. Right there in plain sight was the power that ran the world.

They tracked and hunted down anything that rose up that

threatened to reveal what they were doing. Nothing could stop them. Stall them, maybe. Stop them, no.

Grant turned his pale blue eyes to the man sitting next to him and smiled. It was one of his most powerful weapons. His smile. If you didn't look higher to his eyes and notice they didn't smile, you could easily be lulled into thinking he liked you.

Grant knew that the man beside him didn't know that the smile was hollow. He had long ago fallen under Grant's spell and did whatever he asked. If it was horrible, or dangerous, or made his weekly confessions intense, he didn't care.

Grant trusted him, Hank Blaze. Mr. Blaze to the world. To Grant, he was Hank. He was loyal, and he belonged to Grant.

This time the smile was not a prelude to something terrible for him to do. Grant only wanted to confirm that their golf game was still on.

Ask easy things once in a while thought Grant. That way the harder things become just another errand. *He better not fail me next time, that disaster in the mountains in Idaho cost us some of our best men.*

Grant never used women in his crew. He didn't trust them. They would draw attention to the meetings. Everyone expected men to sit around and talk about nothing for hours on end. Add a woman, and the dynamics of what people thought was happening would change. Besides, women would question him and distract the men from doing what he wanted them to do. He couldn't have that.

One of the waitresses opened the door to deliver the cinnamon bagels he had ordered. A few of the men tracked her with their eyes as she left.

They were rewarded with Grant's cold blue stare. This is not the time or place to be noticed. Remember, they were in a fish bowl on purpose.

What could we be doing wrong in here?
Nothing of course.

****

Sarah's cell phone vibrated and buzzed. It was a text message from Leif saying he was on his way. Still sitting on the floor propped up against the wall holding the invitation, Sarah was worried.

Yes, a moment ago, all she felt was a flood of joy. But, as she sat there, she realized that in that joy there was something else. She wasn't surprised that there was something dark going on, but what was it?

Sarah knew that they were always in danger. And, of course, a wedding, love to be celebrated, would bring out those that hate.

But it wasn't just a wedding. It would be a gathering of many circles. Lots of protection would be necessary. *That we can handle,* Sarah thought. In fact, she told herself, they could take care of all of it, as they always had. Besides, there was no need to plan what to do at the moment; it was time to prepare lunch.

Getting off the floor wasn't as easy as it was getting down, Sarah observed. She and Leif were young in heart and spirit so getting older within the context of a human body was not one of their favorite things. However, she knew that it wasn't necessary to be incapable. It was time to get back into the walking and stretching routine that was so helpful in keeping both mind and body in action mode.

She had been lax of late. Falling into bad habits was easy. Setting up their new home had changed their rhythm, but the extra feeling of unease that had just appeared was a warning that things were ramping up again. Best to be in shape.

The alarm sounded as Leif's car entered the driveway. Although they no longer had the long sweeping driveway of their old house by the stream, there were always unseen eyes watching the house, and the beep of the alarm was a helpful reminder that someone was coming.

Sarah tucked the invitation beneath Leif's place-mat at the table. She couldn't wait to see his expression when he opened it. *I bet the angels in heaven and earth are singing,* she thought. *Love does win, all the time.* They could and would stick with that. It was more than a belief; it was a fact.

Four

The suitcase lay open on the bed, waiting. Every drawer in the dresser was pulled open, and closet doors gaped. Should she, or shouldn't she? Evan would get over it, wouldn't he?

Ava already knew she wouldn't. Leaving Evan would be the worst thing she ever did for herself, but perhaps the best thing for Evan.

Evan not loving her would be more than she could handle. And if he knew what she had done, it was possible that he would stop loving her.

The problem was, Ava already knew that running could make it worse. She had done it before and now, ten years later, it had all come back to ruin her happiness.

What was that thing she had once heard? Doing something in the present to take care of your future self is like giving yourself a gift? Well, she certainly hadn't done that. She had given her future self, the self she was living now, a stinking terrible problem.

But, then, she had only been sixteen. She should know better now. Run away or not? Think, think, think! Think about what happened. How did it leak into today?

Sixteen and angry at everyone. Angry because her dad had

died in a stupid car accident and her mother smothered her with attention and restrictions. It didn't matter if Ava understood why her mom acted that way. It was horrible. School was awful. People stared at her. Poor girl, dad died, mom holds her back.

She wanted her freedom, and she was willing to pay the price. One day, Ava waited until her mom went to work and then grabbed the backpack from under her bed, and the envelope of cash she had saved from babysitting. She had added more cash to the envelope by stealing from her mother's wallet the night before.

Ava paused for a moment to look behind her at the house she had called home and then turned and walked out the door for what she hoped was the last time.

It was only three-hundred dollars, but she would find a job. She was tall, strong from gymnastics, and with the right makeup she could easily pass for eighteen. A friend knew a friend who helped with the fake ID. Ava knew she could get work, and make her way in the world; it would not be a problem.

She figured that once she was settled and old enough to be on her own legally, she would call her mom. In the meantime, her mother was probably better off without an angry daughter in the house.

What happened next was better than some runaways have, and worse than most people ever know about.

Did running work then? Not really. It might not work this time either. But, prepare. I can always run if I have to. The letter writer might not follow up, Ava reasoned.

She closed the suitcase, the closet, and the drawers. As she pushed the luggage under the bed, she caught a reflection of herself in the mirror. Ten years have passed, but I could still pass for eighteen, she thought. But, am I smarter now than I was then? Can I give myself a future gift of being with Evan? Will he love me still if I tell, or do I have to do something to keep my secret?

Either way, can I live with myself? Sadly, Ava thought, *I don't know.*

****

"Ava," Evan called as he entered the house, almost letting the front door slam. At the last moment, he remembered he no longer lived alone and grabbed the handle to let it close slowly.

Still, the anticipation of seeing Ava was more than he could bear and he called again, "Ava!"

Ava, taking one last glance in the mirror to make sure there were no more tears on her face, and that the tension in her eyes was gone, allowed herself to feel the essence of Evan and ran to meet him, calling, "Here!"

She ran to him without bumping into the boxes sitting in the hall. It was time to finish unpacking.

First, Evan.

Breathlessly they embraced, happy to be in the same place at the same time once again. For a moment, Ava tensed as she remembered that she still might have to run away. How could she? Her heart had already left her body and entered his. That's why she would die first before hurting him. She had to fix the problem.

"Hey, what happened?" Evan asked holding Ava away from him to look at her. *Had she been crying?*

"Nothing really, just thinking about all the things we need to do before the wedding."

"And that is what I was thinking, too, so let's do some of that today. We can go out and check the venue, the flowers, and have some lunch out as a treat. Plus, let's talk to the seamstress we read about in the paper. I know you are not happy with any of the dresses you looked at, maybe she can make the perfect one for you."

Who wouldn't love him, Ava thought. "Yes," she said to him with a smack on his lips and a twirl.

Evan laughed. *That's all it is; she is just tense about planning.*

After both of them prepared themselves for going out into public with clean T-shirts and combed hair, they headed into town.

Main Street was five minutes away. It was an easy drive. But first, they had to get down the long curving driveway from their house to the two-lane road that took them into Doveland.

The driveway was a mess when they first arrived. Evan had hired a crew to clean it up and maintain it during the winter. A separate private crew came later. Disguised as guests from out of town, their job was to install cameras and sensors in the trees that ringed the property. They also installed cameras and sensors in the fence around the house. It looked like an ordinary fence, but it could be electrified from within the house, or from their phones or computers.

Cameras were generally turned off inside the house when they were home, but automatically turned on when they left the house. All the protection had been ordered by Sarah and Leif. Hopefully, they would never need it.

That wasn't on either of their minds at the moment. They were off to get things ready for their wedding, but first, they changed the order of what they were going to do. Eat first, errands later.

They pulled into a spot by their favorite restaurant, a small diner with a glorious assortment of local farm-fresh vegetables prepared by a chef who had escaped the city to cook in a small town. Evan loved the burgers; Ava loved the pasta.

To the townies, they were the new couple in town, in love, beautiful, probably filthy rich, having bought ole Mack's place, but kind and giving to everyone they met.

What more could they want, everyone thought as the newest members of town walked through the door. Except there was someone else new there that day. A waiter, a friend of the cook's, who had said that he had also escaped the city to live the rural life.

He smiled as Ava and Evan walked through the door. He knew they would be there, and now they were his.

Five

He watched as they ate and chatted together, unconsciously touching hands as they reached for their drinks. Although attentive when they ordered, even noticing his name tag and calling him Andy, it was temporary. They were there only for each other. It was simply a reflex to look up each time to say thank you as he put the plates on their table.

On the surface, everything looked fine. However, under the table, Ava's foot kept tapping. She was worried about something, Andy thought. Perhaps the letter?

As he placed the bill on the table, Ava glanced up at him, and something changed. Did she know him? How could she? It was only a brief meeting once before. He couldn't change his height, but he had gained weight and grown out his beard enough to hide his jawline.

How could I know him, Ava thought. *He's new to town. I am just a little jumpy. This afternoon is going to be all about Evan and our wedding. For one day, I can put aside my need to decide what to do about the letter.*

The afternoon was glorious. Late May in Pennsylvania meant that although the lilacs had finished blooming and the daffodils were in their last flush of color, other bushes and flowers were bursting into bloom. Most of the leaves on the trees had unfurled a few weeks before, but the many shades of green were still evident. The summer dark green had not taken over yet.

After eating, Evan and Ava walked across the street to the town square. It was a small park, but beautiful and well tended. All the roads that came into town ended at the square, which meant either heading into town or leaving town everyone circled the park. A few benches dotted the area, and they strolled over and sat on one.

"See how that maple tree is not ready to leaf out yet? Instead, it's loaded with thousands of seeds. This year is its turn to produce most of the seeds, which means it will have less energy to produce leaves. Next year, another tree will produce the majority of the seeds."

"How do they know to do that?" Ava asked.

"Plants talk to each other all the time. They warn each other, and they protect each other. They are a community, not individual plants. How they do it, we don't know yet. Makes you wonder which of us is the most intelligent species, doesn't it?"

"It's a community, just like ours, isn't it? Some people wonder how we talk to each other, too, don't they? After all, we don't always use our phones."

"No, we don't," answered Evan as they paused in their talking and passed words and pictures between each other.

"Anyone can do this; children do it all the time."

"Why would someone want to stop this evolution of understanding the depth of who we are?" Ava asked. "What do they want?"

"In their own way, they want what we all want, to be loved. Their wiring gets crossed somehow, and they think wealth is about how much they own that will make people love them more. They believe that if they control the people around them, that makes it a community. If everyone learns how to communicate directly, which is just the beginning of what's possible, that power and control will be over for them. That's why they are so intent on keeping the people of the world distracted and afraid."

Ava shivered. That is exactly how she felt, distracted and afraid. Years ago, when Suzanne had first introduced her to the Forest Circle, she had learned about what they called the Evil Ones.

How many Evil Ones are there, she wondered.

Evan broke into her thoughts. "That's enough of that. Let's enjoy the day, and start planning our wedding. Many circles will be here, and we want to give them an event they will always remember."

There weren't many places to hold a wedding in the area, and none that could be secured, so they had decided to hold the wedding at their farm. It was hardly a farm, since they didn't have animals or crops. Crops were on the list though. More like a family garden. But, animals at the moment, were not part of the equation—yet.

Holding the wedding on their property meant the guest rooms and bunkhouse had to be ready, and the grounds in perfect condition.

A landscaper had laid out the makings of a beautiful garden. Ava wanted a garden overflowing with native flowers that brought bees, hummingbirds, and butterflies. It would be a garden that would grow with them in beauty.

Their first stop after lunch was the landscaping office to check on how the owner felt the progress was going. They had thoroughly vetted him and his team and were comfortable having them on the property doing the work, but once the project was complete, they would change all the locks and passwords.

Satisfied that all was progressing well, they headed to the caterers.

The food was Evan's bailiwick. His dad had been the gourmet in their family and had taught him how to cook. They had spent many happy hours planning and making meals together. His mom always had the most radiant smile as they served her the dinners and appetizers they had cooked together, with her in mind.

I have many things to learn, thought Evan, but preparing food for Ava is something I already know how to do. He had decided from the first day that Ava had stayed overnight with him, that he would always bring her her first cup of coffee every morning.

Even when they traveled, he would roll out of bed first, and sometimes drive miles to find coffee. Handing it to her every morning, he was silently renewing his promise that he would always be there for her, and thanking her for choosing him.

Foodie or not, Evan knew he was not going to be able to prepare the food for the wedding. Instead, he had talked to the chef at the Diner where they had just eaten. Together, they had planned a menu that would suit everyone, from the meat lovers to the vegans in the group. Lovely sugary desserts and no-sugar desserts just as beautiful would top off the menu.

Chef Sam had finished lunch preparations at the Diner and was at his own small kitchen waiting for them. He had converted the bottom half of a century old home to be the headquarters of his catering business and lived upstairs.

It was always like coming home walking into Sam's kitchen. Sam was waiting for them with a freshly brewed pot of coffee and had the menu laid out for them. Ava made a few suggestions, but for the most part, it was perfect. From this point forward, they would come by every few weeks to taste one of the dishes.

By the time they left, Evan was feeling as if heaven had opened up and gifted him with love overflowing. However, he could tell something was not quite right with Ava. She was blocking him from entering some of the rooms in her thinking. Evan wasn't worried. He knew her heart was still not opened as fully as his. He understood that she was afraid. Time would change that.

Before heading home, they stopped at the seamstress about Ava's dress. He, honoring the tradition of not seeing the bride in her dress until the wedding, waited in another room while they planned the wedding dress of her dreams.

It should have been a glorious moment for Ava. She loved to design clothes. But, when she walked out to meet him, although she was smiling at him, her eyes told a different story. *Yes, there is definitely something wrong.*

Six

A wall-to-wall crowd mingled amid the cigarette smoke and sweat that filled the bar. The crowd was mostly men. Men waiting. Men watching the young women in bikinis serving drinks. No pretense. The women had to expect the attention, but anyone looking closely enough would know how much they hated it.

In the middle of the bar, lights pulsed over the stage. The rest of the room was dark and dirty. Usually, she came in the back door, hidden from the drooling, bug-eyed men, until the moment she stepped onstage. Today she had come in the front. Everyone turned to look. What, why? Looking down, she saw that she was naked. She screamed.

Ava woke up to find Evan staring at her. "Bad dream, honey? Do you want to tell me about it?"

"I don't remember what it was, Evan," Ava answered, turning to snuggle next to him, praying he wouldn't ask more questions.

"Okay. Just know that I'm here," he said rolling over and going back to sleep.

"Would you be here if you really knew me?" Ava asked him softly knowing that he wouldn't hear the question. But, she asked herself the question. Would he still want her?

Did she deserve to be with him?

I thought I had left this all in the past. Why do I have to relive this again, Sarah asked herself.

She was only sixteen. Sixteen and angry, the day she left home. Angry, determined, and confident she could do a better job of taking care of herself than anyone else could. Her mom would be sorry that she had denied Ava so many things she wanted. Ava was ready to discover the world, and no one could stop her.

The first day wasn't hard at all. She headed to California, the land of sunshine and people who played tennis all day. She could walk, she could hitchhike. She didn't care how long it would take to get there. The adventure was the thing, wasn't it? No, the day wasn't hard at all. It was when night fell that a small hint of what life might be like took over.

A kind truck driver had dropped her in a small town on her way west. He was heading north next, and it was not the way she wanted to go. Looking back, she knew she was lucky in those first days of her journey. Kind people picked her up, kind people helped her find a place to eat, and kind people pointed her toward small, but clean and cheap motels. Still, after only one day on the road, she had spent more than fifty of her three hundred dollars.

Ava realized that she was never going to make it, and, since she was in no hurry, she decided to work her way across the country. She had experience as a waitress, and she knew she had the look restaurant owners wanted. It would be easy to get a waitress job, work for a few months, and then move on.

The waitress idea was perfect. She enjoyed the freedom and easily made friends, but she hated that she was always lying. She could never tell anyone the truth. Looking back, she could see that was when she started closing the door to her heart. Perhaps, that was lucky because as time passed, it seemed that having a closed heart saved her, or at least saved her from the bad things. But what about the good ones?

Ava thought that maybe if she allowed herself to go back into the memory, she could discover who sent the letter and what they wanted, so she forced herself to concentrate more.

She made it to California, but with only fifty dollars in her pocket. She had two outfits. She wore one and washed the other. All the money she made from waitressing as she passed from town to town and state to state went to food and housing. She slept in the restaurants when she could, but it was often so much more filthy than customers knew, and the owners always freaked out when they found her.

After months of traveling, she looked even older than eighteen. Uncertain work and a constant fear for her safety had aged her. It wasn't the same as when she traveled with Evan. Of course, she could never tell him that some of the towns they passed through for the first time, was not the first time for her.

One time they almost went to a cafe where she had worked. She could see a waitress through the window that had been employed there with her ten years before. Terrified that she might be recognized, Ava steered him away at the last minute claiming the desire for pizza from the pizza place they had seen a few miles back.

The last ride into California dropped her off in Long Beach. Dirty and hungry, she was ready to go to work for real, but first, clean clothes and something to eat. It was going to take a big chunk of her money, but it was necessary.

While her clothes washed and dried, she looked in the paper for a job. This time, she wanted to make enough money to rent an apartment and begin her life. She had sent a postcard home a month ago, letting her mom know she was okay. She owed her that much. Ava had mailed it without a return address so there was no way her mom could find her.

At home, she had long hair. The first day on the road, she had trimmed it into a pixie cut, but couldn't bring herself to dye it. *So many young girls, how would someone find her, even if they were looking for her,* which she doubted.

"Whatcha doing?" a girl, the only other occupant of the Laundromat, asked.

Barely glancing up, Ava snapped, "Looking for a job."

"What kind of job? And don't try ignoring me. I'm bored, and I am going to keep on talking until you decide to give me the time of day."

Ava laughed, and looked up to see that it wasn't a girl, it was a young woman wearing jeans with stylish holes in them, and a tank top that fell casually off her shoulders giving her the appearance of not knowing that she was beautiful. Her hair was a striking shade of auburn, pulled back into a ponytail. She had an easy smile, but old eyes, which focused on Ava as if she knew her.

****

Her name was Mandy. *It probably isn't her real name,* Ava thought. However, that day was the first of many fun times they shared together. Together they finished their laundry, Mandy laughing at Ava's tiny satchel of clothes.

"Are you hungry?" Mandy asked.

Ava was pretty sure she was always hungry, so without thinking of what might happen next, she nodded.

Mandy's car was a beautiful restored white Karmann Ghia convertible. Stick shift. Not that great an idea in the land of traffic and freeways, but it brought her lots of attention.

Mandy craved attention. Everywhere they went, people smiled and waved at the two of them. By the end of the day Ava was exhausted, but happy. She had met a new friend, a friend that knew people. She would be okay.

That night, she slept on the couch in Mandy's one bedroom apartment. It was clean and stylish. Mandy had put together a mix of art deco and mid-century modern. Ava's mom liked both styles, but had never mixed them this way. Ava thought it took quite a bit of vision and taste to pull it off in such a small space, and what Mandy claimed to be an even tinier budget.

Mandy said the apartment was temporary. She was moving to Los Angeles. Why not come with her? Why not indeed, Ava thought. The land of the angels. It was a sign of something good coming her way.

Mandy was generous to her. She paid for food and a few new outfits, and all she asked in return was help moving. Where Mandy got her money was a mystery. But Ava didn't want to look a gift horse in the mouth so just smiled and said, "thank you," whenever she could. Mandy always nodded, and smiled, and sometimes said, "Just passing the good around."

It was insanely hot the day they moved. The sun beat down on them without mercy. The massive amount of concrete in Los Angeles made it so much worse, Ava thought she would scream. Where was the beauty? Where were the people who played tennis all day?

That all changed as they drove to the house that Mandy had rented in Venice Beach. Not in the more beautiful canal area, but in a strip of sidewalk just a block from the beach called Park Place. Ava figured it was another good omen. Park Place—like Monopoly.

Even though the houses were small cottages, with hardly any lot space, Ava knew it had to be expensive. She asked Mandy how she could afford to live there, but Mandy just shrugged and told her not to worry. Besides, Mandy promised she would help Ava get a job, then she could start paying her own way. It was charming, and Mandy's furniture and style made their little cottage feel more like a home than her home had ever been.

Ava was happy. Her life was lovely. Every day the beach was filled with people enjoying California. Tourists who wanted to be part of the "scene" crowded the beach and shops. Ava enjoyed watching them discover her new world, while she stayed in the background as much as possible.

Sitting by the ocean every night as the sun went down was magical. Sometimes Mandy joined her, but usually she was by herself. She loved it. Over time, her hair started streaking from the sun, and she gained a deep tan, something she had often coveted while living through long cold winters.

Always tall and thin, she filled out just enough with all the food Mandy somehow supplied for them. She became even more striking, although she didn't notice. Yoga classes at the rec center, skating on the boardwalk, and long walks along the beach filled her days.

No one knew her age, so no one asked why she wasn't in school. No one bugged her to find out what she wanted to do with her life. She had made it; she was free.

Seven

Looking at him, you couldn't tell, but Hank was thrilled. Grant had given him a job to do that was right up his alley. They didn't call him Mr. Blaze for nothing. It wasn't his real name, of course. Even Hank wasn't his real name. By the time he was ten, he knew he wasn't going to make it in the "nice" world. He started trying out names until he found one that fit.

It was an old story. An abusive father who had no problem beating the crap out of his wife when she was home and not lying in an alley overdosing. After hitting his wife until she couldn't move, he turned to his kids.

If they really ticked him off, he would lock them in the closet and leave them there. Sometimes for days. His sister would curl up in the corner and go to sleep, having learned long before that no amount of sobbing or kicking would change the outcome. Their father would let them out when he dang well pleased.

Which wasn't ever soon enough for Hank. One minute was too long. Hank was different. As his sister slept, he just got angrier and angrier. He screamed and pounded on the door. No one heard or cared.

Finally, he learned to contain that anger until it did some

good, and one day when the door opened, he quietly walked to the garage, got the crowbar, and came back and hit his father as hard as he could.

He could still remember the sound. Not the sound of his father falling. No, he remembered the satisfying crack of the crowbar on the back of his head. Hank reveled in the fact that he did it so quietly, that his father didn't know it was coming. Too drunk to care. Too stupid to notice his son was no longer a punching bag. He was fourteen. He was a man.

His little sister—still asleep in the closet—never heard a thing. He picked her up and carried her past the blood stretching across the filthy linoleum floor, ignoring the smell, ignoring everything but feeling how powerful the blaze of anger had been. He had freed himself. He had rescued his little sister from hell.

Hank didn't try to convince himself that it was the right thing to do. There were probably better options, but he didn't have time to find them. Instead, Hank decided then and there, since he was so good at controlling his anger, and using it to get what he wanted, he would learn to do it even better. He would become the best bad person he could be.

But, first, he had to find a home for his sister. Even though he was only fourteen, he knew, without a doubt, that he could take care of himself on the street. But, his sister. No. She was only eight. She needed love and attention. He could love her, but he couldn't give her enough attention or raise her properly.

So he did the next best thing. As she slept, he packed a bag for each of them. Into hers, he put a few sets of clothes. At the last minute, he remembered that she hid her favorite things under the filthy mattress that she slept on so that no one would take them away from her.

Reaching underneath the mattress, he found a book and a

tiny stuffed animal. The animal was so worn, he wasn't sure what it was, but probably a stuffed rabbit. The pink nose gave it away. He added those to the backpack, along with a note and half of the money he had saved for running away.

In his bag, he put clothes and the rest of his money. He tore apart the house and found a stash that his father had hidden from his mother, and took that, too. No one would be returning to the house. Blaze was his new name. Controlled blaze. This time, his anger would become a fire.

There was no need to do anything to make the fire burn. Trash was everywhere in the house. His dad smoked all the time. Alcohol was everywhere. It would burn quickly.

His sister was still sleeping when he carried her outside. He knew that wasn't good. She slept all the time. But he also knew a place he could leave her where they would discover what was wrong and make sure she had a happy life.

As he walked away with his sister in his arms, he glanced back at the house. A wisp of smoke drifted out of one of the broken windows. It wouldn't be long before his past was gone. He smiled. It was a smile to him. If anyone else was watching, it would have looked like a sneer. Hank experienced a rare feeling of happiness. For the moment, the blaze in him had settled down.

And now, Grant had asked him to use his skill again. Grant was the only one Hank did anything for when asked. It didn't matter what Grant wanted him to do; he would always be ready. It thrilled him to create chaos. He had discovered the joy of eliminating the lives of evil people.

It never occurred to him that he didn't have a right to be the judge of other people's deeds. He knew that even if there were life after death, which he seriously doubted, he would go to hell. Burn, blaze. Who cared?

In this life, he was content. In fact, he lived in a heaven of his own making. He made his own way, did his own thing, and only Grant knew where his true skills lay.

The waitress' eyes had skimmed right over him while she served him coffee. He was just an old white guy. Inside, Hank smirked with appreciation.

He was not really as old as he let himself look. It helped to appear old. He was neither handsome or ugly. Neither fat or thin. Enough hair to not be balding, but not enough hair to stand out. His clothes were the standard sloppy jeans, and a white shirt with an old jacket.

He was invisible. Just the way he wanted to be. He was quiet. He contained his anger. And when he was ready, he did what he wanted to do with it.

What had he done with his life? Only he and Grant knew, and the fact that Grant knew is what kept Hank in line. But, even Grant didn't know of the slow burn that Hank kept, just for those who had personally wronged him. If Grant knew that there was a list slowly building against him, he would be terrified and would probably try to get rid of him.

But he didn't. He wouldn't be able to anyway. Even Grant misjudged the blaze called Hank. For now, though, Grant asked him to do the things he loved best: destroy what needed to be destroyed and leave no trace, just as he had done forty years before.

For a moment, he wondered what happened to his sister after he left her in the free clinic's waiting room. But, he knew, in the spark of love that still burned for her, that her life was better without him.

Eight

"Tom, Mira, we weren't expecting you!"

Leif and Sarah were sitting in the garden behind the house, enjoying the wind moving through the trees. The hawk who had followed them to the new house was sitting on a branch, constantly on the alert. Sarah never knew if he was watching them or watching over them, but either way, she loved to see him perched nearby.

It was warming up in Sandpoint. June had arrived. But where they were on the mountain took longer to heat up. However, if they wanted more flowers and warmer weather, a drive down south into the Lewiston valley brought them a few weeks later into the season. Sarah loved the sight as they would crest the hill and see spread out below trees and flowers a few weeks ahead of them. It was almost like looking into the future. Add in the view of the beautiful Snake River, and it was as if heaven lay before them.

They were thinking about taking that drive when Tom and Mira had appeared. Well, not appeared, per se. Although they looked as if they were sitting in the garden with them, they weren't. In fact, Sarah realized that she had no idea where they might be. Their business of doing unnoticed good, with their private company called, Good Old Boys, took them all over the world.

Typically, they scheduled their visits using a code that only the seven of them knew. Tom, Mira, Craig, Ava, Evan, Sarah, and Leif. It was their Circle. Sarah had started calling it the Stone Circle since they were the ones who had received the stones last year.

Even though it didn't seem possible that the people who didn't want them to exist would be able to track their communication by using remote viewing, they didn't take any chances, hence the use of codes.

Sarah wondered if perhaps they had a remote viewer that could watch without being seen. Anything was possible. That was both wonderful and terrifying. Until everyone chose to use these gifts with integrity and with the intent of good for all, they were always in danger.

Sarah had just finished reading the book *Almost Human* by Theodore Sturgen. It was a fiction story in which a group of people discover the ability to do extraordinary things. But they needed each other to function effectively. Others were not happy that the human race was evolving and wanted to stop them, so their circle always had to be careful.

There are differences though, Sarah thought. These extraordinary things that we do are probably not an evolution, but a revealing. Yes, not everyone seemed to have the same gifts, but wasn't that true about every talent? Some people are musical; some are not. Some are gifted athletes, others, not so much.

Plus, it takes practice to be good at all talents or gifts. Didn't Einstein say, "Genius is one percent talent and ninety-nine percent hard work"?

Tom and Mira seemed to have inherited their gifts from their parents who had been employed by the government in the secret remote viewing department. Mira and Tom had been adopted separately from birth, and only recently found each other.

The fact that they had gifts and abilities was new to them, so they put in a lot of time diligently practicing together. They were becoming quite good at what had come easily to them, projecting themselves where they wanted to be.

So here they sat—or not—in Leif and Sarah's garden, to talk about something fantastic, Ava and Evan's wedding.

"Remember when they first saw each other?" Mira asked. "It was that proverbial love at first sight, wasn't it? Although, of course, it wasn't first sight at all, was it? They have always known each other and have always loved each other."

"Sure. But, we got to see the reunion, and it was absolutely a joyful one." Sarah answered. "Shall we talk about the arrangements for the wedding, or what we're going to wear since that is the terrifying part."

"What, why?" Tom asked. Leif, having been around longer, wisely kept silent.

Sarah and Mira giggled and then turned serious. This was an unexpected meeting after all. Not planned by either of their guests. Someone else had sent Tom and Mira to Sarah and Leif's garden.

Looking out into the forest, Sarah saw Suzanne and Jerry holding hands. They nodded at her and then were gone. So, I am to pay attention, Sarah thought. I'm not wrong to be worried.

****

Suzanne reached for her husband's hand. What a joy to see their children Tom and Mira. What a joy to see them becoming so practiced at the gift of remote viewing. No longer just remote viewing, but literally appearing where they needed to go. Not their physical bodies, of course. *But, then we aren't our physical bodies anyway are we,* she mused.

Well, they were certainly all learning that! Although Jerry had died to the human world, here they were again. Suzanne had merely left it and moved to a different dimension where the Forest Circle lived. Jerry had stayed and waited for her within the Forest Circle with her parents, Earl and Ariel, and her brother Gillian. Just one circle among hundreds of others. Circles that kept the line of light flowing.

We are getting stronger, but the resistance is also getting stronger, Suzanne thought. That's why today she and Jerry had brought their children to Sarah and Leif.

Sarah's Stone Circle needed to pay more attention. While they were getting to know each other again, forces that resisted progress and lived for power had spent their time preparing to stop them. The anger against the knowledge of the power of good was intense.

Suzanne's Forest Circle knew about Grant. They had stopped him before. This time, it was up to their children to do it. Suzanne and Jerry would take care of things building where they were, but the humans in this dimension had to learn to recognize and dissolve the evil that exists here. Ignoring it is not going to make it go away.

Sometimes they needed a reminder. Sometimes they needed a prod. Always, they needed to make the hard choice. To not be apathetic, but to wake up, and take whatever action was necessary.

In this case, it was the action of protection. For Ava especially, who was as loved by Suzanne as much as she loved her own children, Tom and Mira.

Suzanne hadn't yet discovered where Ava's mother went after her death. They had been such close friends. Why had she moved on without letting her know where she was going? Just one more piece of a puzzle that always seemed to center around Sarah and Leif's Circle.

Suzanne sighed, "Our children still wear their hearts."

"Of course, they do," Jerry answered. "It's a reminder that love transcends time and space. We are evidence of that, aren't we?"

They turned to each other and smiled. Yes, it does, they both thought. Nodding at Sarah, they were gone.

Nine

They kept the place as clean as possible, Eric Jones thought as he walked through the clinic's back door, switching on lights as he went along. Still, the smell always gave it away. They tried everything to bring a freshness to the clinic, but poverty and fear kept tumbling in every day, bringing an essence of hopelessness with it.

Even though it was still dark outside, he knew it wouldn't be long before people started arriving. Some just needed some attention. But, many others were desperate.

The desperate ones often hung out in the back of the clinic, afraid to come forward. Eric and the staff had learned to look for them, and guide them to an examination room before they collapsed. They were hungry and often hung over or in need of more drugs that were supposed to keep them from taking harmful drugs. Eric classified any drug that killed someone as a harmful drug, prescribed or not.

Take away the drugs, and they will find another way to kill themselves, Eric thought. The clinic wasn't going to change anything. It was a safe place to come to get help for the immediate problem, but it wasn't going to solve anything in the long run.

They needed help before they got here. Hope had to exist. People needed a purpose. *It's Maslow's triangle of need in the flesh,* Eric mused.

Maslow believed that our most basic need is for physical survival, and after that we deal with safety issues. It's only until those needs are being filled can we move up to fulfilling our need for belonging and love, then esteem and finally self-realization. The people that came here were at the bottom. They were hungry and scared.

Eric wished there was something he could do to make a long-term difference for someone. It was a rare person who escaped the bottom of that triangle. Instead, he patched them up and sent them back out into the streets and into their desperate lives.

When greed and power were running things, only a few got their needs met. However, even the people with all the money, those top one-percenters were still at the bottom of the triangle, when all they were concerned about was their money and their own welfare. They certainly haven't moved up into self-actualization.

Fooling themselves, that's what they were doing, Eric thought. There would be a reckoning someday. But in the meantime, they were harming everyone in their path, intentionally or not.

Switch the coffee maker on, sweep the waiting room, unlock the front door, and get ready to help. However little it is, it is something. I am doing something, Eric thought.

Eric got the sweeper, a gift from a mother who knew her son came to the clinic and not to her for help, and started down the hall to the front room, still switching on lights as he went.

Someone has left all their blankets on the chair. I thought I cleaned up before I left last night, Eric mused.

The blankets moved, and Eric yelped. *Get a pair,* he thought as he crept up on the pile of blankets.

"Good grief, what are you doing here?"

A pair of blue eyes stared up at him. Scared blue eyes. He lowered himself gently next to the blankets and said, "Hi, I'm Eric. Who are you?"

He gently peeled away the top layer of blankets to reveal the face of a young girl clutching what looked like a dilapidated rabbit. Its pink nose gave it away.

They stared at each other. "It's okay." There was no response from the blue eyes.

"Okay, what do we have here?" Eric asked as he noticed a note and an envelope pinned to the girl's sweater.

"Please take care of Abigail. She has no one anymore," it said. A bunch of dirty dollar bills stuck out of the envelope.

"Well, Abigail, I am delighted to meet you. Let's see what we can do for you.

"First, let's move you out of this room into something more private. May I carry you there?"

Getting no response other than a flutter of dark eyelashes that seemed much too long for a child, he picked her up. She was light, either younger than he thought, or undernourished. Or both.

He opened the door of the room he used to get some rest during the day and laid her out on the cot. The room was actually a converted broom closet. The clinic was overcrowded. When he needed to, he turned the closet into a place to get away for a few minutes during the day. He had made the space as comfortable as possible, and the room served him well.

Somewhere along the way, he realized that he had decided to keep Abigail's presence to himself. If he reported her, she would immediately be turned over to social services. He knew they did their best, but rarely did things work out well for a child entering that system.

Eric wanted time to see if he could find her family and if he did, he needed time to determine if she should go back there. Yes, the note said there was no family. But someone left the note. Someone cared enough to bring her to a safe place. Someone knew how to pick the lock to put her inside instead of leaving her out in the cold. That someone might be sorry they didn't have her anymore. He needed to be sure.

He opened his tiny refrigerator and got out a bottle of water and an orange. Still wrapped in all her blankets, Abbie continued to just stare straight ahead.

"I'm going to leave you in here while I do my work, Abbie. Is it okay I call you Abbie? But I'll check back on you throughout the day. I don't want to you to be disturbed, so I'm going to lock the door. It's not to keep you in. It's to keep other people out."

Eric thought he saw a dash of fear in Abbie's eyes, so he stooped next to her and said, "I promise, I will come back for you. I promise you are safe."

A single silver tear formed and dropped down into the blanket. A small nod told him it was okay for the moment.

"Here's water, and an orange. I'm going to find some more food for you. I'll be back. You'll be able to hear all the people talking, but please keep still, so they don't know you're here. I want you to be safe. Okay?"

How many times am I going to be saying okay, Eric thought. He had no idea. But, he did know, that the minute he had looked into those eyes, he would do anything to keep that little girl safe.

****

The door closed softly behind him. Abigail heard the faint chink of the lock as he turned the key. She had heard that sound too many times before not to feel the sudden urge to go back to sleep. But the greater calling of thirst and hunger won for the moment. *Father never left us food or water,* Abigail thought. And it was always dark and cold. And there were never blankets and a bed.

The orange was sweet, and the water helped ease her sore throat. Already things were better than before. Even if he kept her locked in the closet all the time, it was better than before.

Except, where was Tim? Why wasn't he here? Did father hurt him? Suddenly the bigger question occurred to her: *How did I get here?*

There were no answers to any of those questions. There had never been answers to any of the questions Abigail had asked in her short lifetime. Why was mom never home? Why did father always scream and yell? Why is Tim the only one who cares for me? Why am I always locked in a closet?

She could not figure it out. Sleep was the perfect solution to all unanswered questions. It held either nothing or beautiful dreams. Abigail dreamed about people who talked to her. She dreamed about pretty places and a lovely woods filled with people who held her hand and whispered sweet things to her.

This time, falling asleep was different. This time, Abigail was warm, and the room was not dark.

Ten

"Are you two coming to visit in person soon? Because if you do, I'll make you your favorite salsa. We'll even go to Joel's."

"It's tempting," Mira said. "I could use a few days away, and some girl talk. It depends on if Tom needs me though."

"I think that's an excellent idea, Mira," answered Tom. "I believe we can all manage for awhile without you. Besides, I can find you anytime."

They both laughed, recalling when they had first met by remote viewing. Not on purpose. It had scared them so much they were afraid of each other. But exploring that fear had brought them to Leif and Sarah, and then to each other, and finally to their Circle. Mira smiled at him in gratitude. *What a gift it has been to find him,* she thought.

"I've been thinking about something else, too," Mira said. "Could we come up with a name for our Circle of seven? Sometimes when we say 'the Circle' I don't know if we're talking about our Circle or Earl and Suzanne's Circle, and what about all the others that are forming. Concentric circles surely, but what about a name for ours so we know we mean us? Mira pointed to the four of them," and added, "Plus, Ava, Evan, and Craig."

"Good idea," Sarah answered. "Do you have ideas for the name?"

"No, but if we listen, I think one of us will hear it."

"Well," Sarah said, "I have been calling Suzanne's the Forest Circle. I have also been calling our Circle the Stone Circle. What do you think of those names?"

"I like it! The Forest Circle and the Stone Circle." Mira said.

"Speaking of Suzanne, was it Suzanne who brought us here today?" Tom asked.

"I think so," Sarah answered. "Do we know why specifically? I don't believe it's about coming up with a name for our Circle. There must be something she wants us to notice, or talk about, or decide."

"It feels as if it's personal to her," Leif said. "Perhaps it's about Ava? After all, she loves her as if she was her daughter."

"I think you're right," Tom answered. "Something has been nagging at me for awhile about Ava and surprisingly, her mom. What do we know about her? And it worries me that no overt actions have been taken against us since the explosion on the mountain. Those people who don't want us around must have regrouped by now. And the fact that they are keeping so quiet is a dangerous sign."

"Well, let's assume it is about Ava. What about her?" Mira asked.

"Whatever it is, it probably ties into Evan and Ava's wedding. I doubt those people—yes we need a name for them too—are happy about the two of them getting together and perhaps making babies," Mira answered.

"Heaven forbid that we 'humans' uncover and use our expanded awareness to override greed and evil," Leif said.

"That's a funny saying, isn't it? It's not heaven forbidding us; it's those who have lost heaven. You know the "Evil Ones.""

Sarah said.

"Crap. I don't want to say that's a good name, but it is. We will all know who we're talking about anyway. Everyone understands that term," Tom answered.

They all sighed. Too true.

"Still, we need to remember our overriding point of view, that good is stronger than evil. Well, more specifically, that there is only good, and once that fact has been established within all human consciousness, evil vanishes, like the dark," Sarah reminded them.

"Sure," Leif said, "but that doesn't mean we shouldn't be hyper-aware of the dark, or I guess the Evil Ones. We can't be saying these lovely words without staying aware and fighting for the truth of good."

Tom smiled. "It's a good reminder. It's why we're here. Not just here in your garden, but here. There is work to be done. Let's gear up."

Sarah and Mira laughed. "Man talk. Let's gear up!"

Sarah asked, "Mira, will you come visit? Tom, could you drop in on Ava and Evan in the flesh, so to speak. Leif, I know you will do your thing asking the others? Since Evan and Ava haven't been practicing their remote viewing or telepathy, we haven't seen much of them."

"I think they have been busy with other things," smiled Tom.

"As they should have been. And let's not alarm either one of them. Just a friendly, how are you visit. And then check back. Perhaps, Leif, you could check on Craig while you're out there. There's that other project you two have been working on. It would be good to see the progress," Sarah continued.

Tom and Mira looked at each other, "Other project?"

All they got in return was a smile from Sarah and Leif.

"See you in a few days, Mira. Do you want me to pick you up, or are you driving?"

"Hmm. I might take the van from the airport. It gives me a chance to eavesdrop on what people are saying."

"I love that, too. We'll practice that in town when you get here."

"I hope you two are going to stay aware while you do that," Leif said. "It's not something to be joking around about."

"Trust me, I know," Sarah said hugging him. "I can feel the danger, too. We'll be careful."

Eleven

Ava was freezing. Even sitting in the warm sun on the back deck did not stop her from feeling as if every part of her body was in spasm. She longed to run to Evan and into his arms to feel his warmth, but thankfully he wasn't home. Because he would ask questions, and she had no answers. She couldn't possibly tell him she was chilled to the bone because she was terrified.

For the past few weeks, she had lulled herself into a sense of safety. But now another letter had arrived. Did the person who was sending them to her know that she always picked up the mail? Of course, Evan would never have opened it, but he might have asked. No return address was already suspicious.

This time there was a picture. Not the ones Ava had feared, but one even worse. Now it was not just about her; someone else was now more important, and Ava didn't know what to do to make it right.

It took her back to the time she lived with Mandy. She remembered a conversation that started the worst part of her life. "Mandy, I have to get a job," Ava said. "I can't continue to live off of you and your kindness. Or someone else's kindness, since I don't know what work you do, either."

"Look, Ava, you're right. It is probably for the best that you find your own way and move on to someplace else. You don't want to get mixed up in what I do. Perhaps I can help. What skills do you have?"

"Well, I worked my way across the states waitressing. I'm sure I can find a job here."

"Ugh, waitressing. You'll never make enough money to live on your own here. It's expensive. Can you dance?"

"Sure, years of dance lessons and gymnastics. Mom insisted."

"Nice mom. Are you sure you don't want to call her and let her know where you are?"

"Absolutely not. She'll just make me come home."

I wish I would have had called and gone home, Ava mused as she relived the story of what happened next. Instead, Mandy took me to her friend's club, with a stop first at Frederick's of Hollywood to get some cute underwear and bras. We sewed tassels on them to make them look like a costume. Then Mandy took me to see a manager of a club that she knew. He took one look at me, and I started working that day.

I hated it from the beginning. But Mandy was right. I made more money walking around in my underwear than I would have just waiting on tables. There was a no-touch rule. But, that didn't stop the men from trying to grab whenever they thought no one was looking. It was always a tease. I pretended to like it and pulled away just in time.

The girls that worked the club were mostly friendly. We had our own territories, so there was no fighting over tables. During lunch and dinner hours, we took turns dancing on the stage that jutted out into the room.

I pretended that I was doing a play, and the character I was playing liked being up there with people gawking at me. I had a ritual around work. Cry before going to work, work, come home, take a shower, cry in the shower, pretend that I was okay. By then Mandy had asked me to move out. She had done what she promised to do and gotten me a job. She was done with me.

I moved into a little room I rented in a house a long way from the beach. It was probably a garage before it was a room. But, it was mine. I had thought I was free when I ran away. It was a strange version of freedom.

****

"Ava!" Evan called as he came in the door. " Do you want to go out to dinner?"

Snap out of it! Ava told herself as she answered with a cheery, "Yes, I'd love to."

Practice making men happy comes in handy sometimes, Ava thought. *Lots of practice.*

Evan had found a new restaurant, named Laura's. Slightly understated on the outside, but inside was a different story. Clean, modern, filled with the lovely smell of curries. The waitress asked them if they wanted a booth or a table, and in unison they both said "booth." Although waitresses always put the menus on opposite sides of the table, Ava and Evan always moved them and sat on one side together.

They liked sitting together, looking at the same view. Ava smiled at the waitress and glanced at her name tag. She was never going to forget how hard it was to wait tables.

They both ordered the red curry and prayed that it would be good. First, a crisp salad with a light peanut sauce arrived. It was perfect. Their hopes rose. Just as they finished their salad the curry appeared. The smell of it was heavenly and the taste was just as perfect.

"Thank heavens," Evan said. "We found ourselves a Thai

food place right here in the middle of nowhere."

Evan and Ava laughed. It was the middle of nowhere, and they loved it. Quiet and peaceful, and getting friendlier by the minute.

"We'll have a wonderful place to bring our friends when they come visit," Ava said.

"You're so right, and we have a chance to make good on that in a few days. Tom wrote and asked if he could come see us."

"In person?" Ava asked, trying to let the part that wanted to see Tom be the part that asked the question.

Evan laughed, "Yes, in person. He said he needed a few days away from work, and Mira was visiting Sarah and Leif, so Tom thought he would visit us. He thought he might be able to help get the place ready, and I agreed. I could use some help—and some male bonding time."

Ava smiled at Evan. "Sounds fantastic. How thoughtful of him to come help."

Ava might have been smiling on the outside, but on the inside, she was worried. Does everyone suspect that she isn't who she has pretended to be? Is Tom there to make sure that Ava belonged to their Circle? And even if that wasn't the reason he was coming, how was she going to keep the secret away from him? How long would she be able to stay?

As they were leaving the restaurant, Ava caught a glimpse of a couple in the corner. The were looking at each other with adoration and love. She knew Evan looked at her that way. She yearned to be able to feel that complete love for him and share it. She loved him, but the block in her heart was still there. She was terrified that it might never melt.

Maybe I am like this restaurant, Ava thought to herself. *Only backward. I am pretty on the outside, but inside it is an entirely different story.*

Twelve

Eric gently opened the door carefully in case Abbie was still asleep. She wasn't. She was sitting straight up in bed, wide-eyed, and terrified. *The two hours in the closet are obviously not a good thing for her,* Eric thought. *But, at the moment, this is all I have.*

"I brought something," he said holding his arms behind his back. Abbie scrambled farther back into the corner and pulled the covers up over her head. Whoa, I didn't see that coming, Eric thought as he said, "No, look, it's good. It's yummy. Food!"

There was a McDonald's a few doors down from the clinic. Claiming extreme hunger he had rushed down to get himself some food and a Happy Meal.

Abbie sat still under the blanket. "Okay, I am going to have my burger and fries now. Here's yours, if you want it."

Eric placed the box carefully on the cot and sat at his makeshift desk beside it and started eating while making yummy noises and slurping his soda.

Slowly, slowly a hand crept out and touched the box. Two hands and two eyes appeared over the blankets. By the time Eric had finished his french fries, Abbie had the box up to her nose and smelled it.

"Yum," Eric said. "Yours. Do you want help opening it?"

Tiny nod.

Carefully he reached over and lifted the lid. Inside a burger and fries waited for her, and a little toy. One last time Abbie looked up at him to confirm that it was hers and seeing that it was, started nibbling away at the burger.

"Still not sure are you, Abbie? I understand, but I promise you that I am going to help you and take care of you. That is if it is okay."

Another tiny nod.

"Great. Here's what is going to happen. I have work to do today. I still don't want people to know you are here, so I am going to lock my door, so no one comes in. But, I will come back every few hours to see what you need. Let's sneak off to the bathroom first, so you are comfortable. Do you want to go to the bathroom?"

Two more little nods and a hand reaching up to him was the answer.

Never in his life had Eric felt the rush of love he felt for this child he had only met a few hours ago. He had already asked for time off for a few days, claiming exhaustion, to figure out what to do. The clinic wasn't happy with him, but since he volunteered hours long past his shift almost every day, they had to concede.

The bathroom was directly across the hall from his "closet," so it was relatively easy to get Abbie to the bathroom and back without anyone noticing. While he was waiting for her, he grabbed some paper towels and put some soap and water on one and dampened a few more.

Back in the room, he wiped off her face and hands. She let him. Passively. But she let him, her eyes never leaving his face. It isn't possible that I know her already, Eric thought. But I love her as if she was my own child.

Someday she will feel that love, but right now I am happy that Abbie feels safer.

"I will be back when both hands on the clock are pointing at twelve. Okay, Abbie?"

More tiny nods, and a very tiny smile.

Heart full, Eric gently closed the door and locked it.

****

Eric waited until the clinic closed up for the evening. First, he locked the front door, closed all the blinds, and switched off the lights in the waiting room. Eric even took the time to clean up all the trash left from the day, and sweep the floors. He didn't want anyone ever looking back on this day and thinking it was different.

He had checked in with Abbie every few hours, bringing her food, and sneaking her to the bathroom. On one of the visits, he had brought her a children's book that usually was on the table in the waiting room. For that, she rewarded him with an even bigger smile.

I am a goner, Eric thought. *She has stolen my heart without even trying. All these years of looking for the perfect woman to love, a little child walks in and steals my heart. I hope I can still see her after I find who she belongs to.* Eric felt ashamed that he was hoping he would never find anyone. *The note said she was alone. Then who wrote it?*

Hoping to shake off the feeling of already missing her, Eric opened the door for the last time to collect Abbie. This time he left the door wide open. "Ready to go home?" Eric asked.

Abbie turned pale and cowered in her blankets. Well, that settles it, Eric thought. I will never let her return to a home that scares her like that.

"No, I don't mean your old home. I mean your new home. Where I live. It's quiet, and I have a cat. Do you like cats?"

Abbie peeked out from the blanket and nodded.

"Good, because I have one. I named him Buttons. He's gray and has a little white patch under his chin. Shall we go see him?"

When Abbie nodded, Eric finally noticed that she had not said a word the whole time. *Afraid, or unable?*

Holding his hand and dragging her blankets, they slowly made their way across the parking lot to his car. Her rabbit was safely tucked into her sweater, although she kept checking to make sure that it was still there.

While cleaning his little office of any evidence that a child had been there, Eric had found the note and the envelope full of dirty one-dollar bills. He knew he would keep both, and when Abbie was ready, he would show them to her. It was a promise that she was loved even before she met him. Someone wanted her to be safe. Someone would always love her.

Well, more than one person, Eric thought, *because now I do, and that means there will be many more to come as I introduce her to a world of good things.*

As his car neared home, his headlights swept the rows of apartments on the street where he lived. Up until now, this was as good a home as any, but now it wasn't. He would have to change everything. Because he had already decided. She was his daughter, and how was he going to explain that to people who already knew him?

It was time to find a new job and a new home—one that would support and enrich a child. His daughter, Abigail Jones.

Thirteen

I wonder why 3:00 AM is sometimes called the witching hour, Sarah thought as she slowly rolled out of bed. It's such a perfect time to get up in the morning. It gives me lots of time to talk to Leif, meditate, and do all the small but important things I want to do before the rest of the world wakes up and starts moving.

Beside her, Leif was already sitting up. He would be heading outside with his first cup of coffee, while Sarah went to her office to check her messages: messages on the computer, and messages that didn't need computers.

Later, while sitting together on the deck, the one that faced both the meadow and the forest, they would listen as the birds sang their morning chorus.

Nature doesn't care about boundaries, political issues, or the morning news, thought Sarah. *It's hard to understand why people believe that the human species is the most evolved.* "Exactly," answered Leif, even though she hadn't said those words out loud.

Both sighed and sat in silence as the morning light came up over the mountains in the distance and made its way into their yard. They loved the house Earl and Ariel Weiland had given to them. It was considered the center of their two Circles. They still missed their home by the river and the quiet life they had before Mira had called them and asked for help.

"We can't go back," Sarah said. "We chose, and we agreed. We can miss it all we want to, but we are here, and now we have people counting on us. Speaking of which, how is your project with Craig doing?"

Leif paused before answering. "Craig is doing a great job building his healing center. His wife, Jo Ann has been a big help. However, he asked that I visit to do some strategic planning with him, so I thought when Mira comes to visit, I will go to Craig's. That way I won't be leaving you all alone."

They looked at each other. Leif knew that Sarah didn't mind being all alone; in fact, she looked forward to it, as did Leif. The fact that Leif was worried about leaving her by herself meant more than what he was saying.

They both sighed again. Sarah and Leif leaned back into their chairs and listened to the birds as the sun rose in the sky, as it did every day. It was a symbol of the promise of renewal that will always be there—not just for them, but for every living being on the planet. It was not something anyone had to earn; it was impartial and universal.

They looked at each other contentedly and raised their cups in a salute. To each other, and then to the woods.

****

The sun was peeking into the kitchen by the time Leif and Sarah came back into the house. It was still early, but nature was fully awake, even if humans were mostly still in bed. Leif headed to his study to make arrangements to visit Craig.

Typically, Sarah would head to her office to do some writing, meditating, and maybe even a bit of yoga. This morning, she decided to do something different. Sit in the living room and read? Bake something? Go for a walk?

Nothing appealed to her. Although they hadn't changed much in the house since they moved in, they had added a puzzle to the round table that sat in the corner in the living room. Putting puzzles together often helped quiet Sarah's mind. Today, it didn't.

Maybe it's time to make some design changes in the house, Sarah thought. I love to do that!

The house was a small ranch-style home that spread out east to west. The living room and front door faced north, opening out to the beautiful view of Lake Pend Oreille. The kitchen and dining room were open to the living room and faced south over a large yard and small kitchen garden and then into the woods.

The master bedroom with its separate bathroom and Sarah's office was to the east. Leif's study and guest room were to the west. It was a small house but very efficient. The half bath for visitors was near the front entrance and mud room.

Suzanne had updated the kitchen, and she and Sarah appeared to have similar tastes. All the cabinets were a beautiful light coffee color, with crystal knobs that glowed in the sunlight. A large island with white quartz counter-top was where they most often ate their meals.

Leif and Sarah had installed a wood stove in the living room which heated the main parts of the house all winter. Since Sarah liked her office much warmer than anyone else liked their rooms, she and Leif had separate heaters for their personal spaces.

Bored with the puzzle, Sarah walked down the short hall to their bedroom. She loved this room. With a huge closet, a set of French doors that opened onto a side deck to the east, and a very cozy bed, she couldn't think of a single thing wrong with it. Plus, the bathroom was a dream. Someone had spent some time and money making it just what she wanted in a bathroom. *Suzanne again, or maybe Ava,* she thought. Besides a perfect shower, there was a soaker tub. Everything fit into the space without feeling crowded. It was cozy and inviting.

Strolling the halls and walking into all the rooms wasn't helping Sarah's restlessness at all. The bath was calling her. She clicked on the scent warmer, added the vanilla, and headed to the soaker tub. *If all else fails, a meditative time in a tub is often the answer,* she mused. *If nothing else, I will smell fantastic.*

As the tub filled, Sarah added lavender bubbles, lit a candle, dimmed the lights, and stepped in. She loved getting into a bath as it filled. The water knobs were on the side of the tub by her hand, so it was easy to adjust the temperature to be just right.

She kept the water as hot as she could stand and watched the steam rise slowly into the air. There was a vent in the bathroom, but she hated to use it for times like this. It was too noisy, and besides, she loved the mist filling the room. A window set to the side of the tub allowed her to look out into the yard toward the trees that surrounded them on three sides. If it got too stuffy, she could open it a little without moving much at all.

Sarah watched as the sun moved across the property. First touching the tops of the trees and back-lighting some, while making their opposite neighbors appear to be on fire. It's all in the way you look at things, she thought.

Almost asleep, she heard the door open as Leif peeked in.

"Sorry, hon. Didn't realize you were creating a sauna in here!"

"Not! You just can't take the heat," Sarah replied.

They both laughed. It was a common refrain between the two of them, Leif teasing her about the way she loved heat, and she teasing him back about not being able to take it.

"I would like to pop those bubbles and see what's going on in there," Leif said. "But I just talked to Craig, and he said he would like me to be there sooner than later. He has a company plane at the airport already. I have a car coming to pick me up in a few minutes.

It looks as if you'll have a free day to yourself after all since Mira is not getting here until tomorrow. Will you be okay?"

"Of course. I'm just a bit worried about Craig's rush to get you there. And wait. What company plane?"

"Oh, not his. It belongs to the G.O.B. group, but they lent it to him to help get his center done."

"The plane, the pilot—everything? Geez, I am happy those boys know how to make money."

"Me, too. Money for good is always needed. Do you have plans for the day?"

"I didn't. But, since you aren't going to be here, I might drive into town, see Grace, get some lunch, catch up on all the gossip. I don't seem to be able to do anything else."

Lifting wet arms, Sarah pulled Leif down as close as she could to the water to give him a deep hug and kiss. As a parting gesture, she placed a bubble on his nose.

"Let me know when you get there."

"Okay, which way? Text or remote?"

"Better use text. I'll be in town with people."

They smiled at each other. There would always be secrets to keep.

Fourteen

Sarah heard the beep on the driveway letting her know that the car for Leif had arrived, and then heard the beep as it left. A whole day to not do anything at all lay ahead of her. Thinking that there was no need to rush, she stayed a while longer in the tub, letting in a little hot water at a time to keep it steamy.

She let her mind drift back to meeting Grace Strong, when she and Leif were looking for Tom and Mira's mother. They had a sketch of what they thought she might look like using Mira as a model and aging her twenty years. She and Leif went store to store asking if anyone had seen her. Tired and hungry, they ended up in a bakery. Grace had been sitting in the corner of the bakery and recognized the picture peeking out of Sarah's bag.

The story was, Grace had met Ava one day in town. After they had gotten to know each other, Ava had shown Grace a picture of Suzanne and told her that one day people would be coming to look for her. Ava had given Grace an envelope to give to them when she saw them. And that is what she had done.

Since then Sarah and Grace had become friends. Sarah thought that Ava had done a brilliant job of picking Grace to be the messenger. Grace didn't miss anything. She noticed all the comings and goings in town.

Grace kept her finger on the pulse of everything going on. If there was a new person in the area, she knew about it. If someone was sick and needed help, she not only knew about it, she did something about it.

She could reverse her name, and it would describe her perfectly, thought Sarah. *She is strong grace.* Grace gathered people. Grace trusted people, but knew what wasn't right without having to figure out why.

She was the perfect friend. And Sarah needed a perfect friend. She didn't tell her about the Circles or their work together. Instead, they talked about gardens, food, their day, their friends, the town—everything that friends discuss when they trust each other.

Sarah didn't talk about the rest because everyone in the Circle agreed that what it was and what it did was best kept a secret. They were going on the assumption that it wouldn't be safe for anyone they told.

Time to stop ruminating and get some food, Sarah thought. As she pulled on jeans and a T-shirt, and slipped on her sneakers and grabbed a jacket, she texted Grace, "Lunch?"

"Absolutely," was the immediate response.

"Meet me at the new pizza place in thirty?" Sarah wrote back.

"Done," said Grace.

Before leaving the house, Sarah stepped outside to say hello to the flowers, and brush the lilac bush with the tip of her fingers to say thank you for being so beautiful. She checked the bird feeders and birdbaths, waved hello at her bird friends, and returned to the house to set the alarm. The house and the garage were on separate alarm systems; closing the garage door set the garage alarm.

Going down the mountain and into town was always a beautiful drive. Sarah's heart filled with gratitude for having found a place she felt so at home.

The new pizza place was in the same building in which other restaurants had come and gone. *Perhaps this one would make it,* Sarah thought. She and Leif had driven by the restaurant on the way home a few days before, and she had noticed an outdoor patio. That always made a restaurant move to the top of her list. Plus, it was a make-your-own-pizza place, so she could have a pizza with tons of veggies on it without cheese or tomato sauce.

Grace was already waiting for her, just another reason to love her. On time, dependable, sweet, kind, and blunt, what could be better in a friend?

"Okay, spill," Grace said once they were firmly seated outside in the corner of the patio. "I know you, like Ava, keep secrets you won't or can't tell, but the one you're keeping right now, well, you can tell me about it."

"Good grief, Grace, how do you do that?"

"Don't know—have always been able to. Remember when we first met, and I told you that I knew who you were by the picture sticking out of your bag? Well. I did see the picture, but even before I saw it, I knew you were the ones that Ava had told me would come looking.

I know that you have the same secret Ava and Suzanne and her father were keeping up there in the house. Geez, girl, everyone wonders how you ended up owning that house."

Ignoring the implications of what Grace said about knowing, Sarah asked, "Everyone?"

"Sure. One day you live across the lake, and then Earl and Suzanne disappear, and you end up living in their house. What do you expect?"

"So what are the rumors about how we got it?"

"Well, I have helped. I told people that I heard that Suzanne and her dad wanted to travel the world and wanted to make a quick sale of the house. You were an old friend of Suzanne's, and when she discovered that you and Leif lived here, she and her dad decided you and Leif would be the perfect owners of their home."

Sarah was speechless. *All this secrecy and we never took into account what people in town thought about it. And Grace knows we are keeping a big secret?!Now what?*

"Look, Sarah," Grace said, squeezing her friend's hand. "I am your friend. I know your heart. Whatever is happening is okay, and I will do whatever I can to keep people from being too curious. But now, spit it out. What is the secret that you're keeping that you can tell me."

Sarah burst out laughing. Grace made it so easy.

"Thank you, Grace, and yes, I do have a lovely secret to share. Ava and Evan are getting married. Their wedding is going to be in August."

"Yes, I knew it," Grace said pumping her arm in the air and jumping up to hug Sarah. "What joy! I want to help in any way I can."

For the next few minutes, Grace and Sarah were two friends discussing weddings; what Sarah was going to wear and what gift she was bringing.

And then, Grace paused and finally spoke, "You need more from me than this, don't you, Sarah. You're worried about Ava. Why? And what can I do?"

Fifteen

"I swear, Tom; sometimes I rue the day I met you."

"Right. You regret meeting me right there in the womb. You turned to me and burbled, 'Get out!' And what kind of word is 'rue' anyway?"

"No, I didn't say that, but I might have asked you if you were capable of keeping your stuff from being all over the living room," Mira exploded. "And rue is a perfectly acceptable word meaning bitterly regret. Which I sometimes do!"

Tom looked around the living room and saw his shoes, some socks, and a jacket or two lying on the floor and couch. He had gotten used to treating every room like a hamper or closet, he realized.

"Look, Mira, I'm sorry. I've gotten too used to living by myself, as have you. You want everything in the same place you left it; all put away until the next time. I want to leave stuff out to make sure I know where it is—right in front of me on the couch when I go to sit down. Or still in the sink when I want my favorite dish. But, I will do better, I promise when I get back from seeing Evan. He's a neat freak anyway. Maybe he'll rub off on me."

"Neat freak! I am *not* a neat freak," Mira shouted. And

then she saw Tom's face. "Oh geez, I'm sorry too. I know you're worried about Ava and Evan. I am, too. I shouldn't be taking this out on you."

"Hugs?"

"Hugs? Why not."

As they stepped apart, Mira couldn't help getting in the last words. "But, I'm right, you know."

Tom looked at his sister standing in his living room and smiled. He didn't care how many words they had over things they didn't see the same way.

Finding her was the best thing that ever happened to him. He no longer felt alone. He had his good old boys club, but since his adoptive parents had passed away, he had no one he could fully trust.

Now, he had his twin sister. And along with Mira came the rest of the Circle. Everyone of them was someone he loved, trusted, depended upon, and connected with, even when they were not together.

Mira had come to share his home. It was silly for both of them to live in the same town and not be in the same place. So Mira had sold her house and moved in with Tom. Other than disputes about the placement of objects, it was working well for both of them.

They each had their private section of the house. He had added a separate entrance to her wing, so Mira could come and go without feeling as if she was living in a fishbowl. However, they shared the kitchen and the living room space, and that was where this bone of contention took place.

She was right, of course. He needed to be more mindful of living peacefully with another person.

Someday he hoped he would meet his one-and-only—the way Evan had, and this was a good training ground. He snickered.

He wouldn't poke fun at Mira anymore today, but she, too, needed to learn how to live peacefully with someone else.

Mira looked sideways at him and said, "What?"

"Nothing," Tom said.

"Alright, we'll agree 'nothing' for now. We have bigger things to worry about than socks going into the hamper when you take them off—which they should you know. Why do you think Sarah asked me to come visit, and you to go see Evan?"

Mira and Tom stood in the living room staring at each other. It was easy to tell that they were twins. Not just because they looked alike—lean, chestnut-brown hair, green eyes, and Roman noses, but because of the way they leaned into the world.

They were both ready to deal with whatever was in front of them. They had been that way before they met, living with different adoptive parents. But now that they had found each other, it was as if the two of them together more than doubled that intensity.

At the same time they each said, "Ava."

"Yes, something is going on with Ava," Mira said. "What do you think it is?"

"No idea, but we'd best pack and get where we are going, because we won't find out just standing here."

"Do you think I'll see mom and dad when I am at Sarah and Leif's?" Mira asked.

"You know they aren't always there, don't you? If they want us to see them, they'll show themselves. Otherwise, they'll probably be working their own dimension. Plenty of work for them to do there, too.

"Want to switch heart halves before we go?"

Mira smiled at her brother. He was so sappy and sentimental. She loved him for it. Mira and Tom unclasped the necklaces they each wore. On each chain hung a heart half. One said, "love" and the other said, "always."

"When we get back, we'll switch again," they said.

An hour later they were both ready to go and heading to the airport, Mira with a rolling suitcase with a lavender strap and Tom with his backpack. Tom had a short flight, which wasn't leaving for a few hours, but he wanted to make sure Mira got on her plane safely.

If they had turned around and looked at the house as they drove away, they might have seen their parents, Suzanne and Jerry, standing in the yard holding hands in the twilight, smiling at them.

As a neighbor's car pulled into the driveway next door, its headlights sweeping through Mira and Tom's front yard, he saw nothing.

Sixteen

"They are on the move, sir."

"Blast it, Hank. How many times have I told you not to call me sir? We are supposed to be friends, even though I don't know how anyone could be your friend," Grant shouted.

"I always call you Grant in public," Hank replied, keeping his voice low and controlled. He had done it on purpose. He loved to keep Grant on his toes. Sure, he admired the guy, but he was never going to let him control him, and this was one way of letting him know that.

Swearing as many swear words as he could in one breath, Grant nodded and sat down. He knew what Hank was doing, and he still let himself get out of control. He couldn't afford that. He needed to remain the leader.

He settled himself back down into his living room lounger. Anyone looking on would have thought they were watching a guy in his sixties hanging out with his friend, having a beer, and discussing the latest basketball games.

Of course, no one would ever be looking on, because everything about the ordinary country home was secure: soundproof walls, daily sweeps for bugs, cameras everywhere. Everything controlled by Grant.

It made Hank laugh, but only to himself. Grant thought he was so safe, but here he was alone with Hank. But for now, Grant served his purpose. He paid him well. And he got to keep his habit of eliminating people he didn't like—a side hobby that no one knew about, and never would.

The lounge creaked as Grant sat. He gestured for Hank to sit, too. "Okay, what do you mean 'they are on the move?' Do you think they suspect something? How could they? That blasted ability they have to 'feel' stuff is really bad for business. The sooner we stop them, the better."

Hank waited for Grant's tirade to be over before answering.

"Mira is visiting Sarah. Supposedly to shop and have coffee together. Tom is visiting Ava and Evan. Evan said he needed some help around their new house to prepare for the wedding. Leif is visiting Craig to help do something with the new healing center."

"All of it sounds plausible, of course. But, why is Ava still there? Perhaps our campaign needs to be stepped up. I'll take care of that part. Do you have men in place?"

"The permits for the house we will be building have been issued. Construction starts next week. We'll use some locals, but mix our guys in. No one will notice."

"I want you there in town, Hank. I need someone I can trust making sure this all goes to plan. Do you have people watching the rest of them?"

Hank's cold dark stare was his answer.

If only I didn't need him, I would get rid of him, Grant thought. *But he is the best, and in spite of everything, he owes me his life. So, friends, we will remain. For now.*

****

It didn't take long for Hank to pack. He traveled light. Long ago Hank had learned that having attachments only led to pain and heartache. Instead, he avoided any and all possessions that tied him down.

He had rented a tiny ugly house in the most unpleasant part of town—the part of town where no one wanted to know your name and no one cared what your business was or why you came and went.

If he was ever in need of a woman, he picked her up and took her to a cheap motel—never back to his house. Life was ugly. People and their actions made it uglier. Yes, he eliminated the ugliest of the ugly. But, he always did it with an artistic sense. No mess. No fuss. Always looked natural. Sure, fires were his favorite, but they were not always effective, so he became a master of the accident or they-died-in-their-sleep kind of deaths.

No one would look at him twice. He was just a run-down guy, with a run-down car, who worked in construction which explained his truck and tools. But, he wasn't run-down at all. Away from prying eyes, he was a faithful runner, and he used straps and his body weight to stay in shape. Underneath the baggy jeans, he was more fit than most teenagers.

As he packed, Hank thought about what Grant wanted him to do. Something about it didn't feel right to him. *What had these people actually done to deserve what they were going to get?* Grant often asked him to do things that he would never do on his own. But, he could always find something that ended up making the killing feel necessary and right. Not this one.

But, I owe Grant my life. He found me on the streets learning how to survive doing the worst jobs imaginable. He gave me a home. He gave me a job and didn't care where I came from or what I knew. Without him, I might not have made it. Almost forty years—how much longer do I owe him? Hank wondered.

Grunting with displeasure, he picked up his bag filled with work clothes. He'd be driving to this gig. He was going to be the foreman on the construction team they were putting together in Ava's town. Hank checked his house to make sure that if anyone came looking for him for any reason, all they would find was an old guy's house with nothing important in it. He had nothing to lose.

Hank packed as if he would never come back. He always prepared that way. Life had taught him the lesson that every day contained a possibility that it was your last day. Not necessarily a bad thing. What was bad is that someone might guess your secret. That was bad.

He checked his watch; he would be there in the early evening. Time enough for a detour. No one would question why he was driving through that part of the country. It was on the way. He could always say he was looking at the scenery, which he was. Just what scenery was that?

Seventeen

Tom kept checking the map app on his phone to figure out where he was going. He had rented a car at the airport to make the forty-five-minute drive to Evan and Ava's house. He was good at finding his way to new towns, cities, and countries, and he loved the adventure of exploring. Tom was pleased that in spite of having traveled all over the world, this part of Pennsylvania was new to him.

It was a lovely drive. The day was perfect. Beautiful white and gray clouds scuttled across the sky. All the trees were sporting their summer green, gardens were blooming, and the rolling hills were dotted with farmland and forest.

The app on his phone alerted him that he had arrived, but there was still no house. He wasn't worried. He could always call if he got lost, but the GPS was almost always right. With no traffic on the road and not having seen a car for at least ten minutes, he pulled off onto the shoulder, gravel spitting up into the underside of the car, and looked around.

Scanning the two-lane road he was on, Tom noticed a mailbox and an opening about ten feet ahead. Thinking that there was nothing to lose, he moved back onto the road and turned into what appeared to be a driveway. Within one turn, he was treated to a view of a beautiful farmhouse set on a slight rise. Woods surrounded the house, but left lots of room for a long rolling lawn in front, a flower garden, a porch that took up the whole front of the house, and what appeared to be a vegetable garden on the right.

The driveway curved around more than a few times before it reached a large gravel parking area to the side of the house.

Evan sure knows how to pick them, thought Tom as Ava and Evan burst out through the open door. Tom pulled the car into the parking lot and started smiling. He hadn't realized how much he had missed his friends. Seeing them on a computer screen or with remote viewing was definitely not the same as seeing them in person. As he opened the car door, Tom smelled the trees, the clean fresh air, the burst of blooms from the flower garden, and he smiled even wider.

Hugging Evan and Ava at the same time, he said, "Dude, you picked heaven on earth. This place is beautiful. I could live here!"

"Why not, Tom? We can't wait to show you around! First, though, let's get you settled. Then we can catch up. Are you hungry? We put together a little lunch, but later we can take you to one of our favorite restaurants in town."

"Town? There are things to do in town?"

Ava giggled. "Sure there are, you'll be surprised."

"I already am. I thought you lived in the middle of nowhere."

"Well, in a sense we do, at least compared to the city. But, small towns have their charms, you'll see," Evan answered.

As they stepped up to the broad front porch and opened the door into the mud room at the front of the house, Tom turned to look back over the driveway and lawn. "The first line of defense, Evan? You sure can see everyone coming from this direction."

Evan nodded. "There is more, of course."

As he spoke, he and Tom stepped into the living room. The living room, dining room, and kitchen were actually all within one big space. Warm and inviting, it spoke volumes about the couple living there.

"Wow."

The wows continued as Evan led Tom to the guest room.

"A guest room with its own bathroom?" Tom sighed.

"Yep, and there are two more like that in this wing of the house. And then there is a bunkhouse out back. Plenty of room for everyone when you all come to the wedding. How much time do you need to freshen up?"

"Fifteen minutes? I am looking forward to lunch and catching up on all your news."

"Okay, we'll be waiting for you in the back of the house. Just follow the hallway away from the living room and you'll find us."

Fifteen minutes later, Tom followed the hallway to a large screened porch with French doors opening to a deck and pergola. A wooden picnic table was set for lunch.

Tom watched Ava as she brought food from the kitchen. She looked beautiful, if much too thin. Other than that, what was different? She was tense. *Could it be the wedding?*

Ava lifted her gaze as Tom walked across the porch. Same eyes. But, not as soft as before. *Yes, something is going on, thought* Tom.

Crap, Ava thought. *He knows something. What am I going to do?*

From across the deck, Evan watched Ava attempt to relax as Tom arrived. Perhaps the two of them together could uncover the problem with Ava.

"I am so glad you're here, Tom. We have so many things to do before the wedding, plus I want to catch up with you about what's going on with G.O.B. Are you still doing good all over the world?"

Tom laughed. "In a way. As you know, we were always a loose-knit free-spirited group of guys. No real planning. It's just that wherever we went, we tried to do something good before we left. Sometimes big things, like the water deal you helped us with, sometimes small, like paying for all the groceries for the next ten people in line behind us.

"But, once Mira started helping us, we became a little more organized. Now we have team—not just guys—going out whenever we hear about a problem. But, I don't want to hinder the free movement that we had in the past, so no real hard-and-fast-rules."

"Do you still pick people based on seeing a light shining on them?"

"Other than you, Evan, yes. I think that will keep people out who are using the cover of good to do evil, which is, as you know, more common than we ever thought."

Ava heard what they were talking about as if she was in a trance. She served lunch, smiled, and answered when spoken to, but her thoughts were far away on when she was sixteen and stupid—and what she had done.

Eighteen

The bar was always dark and it smelled like sweat and old food. But it was a job, and it paid enough to have a one-room apartment in a duplex. She was pretty sure her one room used to be a garage which was why it was so cheap, but she could afford it and still buy a few groceries.

She practiced flirting with the male customers and making friends with the female customers who came with them. Ava made sure that both parties always knew she would not be going home with the men and she wasn't a threat to the women. As she got better at this delicate balance, her tips increased, some of which she reported to the IRS, and some she didn't.

If she had reported them all, she wouldn't have had enough money for groceries. There was food at the bar that everyone knew how to get without anyone knowing. But it always tasted like the bar, so she had stopped eating it.

The hours were horrible. Ava started before lunch, and sometimes the shift wasn't over until after midnight. Then she'd have to drag her tired ass out to the parking lot and look for the junker car she had bought for three hundred dollars, hoping that no one was waiting for her, either thinking she wanted to see them or even scarier, knowing that she didn't.

The car ran, and that was about it. It was a stick-shift green Volkswagen, probably older than she was. It would pop out of second gear and into third without her shifting, so she kept a brick in the car that she wedged between the gears after she got going. Since she lived only a few miles away, second gear was enough to get her home.

There was a backseat, but no way could she put anything there because there was a hole in the floor that things might fall through. Ava had found some boards lying on the side of the road so she had put them on the floor. The boards kept the road from being visible, and rocks from flying up into the car, but they rattled all the time.

Yep, freedom. This is what it looks like, Ava would think. The idea that things would get better, along with her stubborn pride and ego, wouldn't let her go home.

Instead, home was the garage-turned-apartment with its tiny bathroom, and a pretend kitchen that held a small refrigerator and a hot plate.

Before disappearing from her life, Mandy had brought over a futon from her house, and that served as the bed, the couch, and the chair.

Outside Ava's door, there was a patch of dirt. She had bought a pack of morning glory seeds and planted them, watered them with a cup of water every day, and prayed they would come up. She needed beauty in her life.

The fact that the seeds had sprouted and grown into a huge flowering vine both buoyed her and sunk her into depression. Beauty from the flowers and sadness from the awareness that she had lived in that dump for long enough for that to happen.

Every morning the flowers bobbed their happy blue faces at her as she opened the door to go running. Running was freedom. It didn't cost money, it kept her energy up, and sometimes she would briefly catch the feeling that she could do anything.

She'd head to the beach and then run a few miles down the waterfront to get a cheap cup of coffee and watch the waves. Something about the ocean both calmed and excited her. So changeable: peaceful one minute, pounding surf the next.

After coffee, she'd run back to her room, shower and get ready for another day of flirting and teasing and pretending that this was exactly what she had wanted all along.

One day, Ava realized that it was September and her birthday was only a week away. She would be seventeen. Almost the age showing on her ID. Funny that. Someday she would be the age she pretended to be.

There was no one to tell.

Mandy had disappeared out of her life. None of the girls at the bar wanted to be friends. It was a competition, not a community. She felt she was being ignored because the manager kept telling her that she was too wholesome looking. Too girl-next-door.

It was up to her to find a way to celebrate. She asked for the day off, and since it was the middle of the week she got it—but not without promising to pick up extra shifts when she could to make up for it. Plus she had to give the manager an extra sweet smile to make him feel important.

Men. Easily manipulated. She was beginning to hate them.

Once, she had a boyfriend, but he thought the girl with bigger boobs was cuter, so she was happy to let him go. Now, the thought of dating anyone she met disgusted her.

She had major doubts that any man wasn't driven by only one thing, no matter how nice they tried to appear. Every night, she saw the ugliest of the ugly. She wanted nothing to do with them.

******

"Earth to Ava," Evan called. "Geez, Ava, where have you been? Tom asked you a question."

Ava glanced up to see both Tom and Evan staring at her as if there was something wrong. *They aren't using the spidery senses, are they? I'm in trouble if they are, and I have got to stop thinking about this stuff while they are around.*

"Oh, so sorry! I guess I was daydreaming. You know how much I like to design things. I was thinking where everyone would be sitting during the reception."

A brief hint of disbelief flitted across Tom's face but he immediately corrected it. Ava doubted that Evan had noticed.

"So, the reception is going to be here?" Tom asked.

"Yes! But the wedding is going to be in a little church in town."

As Ava started describing where the wedding would take place, what kind of food they were planning, where everyone would sit, and what the table decorations would be, her face lit up more and more with happiness.

Well, whatever is going on, it has nothing to do with how Ava feels about Evan, Tom thought. *I'll play along, and see what I turn up. Nothing can stop this good that is going on. They can try, but it won't work.*

"That sounds perfect, Ava. I know the rest of our Circle will be here, plus probably Suzanne and Earl's Circle. What about your mom? We have never talked about her. She passed away I know, but do you ever see her? Is she part of a different Circle?"

Evan threw Tom a warning glance. Too late. Darkness had already flitted across Ava's face. Almost indiscernible, but the light had gone out of her eyes.

"I am so sorry, Ava; I just thought we never had time to talk about it, which is why I didn't know. Plus, I understand that there are many Circles, including the one with Evan's parents. I just assumed."

"It's okay, Tom. I wish I could tell you, but I don't know. She died almost six years ago. She knew she was dying, so she made sure I had a home waiting for me. As you know, I went to live with her best friend, Suzanne, but I never saw my mom again. I tried to bring it up with Suzanne, but she always diverted my questions. I figure mom has already gone through to the light."

"But, you know that she loved you, don't you, Ava?" After all, she made sure you were taken care of, right?"

"Sure." Ava sighed.

And to herself, Ava wondered if her mom was punishing her for what she had done.

Nineteen

Was this the same town? Hank wondered. Some things remained the same. The downtown had the same old brick buildings. The vibe was still quiet. The sidewalks were still the same ones that traveled from the center of town in each direction until petering out into woods or farmland.

On the other hand, the buildings were no longer covered with dirt and grime, but now had painted window frames and tiny gardens; some had a bench or two out front. The sidewalks were not cracked from one end into the other, making the game of not stepping on a crack or break your mother's back almost impossible.

The old trees whose roots had buckled the sidewalks were gone, but new trees were growing in their place, not as big, but just as pretty. Hank figured that in early the spring, the trees were probably the flowering type. He thought about how much he liked the spring colors of leaves with all the shades of green. They were just as beautiful as the fall. Plus white apple blossoms and the pink cherry blossoms were undeniably beautiful.

Good God, I don't have time to be thinking about pretty trees, Hank thought. *I am on the job. I gotta get there. Time to find that frigging cemetery so I can spit on his grave.*

As he drove down Main Street, he realized that although it was still quiet, there were more people about than he had ever seen. Some restaurants had a few tables and chairs set out under umbrellas, and there was a trendy coffee shop on the corner.

He tried not to stare.

He was on his way through to the next town. He was not interested in this one. Plus, he certainly didn't want anyone recognizing him.

That someone might was close to impossible. After all, he had left more than forty years ago as a boy. But this was no time to be fooling around. He was already taking a chance by going to the cemetery.

A few miles out of town, he made a quick right onto an old dirt road. He hadn't even had to look up where to find it; his young self seemed to guide him. The cemetery was much farther down the road than he remembered.

Just when he was beginning to believe that he hadn't remembered where it was, he could see it on the rise up ahead. Hank wasn't completely sure if this was where that bastard was buried. But it stood to reason that someone would have seen to his burial, and this is where they stuck all the poor people.

He pulled his dusty truck into a stand of trees, making sure that it couldn't be seen from the road. As he stepped out, he felt goosebumps go up the back of his neck. Instinctively, he ducked down behind the wheels and glanced around. Nothing. Just a hawk sitting on a tree a few hundred yards away.

For years he had the feeling that someone was following him. He always took precautions, and he never found anyone, but the feeling remained.

Not that anyone would know to follow him. He was just a middle-aged guy, who looked older than he was, and who moved around from construction site to construction site.

He always kept out of trouble. No one ever knew the pain he caused, and he tried to never make either an enemy or a friend. He was always neutral. And yet, there was the feeling of being followed.

Shaking it off, since there was no one in sight, Hank started up the grassy hill to where he could see flat white stones in the ground. Little had been done to keep the graves from being buried in weeds and grasses.

The gravestones were almost all hidden under moss and sticks which had fallen from the trees. Hank tried to ignore the birds singing, the blue sky, and the rustling leaves because they were bringing up old feelings that he had long buried: feelings of love for the land and nature.

Considering the job Grant had asked him to do, he couldn't afford any notions of caring. Once he found the grave, he knew that the hate that had driven him all these years would burn again. He had to find it.

It wasn't a big graveyard, but trying to find one plot without disturbing the others turned out to be more complicated than he thought it would be. He had to be careful. No one could know that he was here. No one could know that he was looking for this particular grave.

How hard can it be to find him? His grave probably gave off an evil light, Hank thought. Twilight was fading; this had to happen soon, he couldn't turn on a flashlight. He might be seen.

What I need is someone to show me where this bloody grave is. Out of the corner of his eye, he watched the hawk leave his perch and fly low over the graveyard and land about twenty feet away from a grave at the end of the row.

Seriously? You want me to believe that you are showing me?

Thinking that he had nothing to lose, Hank trudged over to the grave as the hawk lifted off to land on his perch in the trees.

It was hardly visible, but there it was. Frank Sampson. *It should say bastard,* Hank thought. *Relief flooded him. He really is dead; I have nothing more to fear from him. He's gone.*

After spitting on his grave, Hank spun on his heel and headed back to the car. *No more screwing around. I have a job to do.*

Pulling away, Hank glanced back just in time to see the hawk leave his perch and fly back into the woods. Ignoring the goosebumps, he drove away feeling lighter than he had in a long time.

Twenty

After lunch, Evan asked Tom if he wanted to go for a walk through the property. Ava begged off. Lately, she felt as if she was carrying the weight of the world on her shoulders.

"I'm going to take a nap, Evan. Plus, I know you two. You're going to climb some trees and explore as much as possible. I'll let you two have a go at it while I am having a beauty sleep."

"Hon, if you get more beautiful I'll have to start wearing sunglasses all the time," Evan said.

Ava smiled and hugged Evan. She waved as they walked off to get some hiking boots for Tom. But, first Tom circled back around to hug her, too. "He loves you over-the-moon you know." And with a gentle kiss on her cheek, he quickly walked away to catch up with Evan.

Standing as still as possible, waving with a smile on her face, Ava maintained her composure. She knew how lucky and blessed she was to have Evan and her friends. She knew how much his heart had been given to her. She knew how deeply he loved and cherished her. Everyone could see. It had happened right away for him. He didn't have any barriers in place.

She did. She loved him, but something was missing. It wasn't him. It was her, as trite as that sounded. A few weeks ago they had gone out for dinner and watched a couple dancing together. The couple held each other's gaze with their open hearts shining through. Everyone watching knew that they were seeing pure love.

Ava had looked down at her soup so Evan wouldn't see the tears gathering in her eyes. She wanted so much to feel that love. Ava wanted her heart to be open and free. She wanted to be able to look at Evan with that complete look of love.

But now it seemed even more impossible. Maybe it was for the best. Perhaps what she was going to do might not hurt her as much. But Evan was an entirely different story.

Ava wasn't kidding about needing a nap. However, instead of heading for their bedroom, she lay down on the couch. It felt more like a nap that way, and she didn't want to see their bedroom and all the evidence of their commitment spread out before her.

Sometimes Ava's need for a nap seemed to be driven by outside forces, as if someone—or something—was calling her away. That was the case this time. Even before her head hit the pillow, images started to appear before her, and she was gone. Gone to that world, or in this case, that time.

Her birthday arrived. September in California wasn't at all like September in the east. It was warm and sunny. She decided to do everything that she could that would make her happy that day. There would be no ruminating about work. No thinking about home.

She had taken care of her thoughts of home a few days before, by sending her mom a postcard telling her that she was doing fine and wishing her a happy birthday. After all, she was the one who had given birth seventeen years before.

Ava hoped that was enough to keep her from worrying. Shaking off any residue of doubt, Ava pulled on running shorts and shoes and headed outside, brushing the morning glories with the tips of her fingers on the way out.

First a run, then maybe a yoga class at the pavilion, sponsored by Parks and Recreation, a lovely lunch on the boardwalk, and then a movie.

Some people wouldn't have thought of this as a good day, spent by yourself, no one to celebrate with, but to Ava, it sounded like heaven. She loved being by herself. Surrounded by so many people during her work day, she counted the minutes until she was alone.

Ava would never forget that day. It marked a turning point in her life that changed everything.

At first, it was exactly as she imagined it would be. Her body felt light and free as she ran to the beach. It was the middle of the week, and the end of the tourist season, so there were fewer looky-loos, fewer people attempting to look hip and happening, which only managed to make them look stupid.

After the run, the hour long yoga class felt fantastic. She had danced and done gymnastics as a child, and the joy of moving and feeling flexible stayed with her. As they lay on mats at the end of the class, she tried to practice what the instructor was saying. "Breathe in the light, breathe out the negative."

If it was only that easy, thought Ava. *No negative thinking today. Today, I celebrate. Today I look for what is good.*

The next decision was where to have lunch. Without much spare cash, it would have to be somewhere not too expensive.

Ava had run home, changed, and was standing outside two different restaurants trying to decide which one when it happened. She knew which one she wanted.

It beckoned her, but the prices on the menu were far above what she could afford. Plus she had also promised herself a movie.

Lost in thought, Ava was completely startled when a voice said, "Maybe I can help you decide?"

Clasping her hand to her chest in surprise, she turned so quickly that she almost bumped into the man with the voice and the question. He caught her as she tipped off balance, and said "Didn't mean to startle you. I just saw you standing here and thought I could help you decide."

Righting herself, Ava finally glanced up to see who had spoken and was now holding her shoulder. It was a pleasant sight. He had a quick smile, dimples, and a head of sleeked back blond hair.

"I'm Rick," he said as he stuck out his hand. "Ava, she answered."

****

Lunch flew by. Rick had decided for her that the more expensive restaurant was where she wanted to eat. He was right, of course, and she was too embarrassed to tell him that she couldn't decide because it was too expensive.

"What about keeping me company?" he said, and Ava, only slightly reluctant, agreed.

"So, what are you doing out on such a beautiful day, Ava?" he had asked, and Ava, tongue loosened by the wine he had ordered and said would pay for, told him. Once she started talking, she couldn't stop. She told him about living in a tiny disgusting apartment, and her job and how much she hated it, and finally she told him that it was her birthday.

It was easy to talk to him. He was a stranger. She would never see him again.

He listened well. Rick nodded and smiled. Finally, she put a stop on it. She managed to keep her secret about running away, by making up a story about being eighteen and moving to California to become some a star, like every other young pretty girl.

"I am so sorry for all that talking" Ava said. "I don't know what I was thinking. I blame the wine. Now, tell me about you."

Later, Ava would realize that although he started talking, he never told her anything of substance. To be fair, she hadn't told him anything of substance either.

****

The next day, Ava was back at work and hating it even more than before. The contrast of how she spent her birthday and the dark, ugly, and stinky bar with the pawing men was painful.

A few weeks before, the manager of the bar had added a noontime act. Each waitress used to take turns going up on the stage to dance during the lunch hour. But lunchtime had become so busy there were not enough girls to spare for dancing.

With the new act, every day a different girl would come to the club just to dance. They spent the hour on stage and left.

That day, Ava happened to be in the bathroom at the same time as one of the girls who had come to dance. Ava, always slightly clumsy, had bumped into her as they both went to get towels to dry their hands.

The girl smiled at her and Ava gathering her courage and asked her, "Do you like coming in and dancing?"

The girl paused and smiled. "Are you sick of men pawing at you?"

Ava answered, "More than sick of it."

"Well, the good thing about coming in this way, is they can't. I can still see them drooling and acting like fools, but other than giving you money, they can't touch. Plus, a bunch of the clubs have to have someone escort me back to my car. And the money is much better."

They stared at each other as the girl waited for Ava's response. Finally, Ava asked, "Could I do something like that?"

"Well, you have such wholesome look, I'm not sure if it will go over, but if you do well here, it might. Plus, some clubs want college-aged, girl-next-door looks. You need an agent to get into them, though."

She paused. In hindsight Ava knew why she paused. Later she would find out that most of the girls and women she met dancing at clubs never got free from the life. But, at that moment, it sounded like freedom, so she begged, "Could you introduce me to yours?"

The girl—Ava never did learn her name—grabbed a paper towel and asked Ava for the pen she kept in her apron and wrote down a name and number. "If you are sure this is what you want, call him."

During her five-minute break that afternoon, Ava called the Tip Top Agency and asked for Joe. After asking a few questions about her age and the size of her boobs, he scheduled an appointment with her for her next day off.

He told her not to wear a bra to the meeting. They would be taking pictures and he didn't want bra-strap lines. That took Ava aback for a moment, but then she remembered what she wanted and let her concern fade into the background.

For the next few days, Ava was happier than she had been in a long time. She had met a nice man who had paid for her lunch after learning it was her birthday, and she was going to change her life for the better on Monday.

Ava knew Joe would want her. She had a way with men.

Twenty-One

Tom and Evan returned from their walk buzzed and excited about all the nature that they had seen. They wanted to tell Ava all about it, but over dinner, in town.

By then, Ava was even more tired than when they left. The sleep she had was too busy with memories. But there was no way she was going to let the two of them know there was anything wrong. So after everyone had freshened up, off they went to the village in Evan's car. They could have walked the few miles, but decided that Tom and Evan had hiked enough that day. Ava was grateful, too tired even to contemplate walking.

"So what's your new town like, and do you know about the name, Doveland?" Tom asked.

That was a question that neither Ava or Evan could answer. "Is it about doves do you think?" Tom asked.

"It would be kinda appropriate for us," Evan said, looking at Ava.

"Doves mate for life. And when you get to know them, you can always tell which couple goes together. I used to love to watch the doves when I was a boy. They walked as couples through the garden. One would pause and look at things, and the other would keep watch for any kind of danger. Their coos are so calming and reassuring.

"One time, I found a dove that had died and the other one kept walking around and around cooing, trying to call her back. Even after I buried her, he would come every day for a long time to the spot and coo.

"I love the example of birds, and animals, who demonstrate the idea of *Pragma*," Evan said.

"*Pragma?* I have never heard that word," Tom responded.

"*Pragma* is one of the six Greek words for love. It is the mature love. And to me, the one that lasts and the one I want to epitomize in everything I do," answered Evan, once again looking at Ava.

"Wow," was both Ava and Tom's response. Ava thought that they each had different reasons for saying it though.

****

Doveland, thought Ava. *Who would have thought I'd move someplace that represents mature love to Evan?*

Like many small towns in the east, Doveland's town square was a park. Four roads, one for each direction, headed to the park. To continue on the same road, you had to circle the park first. That meant everyone coming to town circled the square sooner or later. Usually, there would be people sitting on benches waving at friends as they drove by to head out again.

In the summer on Wednesday evenings, local musicians would play, and on Saturday mornings, there was a small farmer's market. It reminded Ava of the one in Sandpoint, which always made her think of Sarah and Leif.

Ava and Evan decided to take Tom to the Diner, located on the north side of the park. As they parked, Evan pointed out Laura's, the other restaurant that they loved.

"We wanted to bring you to the Diner," explained Evan, "because the cook is the one who is catering our wedding. But we will visit Laura's before you return home. They make a fantastic red curry, even though you might not associate the name, Laura's, with red curry."

Evan held the front door of the restaurant open for Tom so he could get a complete view of the Diner. It was busy enough to have a pleasant buzz, but not too busy to feel crowded.

"I have a feeling that I am going to be saying 'wow' a lot while I am here. This place is fantastic. An upscale old-time diner. You can't tell that from the outside, can you?"

"It's a simple style, but we love it," Ava said sliding into a booth. They didn't have to ask. Andy had seen them as they came in the door and knew where they loved to sit.

As he handed them the menus, he introduced himself to Tom.

"Have we met before?" Tom asked. "You seem familiar to me."

"One of those faces, I guess." Andy laughed. "I'll be back in a minute with your drinks. Ava and Evan, do you want ice-tea?"

As they nodded, Tom added, "Me too."

"Are you sure we don't know him?" Tom asked.

"Although he does seem familiar, I know I hadn't met him until we started coming here," answered Ava.

"Now he feels like an old friend. We asked him to manage the servers at the wedding. I'll ask Sam, the chef, to come out later, but in the meantime I realize I'm starving, and they have fantastic portabello mushroom burgers here."

Seeing Tom and Evan's face, she added, "And regular burgers too!"

As they ate, Tom kept feeling as if someone was watching them: spider-sense, almost the same as when he first felt Mira remote viewing him before they found each other. He wished he was skilled enough to tell if it was a good sense of being watched or a bad one.

In the corner, a group of construction workers finished their dinner and got up to pay the bill. Tom watched as they chatted with the cashier and headed out to their respective trucks.

"Are those the people who worked on your house, Evan?"

"No, they aren't. Ours came to town just to work on our property. Sarah and Leif sent them, since we had some unique equipment installed. I heard that there was a group of new construction workers in town building a home a few miles down the road from us. Perhaps that's the group.

"Why are you asking? Is there something wrong?"

"Maybe," Tom answered.

Twenty-Two

Sarah never responded to Grace's offer to help. She had squeezed her hand and told her she needed to think about it. Grace, living up to her name, smiled and said she could wait, and she would be there if and when she was needed.

To tell Grace anything other than what she was thinking was a decision that needed to be brought forward to the whole Stone Circle. Plus, she needed to listen within to any messages about what she should do before bringing the request to them.

Before heading home, Sarah stopped at the store to get a few things.

Mostly she ordered online, but sometimes shopping in person was like going on a treasure hunt. The farmer's market would be open on Saturday, and that would mean fresh vegetables that they weren't growing in their garden.

Plus, crafts people who had been making unique items all winter would be there to sell them. Perhaps she could pick up something special for Ava and Evan.

As she pulled into the driveway, Sarah got a glimpse of what she called her sentinels in the trees. Her heart filled with gratitude for the lovely souls who had agreed to watch over their home at all times. Installed alarms were fantastic, but nothing would ever be as comforting as knowing that she was always being watched over.

If only everyone knew, thought Sarah. *Everyone is always being watched over; everyone is cherished. Even those who seek to stop the awakening of humanity are watched over.* Sarah believed that the fear that keeps some people caught in the urge to kill and destroy anything they don't understand must eventually be dissolved. But until then, diligence and awareness are always necessary.

She waved and laughed. She always waved at trees and flowers. Sometimes there were people who waved back, too.

After dumping the groceries on the kitchen counter, Sarah grabbed her clippers and went out to cut some roses for the living room. The smell was heavenly, perfect for Mira's visit.

In the middle of putting them in vases, she started feeling the call. Leif was practicing remote viewing again. He had gotten much better at it these past few months. Although still not an expert at calling, Sarah was getting better at receiving.

Plopping into one of the comfy chairs in the living room, she answered him with a big air kiss.

"You're already there?"

"No, I am trying this as we are flying. Fast plane, though. Tom sure knows how to take care of his friends," answered Leif. "I see you have been flower arranging and shopping. How was your visit with Grace?"

Sarah told him what Grace had said. "Do you think we should bring her more into the loop?"

"We need to think about it, and have a group decision. Not just for us, but for Grace's safety. We put her at risk by telling her more."

"But, aren't we already putting her at risk by not telling?"

"Good point. I'll talk to Craig when I see him, and you talk to Mira. Gotta go, here comes food. Love you!"

Sarah barely had time to say goodbye before he disappeared. *Almost like the Cheshire cat.*

****

That night, Sarah dreamed: She was in a home she had never seen before. A small baby was crying. In her dream, Sarah reached for the baby, but it vanished and in its place was a yellow rose. The scene changed, and Sarah stood in a graveyard and watched a man spit on a grave. A hawk circled over him and then was gone.

Opening her eyes, she saw it was 3:00 AM, time to get up. Trying to pull the dream back was futile. Perhaps later in meditation, she would learn more, but for now, she needed a bit of stretching and some coffee.

Today Mira would arrive, and perhaps she would have an idea what to do about Grace. Maybe she would also have some insights into the dream.

Since Mira was arriving by shuttle from the Spokane airport, there was nothing for Sarah to do but wait. She checked the guest room and bathroom to make sure that all was in order, spent some time deadheading any roses that had finished blooming, and did a few yoga stretches. Sarah stayed on the mat to do her meditation. She had discovered that she was less likely to fall asleep while meditating if she was sitting on a yoga mat rather than a chair.

Sarah had also discovered that when she wanted some deep insight, it was the time she was least likely to get it. It was when she least expected it that ideas would appear.

With still a few hours left and nothing to occupy her mind Sarah succumbed to her favorite pastime, reading. She grabbed a book and an apple and headed to the living room, her comfy chair, and a few uninterrupted hours of pure joy.

Many chapters later, she glanced up from the book and the world that she had lost herself within, and realized that she had spent more time reading than she thought. There was only time for a quick shower. Mira was due soon, and she needed to get to town to pick her up.

Showered, in fresh clothes, and fully rested, Sarah waited for the shuttle. Her heart leaped with joy when she saw Mira emerge from the van. A young man had hefted her suitcase down for her. *Kindness in action.* Another one of the things she and Leif loved about the town when they arrived. Everyone actually looked at you on the street, smiled, and said, "Hello."

It's the small things that make life beautiful, Sarah thought as she hugged her friend. Such a different feeling from the last time Mira had come to town. So many things had changed, and at the same time, so many things remained the same.

"Want some lunch before we head up the mountain, Mira?" Sarah asked.

"Oh, you don't fool me, Sarah," Mira said. "You want to have lunch in town because you have someone you want me to meet, don't you?"

"Got me. Yes, I do. If I text my friend Grace, we could have lunch with her, if that's okay with you."

"More than okay. I am ready for a new friend and an intriguing mystery."

After a brief text exchange, Sarah said, "Let's put your suitcase in the car, and walk over. She's on her way now to the restaurant."

"I love her already. A quick response for one in need."

"I think you have just summed her up perfectly."

And off they went to meet Grace, arm in arm, looking very much like a mother and daughter who admired and respected each other.

What are they up to? wondered the man watching from the building across from the shuttle stop. He pulled out his burner phone, tapped out a number, and related what he had just seen. He listened and snapped the phone shut and continued his watch.

****

Sarah led Mira to their favorite Thai restaurant. "Yum," Mira said.

"I thought you would like coming here again. Grace likes it too. On the other hand, who doesn't?"

Grace was waiting for them in the booth by the window. After introductions and a quick order because they all knew what they wanted, Sarah told Mira what Grace had been doing for them.

"I'm not doing anything special. I just pay attention to who is in town that wasn't here last week, or who in town acts differently. If there is something I can do to help, I am always available. My husband passed away years ago, and we didn't have any children. I have always been a free spirit, ready to roam wherever I am called to go."

"I thought you had been in Sandpoint forever," said Sarah.

"I do give that impression, don't I?" Grace answered.

"However, I traveled all over the world when I was younger. You know, the walking, backpack, stay-at-hostels kind of lifestyle. I earned my keep as I went along. On one of my trips, I met my husband, Jim, who was doing the same thing. He was writing for a travel magazine, and that earned him just enough to fund his trips. I tagged along. We got married.

"Our trips calmed down over the years. Instead of backpacking, it was trains and hotels. After Jim passed away, I came back here. We had visited on a vacation, and I thought it was beautiful. Jim had taken good care of me while he was alive, and left me insurance money when he passed away, enough to keep me comfortable. But, I'm feeling restless again. Thought perhaps you two might have a new adventure for me."

Sarah and Mira exchanged glances.

"Oh, you're wondering how I know. Well, as I just finished telling you I am a wanderer, but I am also a busybody, and proud of it. Your friend Ava must have known that about me. Otherwise, why would she tell me to watch for you? And, as I told Sarah, I knew it was the person who Ava had told me about even before I saw the picture sticking out of her bag. When you have been watching people and how they behave as long as I have, you know things.

"Like, do you know that you are being watched as we speak? That man followed you from the shuttle stop."

Grace tilted her head to point across the street at a man sitting on a bench, smoking a cigarette.

"He looks like he belongs here, doesn't he? Nope, he's new. I thought I would go chat him up later, you know, welcoming committee and all that. I'll let you know what I find out. And, no, this isn't because you said I could help, it's because that's what I do. Travel, and stick my nose into other people's business. Who is afraid of an old lady? I'm invisible most of the time. Old outside, young inside."

Sarah and Mira looked at each other and started laughing. Grace joined in, and soon they were giggling like schoolgirls, or more like old friends. As Sarah watched Mira and Grace laughing together, she thought perhaps they were.

Twenty-Three

Ava watched Tom and Evan enjoying their food. She could barely touch hers. Lately, nothing tasted good. She was much too tense to eat. But when Tom asked her if there was something wrong, she lied and told him that she had eaten too many snacks while he and Evan were out walking.

Now she was lying to people she cared about, but even worse, lying to people who internally could tell the truth from lies. Ava saw them exchanging glances, and felt their questions, but she had nothing to give them. The pain and sorrow that had followed her all these years was becoming more than she could handle.

After her mom died and she went to live with Suzanne, she thought she would not survive the first year. Suzanne and Earl believed she was mourning her mother, but it was so much more. It was as if all that had happened to her had piled up and buried her.

However, with Suzanne and Earl's gentle compassion, and eventually their introduction into their mission of gathering the Stone Circle, she began to heal.

When Ava met Evan, her closed heart opened a tiny bit. Without being told, she knew they belonged together and had for lifetimes. She had hoped that, over time, her fear and distrust would melt away and leave her with the fully open heart she so wanted to give to him.

Now, the past had all come rushing back. Ava had no idea where her mom had gone. Sure, she knew she passed away, but others who'd passed away were visible to the two Circles—at least some of the time. Had her mom decided to desert her—to punish Sarah for abandoning her for those two years?

But, I didn't know mom was sick when I left, Ava moaned within.

Another thought struck Ava: *What if she knows about the letters?*

Pure panic flooded her thinking. *Of course, she does.* Where she is, she can see time as it is, always flowing with all information always available. An infinite present.

"Ava, what's going on?" Evan asked.

Breathing heavily, Ava gathered herself as best as she could and said she was just stressed and needed air.

"I'll get the bill," Tom said as Evan helped Ava up from the table to stumble outside and across the street to a bench in the park.

Ava put her head between her knees as Evan knelt beside her, patting her on the back and murmuring words of encouragement.

"Is this about the wedding, Ava? I can take care of all the details if it's stressing you out. In fact, I can get the whole Stone Circle here to help."

Ava sat up and looked at Evan. He was her beloved. His face was drawn and he looked worried, a lock of his hair hanging down over his eyes almost hiding the pain hidden in them.

What could she do? Gathering herself, she whispered, "No, Evan, I will be okay. I probably just need more sleep." She put her hands on either side of his face, gently kissed him, and whispered, "You are my one and only."

"Okay," Evan said helping her up. "Let's go home and get you tucked into bed."

Over her head, Evan locked eyes with Tom. She hadn't fooled them. And he knew that she knew she hadn't.

****

Evan kept his word. As soon as they got home, he walked with Ava to their bedroom, waited for her to wash up, and tucked her gently into bed.

"You know you can tell me anything, don't you? You can't say anything that will make me stop loving you. No matter what comes, we can face it together."

"I know," Ava whispered. "It's nothing. I just need some sleep."

Even leaned over, kissed her on the forehead, and turned out the light. "Okay, just call me if you need me. Tom and I will be downstairs doing the guy thing of watching baseball on TV."

Ava giggled. "Baseball, are you serious?"

"Pretty bad isn't it when we have to resort to watching baseball, but I think we could use a guy night. Beer and bonding. And there is no way I am going to leave you alone tonight."

As Evan slowly closed the door to the bedroom, he glanced back at Ava. Her beautiful eyes were closed, and her hair was draped over the pillow. She looked like she was at rest, but the light from outside, seeping through the curtains, highlighted tears under her lashes. *What could be wrong?* He knew Ava loved him. She knew he loved her. It was time for him to get some help.

He told Ava that he and Tom were going to watch baseball. A game might be playing in the background, beer might be in their hands, but they were going to be doing some serious talking and planning.

It might be time to ask Leif to look into the past and see what he could find. Evan didn't like snooping. People have a right to move forward and let the pasts remain in the past, but something was definitely wrong with Ava. He couldn't lose her. Perhaps he could help if he could find out what was bothering her.

Evan spoke the truth. He would love Ava no matter what.

"Are you sure?" Tom asked after Evan told him the plan. "No matter what she is hiding, you will still love her?"

Without a moment's hesitation, he said, "Yes. No matter what. But that doesn't mean I'm not afraid of finding out. But finding out can't be worse than the fear of what it could be that I'm making up in my head."

"You're lucky, Evan, to find someone with whom you want to be with in this lifetime. It's a gift, isn't it?"

"It is, even if some of this gift feels as it has a poison wrapper around it. I'm going to have to be careful as we do this. I don't want to let anything contaminate my love for Ava. And you and I know how doubt and suggestions can act like the worst poisons of all."

"That, we do," answered Tom. "Shall we call Leif, and maybe Craig, since they are together?"

"Good idea. Do you want to use the phone, the computer, or remote viewing?"

They both laughed. "Good thing no one can hear us, they'd probably think we were crazy."

Tom said, "There are other reasons why we don't want people to hear us, aren't there?"

Looking around, he asked, "They can't, can they?"

A long look passed between them.

"What about the new guys in town," they said to each other— but not out loud. "Yes, it's time to call Leif."

The answer as to which way to call was clear.

Twenty-Four

Ava didn't sleep. She knew she wouldn't. She was so tired she thought she would drop over from exhaustion. Still, she knew she wouldn't rest. She wasn't sure she would ever sleep again.

Instead, she forced herself to remember what happened.

She was right. Joe was easy. Tip Top billed itself as a modeling agency, but they didn't place models in magazines. They put them in bars and clubs. However, like any modeling agency, they needed pictures. But, they weren't head shots. They were full body topless photos.

Ava was outwardly okay with it; she needed the job. But inside she cringed thinking what her mom would say. Joe promised her that if she ever stopped working for him, he would destroy the pictures, so she let him take all the pictures he wanted.

He said that the best pictures would end up in his portfolio book, which he showed to bar owners and club managers. They would flip through, point to the women they wanted, and he would schedule the dancers.

And since it was dancing, he had to show her how to do it.

Ava almost laughed as she thought about that part. Joe was a small man in his early fifties. He looked like a successful businessman with his glasses. The fact that he had a big belly and was not graceful at all didn't stop him from prancing around the room, displaying the correct way to dance onto the stage, and the provocative way to eventually take off your bra.

Joe wanted to teach her how to strip entirely, claiming that some clubs would demand it. That was the line that Ava drew.

"No stripping," she said.

He said, "You aren't completely naked, there is always something covering you—it's an illusion."

Ava said that didn't matter. It was bad enough she had to take her top off and pretend to enjoy it.

Joe shrugged and appeared to let it go.

The next day, Ava told the bar manager she was quitting, but perhaps they would see her as she came around to do the noon-time dancing shift. The manager sneered and said that it would never happen while he was there. Ava didn't care. She was tired of crying before she went to work, trying not to cry while she was working, and sobbing herself to sleep every night.

She kept telling herself that she was happy to be on her own, that she didn't miss her mom, and that whatever she was doing to be free didn't matter. The irony of it wasn't lost on her; she just ignored it.

Joe's assistant called her the next day and gave her the schedule of where she had to be that week. Joe ignored her after that. He got what he wanted. He had his pictures. To the assistant, Ava was just another body to book.

The first time out, Ava was petrified.

But she did okay, or so the manager of the first club told her. She could still see the drooling men. She could still smell the disgusting scent of the bars she went to after that.

What made it bearable was that she was only there for an hour or two at a time. Usually someone who worked at the bar walked her to her car, especially if it was a night-time gig.

After a few weeks, Ava just felt numb. Once, driving down the freeway to a bar and passing under the graceful overpasses, she started crying, and asked herself how she could have possibly gotten herself into this situation. *Is this why I ran away?* Since there was no answer, she gathered herself together and drove on.

Ava discovered that she was always at risk of not having a job. After dancing at a club or bar, she was evaluated by the manager or owner, and they told Joe if they wanted her back again. Surprising to Ava, some places didn't want her to return because she wasn't sexy enough.

The Top Agency took that in stride and found her jobs in places that younger men went to and were close to colleges.

Her act was still only taking off her top and down to her bikini underpants, but she started going onstage in clothes that looked like any college girl. Once she had that act down, she had plenty of work.

Once in a while, she danced at night with other girls, like a show. Waiting to go on, they would sit together and tell stories. Ava was always the youngest one, even younger than they believed she was, so she didn't have any stories to share.

Instead, she listened. One thing she discovered was that most of the women not only danced because that was the only skill they believed they had, that and their looks, but because they hated men.

It didn't make any sense. All the women had boyfriends of a sort. One girl showed Ava the scar on her stomach which she said came from her boyfriend shooting her.

"What happened after that?" Ava asked. "Did he go to jail?"

"No," was the answer "He said he was sorry."

Ava didn't understand how one could hate men, dance to prove how disgusting they were, and still let them be part of their life. She didn't want to be like that. She wanted to like men. She wanted to dance just to earn enough money to move out into the world and do better.

And to prove that was what she wanted, she had been delighted when she ran into Rick again at the farmer's market and had said, "Yes" when he asked her out.

Yes, with reservations. Only lunch, until they got to know each other better. Rick agreed. Ava was sure that made him an understanding and kind man. After a while, lunch didn't work well since she was often working in the middle of the day and she got tired of lying to him why she couldn't.

There was no way Ava was going to tell him that she was taking her clothes off in bars and clubs. He was charming, well dressed, and would likely never go to someplace like that, so she wasn't worried about him walking in one day and seeing her.

Instead, she told him she taking some classes during the day, and he believed her.

Twenty-Five

It didn't take long for things to get serious with Rick. Ava was tired. Rick treated her well. He always paid when they went out to eat, and he was always careful about getting her home early for what she called her beauty sleep. He was so polite that Ava was beginning to worry that he might be gay because he never even tried to kiss her.

Ava got very good at telling stories. She made up a whole family that lived in Montana and a mother she called every weekend. Her parents gave her just enough money to get by while she was in school.

Rick would smile and nod, and Ava would then ask him to tell her about him. Which he did. Rick told her about his family and growing up in Iowa, and his mom who was still alive, and that he, too, talked to every weekend. When Ava asked him what he did for a living, he said he was a trader. What kind of trader? His answer was always evasive, so she never could get a handle on what kind of work he did.

She grew to like the way he looked. He said he was twenty-nine, and since she claimed to be eighteen, she convinced herself that eleven years wasn't that big of an age difference. He always dressed in sports coats, even on hot days, and he had loafers with tassels. Ava thought they had gone out of style years before, but he made them look classy.

If Ava stopped to think about it, she wasn't sure what she liked about Rick. His dimples and sleeked-back blond hair helped him stand out a bit in a crowd, and she had liked that. He didn't sound as if he was from Iowa. In fact, he didn't have any kind of accent at all. His brown eyes were neither cold nor warm. Later she would realize they were blank eyes, but at the time it didn't register.

Once, she had him pick her up at a dance class she had started going to. He didn't see her watching him as he walked from the car to the studio. She noticed that two of his teeth were just a bit longer than the rest. A little voice inside of her said, "Why are you dating a wolf?"

But he was there, picking her up, being charming to her and everyone at the studio, and whisking her off to a nice dinner, and she forgot.

One night, he surprised her by putting his arms around her and drawing her close for a kiss. Ava was so surprised, and to be honest also relieved that he found her attractive, she returned it. As she unlocked her door, he pushed his way in and pinned her against the wall.

And then he stopped, apologized, kissed her gently and left saying he would call the next day. Which he did.

As Ava lay in her bed thinking about her past and how Rick had seduced her by slowly reeling her in, she felt nauseous. Finally exhausted, she fell into a restless sleep, but not before thinking that it felt as if there was someone was in the room with her. *Impossible*, she thought as her eyes closed. *Impossible.*

****

Leif and Craig levitated in the air in Evan's living room. "Cut it out, guys," Tom said. "It still freaks me out to see that. At least pretend that you are sitting."

Leif and Craig laughed and lowered themselves to look as if they were sitting on the couch. Even though no couch cushions compressed, it made the whole scene appear more normal.

"Where's Ava?" Craig asked.

"Upstairs, hopefully sleeping."

"So the uneasy feeling we have all had around Ava is for real?" Craig asked.

"Yes. Something is going on. I've tried to talk to Ava about it, but she has shut me out and says nothing is bothering her. She knows that I can tell she's lying and she is doing it anyway.

"Plus, there is some new construction going on in town that brought in a new crew. Something doesn't feel right about that, either.

"Leif, I was wondering if you could do some of your stealth checking into the past. And Craig, since you're in the middle of building your center, perhaps you could check on the construction guys? All of this could all be a false alarm, but I don't think so."

"I don't think so, either," Tom added. "Something is bothering Ava, and something is swirling around that doesn't feel right. It's been a while since we have had direct problems with the Evil Ones, but it would be stupid to think they have decided to leave us alone."

"Okay, we'll do it, and of course I'll talk to Sarah and Mira about it, too," Leif said.

As sober as the discussion was, there was still joy in meeting together, and as they air hugged, they all laughed at how silly it looked and felt.

Just before leaving, Leif added, "One more thing. There is

someone else hanging around Ava. I catch a glimpse once in a while. But, they do a good job keeping out of sight. I can't even tell if it is a man or a woman. I'll keep a lookout. But I don't think they mean harm. However, it could have something to do with Ava's upset."

"Seriously? Oh, God, what could it possibly be?" Evan moaned as he sat down hard on a chair, his head buried in his hands. "I don't want to lose her. Please help."

More air hugs and promises that all would be well, and Craig and Leif were gone.

"It's time for us to head to bed, Evan. We won't be able to solve anything if we're too tired to think straight.

But, before we do, let's remember what we know to be true. Good fills all space.

"Everything else that is going on that is not good is an illusion of some kind, projected by fear and misunderstanding. When we clear that up, we will see the underlying principle of good has been there all along."

Evan heard Tom as if in a dream. It was just words, but he clung to them as a life raft. Tom was right. They needed to start with the power of good, and they both needed to rest. Plus, Ava was upstairs sleeping. He couldn't wait to snuggle into bed with her, where everything felt right as he held her in his arms.

Twenty-Six

The next morning, as he always did, Evan brought Ava her coffee in bed.

"Feeling better?" Evan asked as he handed her the cup.

Ava nodded yes and smiled. *She's good,* thought Evan. *Her smile almost reaches her eyes.* He pretended that it did, and sat down on the edge of the bed.

"Tom says he has some computer work to do, so we have the morning to ourselves. Do you want to go the nursery and get some flowers for your garden?"

Ava's heart almost burst open. Almost. Instead, it squeaked open long enough to feel what it would be like to be able to be fully present with someone. *Evan is beautiful, inside and out,* Ava thought. *Honest, full of integrity, and courage.* She didn't deserve him. And he didn't deserve to have a wife that lied to him either.

In that fleeting moment, Ava saw the possibility for their life, but it shut down almost before it began.

Both pretended that it didn't happen.

"Yes. I would love to get some flowers," Ava said with as much joy in her voice as she could find. "Let me take a quick shower, and I will be ready to go.'

Evan had a lovely blueberry-and-almond milk smoothie

waiting for her when she came down to breakfast. As he rinsed out the blender, he asked her if she wanted to drink it outside, or on the go.

Ava decided to cast all worries to the wind, at least for the morning. No letter, no past, just her future with Evan.

"Let's take it with us. I can't wait to get there!" Ava answered with genuine joy in her voice.

The nursery was perfect. Set near a stream with paths that wound between a wide variety of flowers, bushes, and trees, it was like walking through a world-famous garden, but one you could buy. They decided to start shopping in the section with all the plants native to the area. Ava wanted to plant a garden that attracted birds, bees, and butterflies, but didn't require much maintenance.

For Ava and Evan, the next few hours were bliss itself. They picked out plant after plant. They also selected trees that they would come back in the fall to get. A few months before, the nursery owner had told them that you should never plant or replant trees in months that didn't have an R in them. Since they were almost to the end of June, they had a few more glorious months to enjoy summer, and plan out where they wanted to plant the trees.

The nursery had a small, but lovely, coffee shop, with a generous selection of delicious scones and croissants. *Somebody must be reading my every wish,* Ava thought as she and Evan sat outside with their coffee and treats. Ava remembered what Sarah had told her about her trip to Paris and how much she had loved drinking cappuccinos and eating croissants.

She knew that if she told Evan she wanted to go to Paris, he would glow with the anticipation of planning the trip. But, at the moment, being at home with him was what she wanted most. Ava's vision of heaven was to be able to sit on the porch or deck in a comfortable chair reading a great book. And then to be able to glance up and watch the birds in the birdbath and the bees and butterflies enjoying the garden. Their new home was exactly the home she had always wanted.

Ava was doing an excellent job of staying in the moment, enjoying Evan and the nursery, and planning their garden, until a little girl, about eight years old, walked by and smiled at her.

She was beautiful. Her long brown hair bounced as she walked and hopped across the flagstones. Her bright blue eyes sparkled, and dimples appeared when she smiled.

Ava's heart stopped.

I am just pretending, Ava thought. *I can't keep this up. It's time for me to go.*

"Ava?" Evan asked. "Is everything all right? Do you feel okay?"

"I'm so sorry, Evan. My stomach is acting up again. This has been a beautiful and memorable morning. I could not have wished for a better time. Thank you for it. But, can we go? I think I probably just didn't get enough sleep last night."

"Of course," Evan answered keeping his voice as cheery and even as possible. *What just happened? Who was that little girl that smiled at her,* he wondered. *How could that make her upset? What could be going on with Ava and this child?*

While they were having coffee, Evan had asked one of the workers to load their plants into the back of the Toyota pickup truck that they had driven to the nursery. They had purchased the truck, along with multiple pieces of garden and yard equipment, when they first moved in.

Both of them were amazed at how many kinds of gear they needed to keep their garden and lawn happy. Having been nomads of a sort for most of their adult lives, they had no idea how much went into running a home in the country.

The truck was a great buy. Evan used it all the time to haul landscape timbers and plants to the house. Most of the time, Evan would send workmen to pick up the supplies in the larger trucks and trailers, but for visits like this, they wanted something to be able to haul home their treasures.

"Don't forget, we have to cover these plants," Ava teased. "Remember last week when you brought home that beautiful lilac bush, uncovered on the back of the truck, and all its leaves were stripped off in the wind?"

They both laughed as Evan said, "You won't ever let me forget that, will you?"

"Nope," Ava answered.

"I notice that it seems to be recovering though," Evan said. "I hear you outside talking to it every morning, telling it that it will be okay."

"I do! And it will probably be even better if you also apologize to it for your mistake."

"I promise. I'll do it as soon as we get home. After lunch, Tom wants to go hiking up Nittany Mountain and visit some of the small towns around here. Do you want to come?"

Ava pretended to ponder her answer. Instead, she knew it was the perfect time to do what she needed to do.

"Mind if I beg off this time?" She asked. "I need to do some writing and napping, and maybe even some reading while you are gone."

Evan smiled and assured her that it was okay, even though his heart told him that it wasn't.

When they got home, they both kept up the decision to have a glorious morning and pretend that there was not a cloud hanging over their life.

Once the plants were unloaded, they planted many of them and left the bigger ones placed in their pots where they wanted the gardeners to put them when they came the next day.

After they had watered everything well, Ava made a beautiful salad, and they sat outside on the deck eating it. Tom had gotten up much earlier and had his coffee, so he joined them for lunch.

"It's beautiful here," He sighed. *Yes,* they each thought, *it is.*

Twenty-Seven

Ava kissed Evan goodbye. Tom, too. The men were headed out for their walk. The afternoon was bright and clear, with soft white clouds slowly moving across the robin's-egg blue sky. A mid-summer wind rustled the leaves in the trees. Sprouts and stalks of all kinds waved from the vegetable garden, promising a long harvest of fresh vegetables.

Evan wore Ava's favorite blue and green plaid shirt. Tom kidded him about blending in with the mountain. Both Tom and Evan wore old broken-in hiking boots and pants. They each had fanny packs with a few snacks and a bottle of water tucked inside.

They also had light jackets wrapped around their waists. They knew that the mountain could cool down quickly and they wanted to be prepared.

"We are probably slightly over-prepared," Evan said, laughing.

"You think?" Tom replied. "But, preparation is the key to everything, isn't it?"

Yes, it is, thought Ava. She drank in the sight of both them. Had Evan given her an extra-long hug? Did he know? Was she ready?

Shaking away those thoughts, she gave Evan another kiss, and whispered, "I love you." In her mind, she added, *remember that I love you, but please forget me.*

Evan whispered back, "And I love you."

"Kids," said Tom. "Stop already; it's time to get going. By the time you two finish smooching and whispering, the sun will be going down."

Everyone laughed. Ava hugged Tom again, too. "Love you, too, big guy. Have fun today. See you at dinner! Maybe Thai food tonight?"

"Yes," both Tom and Evan answered in unison.

They both turned to wave at Ava as they got into the car. Evan thought again how lucky he was to have found her. Her long brown hair had come unclipped and was flying in the breeze. On her head was a baseball hat that said Penn State. They had picked it up when they visited a few weeks before. Even from a distance, he could see her blue eyes watching his every move.

Ava waved until the car was out of sight, and tried to burn every last memory of Evan into her brain because it was going to have to last her for a lifetime.

Gotta move fast, her internal voice told her, but she took her time to look at everything she loved about her life, the rolling hills, the beautiful house designed just as she had imagined. The birds were singing in the trees, and coming to all the feeders that she filled every morning.

Who would do it now, she thought. *Evan will, won't he?*

Tears rolled down her face. *I can't believe I am crying because I will miss my birds.*

She knew it wasn't that. It was everything. She would miss everything. She prayed that Evan would forgive her, and move on to be happy. She knew she wouldn't be.

Get going, her internal voice told her again. *You don't have all day!*

Back in the bedroom, Ava pulled out the suitcase she had started to pack before Tom came to visit. Thinking it through, she grabbed her backpack instead. It was important to take just what was needed, and nothing more.

She made sure that the letters were safely tucked away in one of the pockets of the bag. She didn't want to leave a single clue. She took her phone, but removed the chip. She would destroy it later. She knew Tom could hack into it if she kept it.

In the small room that she called her office, she found the cash that she had been accumulating all along. *Perhaps I knew I would have to run one day,* Ava thought. But, then she realized that she had always been afraid that Evan would leave her and she would be without anything. Old fears. And now she was leaving him.

Her mind wouldn't let her alone. Questions kept rolling through. *Would Evan be okay?* What could she say to him that would make him let go, and not look for her? It would be impossible to lie and say she didn't love him. She knew she did, and so did he.

Sitting down at her writing desk, Ava grabbed a plain piece of paper to write a note. Nothing but tears came. *Write something. I have to write something.*

"I am sorry, Evan. I have to go. Please don't look for me. Please find someone else and be happy. You deserve someone so much better than me."

It wouldn't stop him, she knew, but it might give her some time while he tried to reason through what was happening.

Ava folded the paper, placed it in a plain white envelope—no place for sentiment now—and took it into the bedroom. She put it under his pillow. He would sleep there and find it.

In the meantime, she hoped he would just think she had gone shopping.

Tom and Evan had taken the truck, so she would take the car and leave it someplace to the east, and then start hitchhiking. The other way. Going west.

Ava gazed longingly at the bedroom. She loved this room. Painted a soft gray, with a big king bed and a white comforter, it was probably her favorite place in the house. White curtains blew in the breeze, framing the view of the mountain where Tom and Evan were heading.

What was she forgetting?

A picture. She needed a picture. Ava kept a picture on her desk of Evan and her that Sarah had taken before they had all scattered to different parts of the country.

She lifted it and touched their faces, remembering how happy they all had been to find each other. She took it, and the picture of all of them together. Sarah, Leif, Ava, Evan, Tom, Mira, and Craig. The Stone Circle. She was going to break it. At least she could remember what it once was when it was whole.

Slinging the backpack over her shoulder, she headed down the stairs, almost tripping on the top step because she kept looking back. *This won't work,* she told herself. *I can't let myself regret leaving.*

Before heading out the door, Ava went into the kitchen to grab food bars and water.

The perfect kitchen, the perfect house, the perfect group of friends, the perfect man in her life—and she had messed it up so long ago. She was paying for her sins, but at least she could stop them from harming the ones she now loved.

As she opened the door of the house to leave, she turned to take a mental picture and then remembered the cameras. There were cameras that would show her leaving.

She ran back upstairs and went into Evan's office and turned them off. Then she destroyed the last thirty minutes of recording. Evan would check later, but at least he would not see what she had been doing.

Ava raced back downstairs. She had wasted enough time. She grabbed the backpack and almost tripped down the front porch stairs. *Be careful,* she admonished herself. Ava put the backpack on the front seat of the car and headed to town.

Moving so quickly, and so caught up in her fears and sorrow, Ava didn't notice that once again, someone was watching her. Someone who could follow her wherever she went.

She wanted to drive quickly, but knew that it would only draw attention to herself.

Weeks before she had noticed a place on the road that led to the highway where hunters parked during hunting season. She planned to pull off there and leave the car hidden behind some trees. If someone saw it, they would think the owner was out walking in the woods.

She had turned off the tracking system in the car. She had learned how to do that online and hoped that would keep Evan from finding the car right away.

Her plan was to walk north to the highway and thumb a ride west. Back to the past. Back to fix what was broken and start again.

An hour later on the mountain, Evan and Tom broke through to an open clearing and Evan's phone pinged. He paused to glance at it and then stopped so suddenly Tom almost bumped into him.

"Geez, man," he started to say and then noticed Evan's face. "What's wrong?"

"The cameras are off at the house, and Ava's find-a-friend app is not working on her phone."

Neither of them waited a moment. They both turned and started jogging back to where they had started. Both wondered what had happened.

Had someone taken her?

Evan was afraid of something even more frightening. What if she left because she wanted to, what if she didn't really love him?

Impossible, his heart told him, but he ran even faster. Tom kept up. Both hearts pounding. Both ready to do whatever it took to make sure that everyone in their Circle was safe, beginning with Ava.

Twenty-Eight

Later on, Evan would wonder how they got down the mountain so quickly. What had taken them two hours to ascend took only an hour to get down. Roots tried to trip them, tree branches swung back into their faces, and mosquitoes decided that a moving target was better than a still one.

At one point Tom paused to catch his breath and wondered if they were overreacting. Looking at Evan's face, he decided that it didn't matter. His friend was in full-blown rescue mode—or perhaps panic mode—and he would support him no matter what. Eventually, they reached the car, and exceeding the speed limit on the way back to the house pulled up to the house with a screech.

"The car's gone, Evan!" Tom shouted. "Maybe Ava just went shopping?"

Evan didn't stop to answer. He just threw open the door and ran into the house. Nothing was disturbed. It was calm and peaceful. *Maybe I am overreacting.* Not stopping to take off his boots, sweat dripping down his face, he ran from room to room.

Nothing looked out of place. The coffee pot was still on, waiting for the next person. The dishes had been washed, and fresh flowers were arranged on the table.

He raced upstairs, looked into both of their offices and saw that nothing was disturbed. In the bedroom, the bed was made, the windows were letting in the fresh breeze, and Ava's toothbrush was in the medicine cabinet in the bathroom.

Sighing heavily, he clunked back downstairs where Tom was waiting for him with a cup of coffee at the dining room table.

"Are you okay?" Tom asked.

"No. But I can't see anything wrong. You may be right; maybe Ava just went shopping."

"You don't think so though, do you?"

Evan shook his head.

"I need to check the camera; perhaps it will tell me something."

Tom and Evan carried their coffees upstairs to Evan's office. Tom sat by the desk while Evan's fingers danced over the keyboard. The longer he fiddled, the darker his expression grew.

Finally, sitting back and pushing the chair away from the desk, he said, "The cameras were turned off, and I'm missing the last few hours of recording. Ava's phone is off, and the satellite system on the car is turned off. Go ahead, try and tell me that this is all a coincidence and there is nothing wrong."

"I can't. But, who did it? Did Ava do it? Did she leave a note? It doesn't look as if there was a struggle, so she must have gone willingly—either by herself or with someone else."

"A note? I didn't see one, but I wasn't looking for that."

Both men jumped up and once again searched the house.

Not finding anything, Tom met Evan back in Ava's office staring at her desk. Something was different, but what was it? Pictures—she had taken the pictures.

Turning to Tom, with tears running down his face, Evan said, "She took photos. She left because she wanted to, she is gone."

****

"Look, Evan, even if she left on her own, she didn't leave willingly. You know something has been wrong the last few weeks. We've all felt it. That's why Sarah asked me to come here.

You know that Ava loves you. Everyone knows it. From the moment you two set eyes on each other, it was evident. It was, and is, a shining example of love transcending time and space. It was two souls meeting again. No matter what this looks like, it is not what Ava wants."

"So, you're saying that Ava is in trouble, aren't you?"

"I am. But we will find Ava and make it right, I promise."

Evan looked into Tom's eyes and saw his passion for proving what he was saying, and he believed him.

"Okay. So what do we do?"

Tom slapped Evan on the back, "Yes, that's the spirit," he said.

"The Circles are the answer. We all have contacts. We will find Ava. We will make this right together. First things first. Everyone needs to know. Conference call, this time," Tom added in a whisper, "If someone is watching they will expect this, we don't want to give them someone out of the ordinary."

"You mean we will keep that part out of sight?"

"That's exactly what I mean," answered Tom as he texted the message to meet to everyone on the conference line they used. He headed into his bedroom and grabbed his computer. Then he went back downstairs and placed it on the kitchen island. By the time he got logged on, everyone was already there.

Sarah spoke first. "You don't need to tell us, Evan. We know there is something wrong around Ava. What happened?"

Evan tried to speak. Failing, he glanced at Tom, and Tom

took over. He explained exactly what they knew and then paused.

Nobody spoke.

"Is it them?" Mira asked. "Have they done something to scare her?"

"I think we can count on that being the case, but what was it? Actually, I don't care what it was; I just want to find her, bring her back, and keep her safe forever," Evan said.

Leif spoke up. "We will, Evan. We will find her. We have many resources, and I will make sure that everyone is working towards this end. However, are we sure this isn't just a distraction?"

"Distraction from what?" Evan said, more forcefully than he meant to. "Even if it is, it doesn't change the fact Ava is gone. To me, everything else pales in comparison."

"We understand, Evan. We do. But, what you just said makes me think it is a distraction, because if we are not aware and careful, there may be something else in the works. It doesn't mean we won't find her, though. We will put all our effort into it. It just means we can't be naive about it."

"I apologize," Evan said, still looking as if his world had shattered into a million pieces.

"No need," Leif responded. "If it were Sarah missing, I would be feeling the same way. But then, you all would be here to help, and that's the point. We are. We will."

On camera, Sarah glanced at Mira who nodded back.

"Mira and I have agreed on something, but just in case someone is listening, we will tell you about it later."

Someone is listening. Hank thought. He had watched Ava pull away, and watched the tracker he had put on her car head north. She would be easy to follow. The call to the Stone Circle didn't surprise him.

They reacted just as he wanted them to. Except, they thought about a distraction. They were even smarter than he thought. He needed to be much more careful. *And what was Sarah talking about?* More eyes and ears were needed. He would take care of it.

****

The next morning, Evan poured another cup of coffee. "Who's that for," Tom asked.

"Ava. No matter where she is, I am still ready to bring her her first cup of coffee for the day."

"We'll find her Evan," Tom said reaching out to touch Evan on the shoulder—a small comfort to try and ease an enormous hurt.

Both men were outside on the deck, watching the sun come up. Evan had been there all night, wrapped in a blanket. He couldn't bring himself to get into their bed without Ava being there.

"There are so many terrible things about what's happening," Evan said. "But the worst thing is, I can't feel her. I have her in my heart, but I can't feel her. Which means she has left me completely. Maybe I'm a fool; maybe she never loved me. Perhaps all of this has been some kind of joke to her."

"You can't believe that, Evan. For some reason, she thinks this is best for you. For all of us. When we find her, all will be well. When—not if."

Evan looked at Tom. Wanting to believe him, knowing it was probably a lie. His life was over. Ava was gone.

Twenty-Nine

Mira and Sarah swiveled their chairs away from the computer and looked at each other. They had spent a lovely day with Grace. First lunch, then a walk through all the stores picking up pieces of art to admire, looking at dresses and tops, enjoying every moment of window-shopping.

They never lost sight of the man who watched them, even though during the afternoon he switched with another man. But they didn't let it distract them from having a delightful girl time afternoon. They would often disappear into a dressing room to try on something and whisper about what they wanted to say without anyone hearing.

By the time the day was over, all three were exhausted. Mira and Sarah hugged and kissed Grace goodbye and headed up the mountain towards home. Grace stayed behind. She said she had something to do before she, too, would go home for the evening.

Once again, she reminded them, that she might look old, but she was young at heart and certainly ready for an adventure should they have one for her.

"Do you think that this is the kind of adventure Grace meant—and is ready to take?" Mira asked.

"We certainly would be asking a lot of her. Not only would she move to some place she has never been before, but we would also be putting her in danger."

"We would. Let's get some rest, and do some quiet thinking about this, and decide whether or not to ask her after that."

"I'm heading for a long bubble bath," Mira said. "It's always a great place to think."

Sarah remained behind at the computer. She would need more assistance to pull this off if they were going to ask Grace to help. Pulling out her burner phone, she grabbed a hat, and stepped into the yard and made a phone call.

The lounge chair that was still in the sun called her. Sinking into it, she pulled the cap over her face to keep the sun off and let herself drift off into sleep. As she lifted out of her body, she saw Suzanne step out from the woods.

They air hugged. Not having a material body was freeing, but hugging was difficult. But the habit was ingrained, and they loved the custom, so they still tried.

"We heard," Suzanne said. "That was a wise call to make. We'll take care of what we can, but now that we are a Circle elsewhere, we have to be there, too. However, we are talking about Ava and Evan, so whatever you need, we will be there."

"How can I be sure I'm doing the right thing?" Sarah asked.

"You can't be sure, my dear," Suzanne answered. "But you have to move forward with the best choice you have at any moment. Don't forget that everything will work out for good, when you love good, act from good, and base all your intents on your highest understanding of good in every moment.

"Even if you make a mistake, it will still take you down the path of a right outcome. We trust your heart, Sarah. You and Leif were chosen because of who you both are, and what you have learned over so many lifetimes. This problem is just another one to solve and gain more wisdom from. Keep trusting your heart, it always knows."

"And good always dissolves the darkness," Sarah heard as she began to wake up. She could feel her spirit settle back into her body. Inside the house, the phone was ringing. Sarah heard Mira pick it up, say "hello," and then call out to Sarah; "It's for you."

"It's Grace," Mira said. "She wants us to put her on speakerphone."

Mira and Sarah exchanged a look as Sarah stepped up to the phone. They had kept a land line in the kitchen in the case of an emergency. Long ago, Sarah had given Grace the number. She had never called before. Was this an emergency?

"Hi, Grace," Sarah said. "What's up?"

"Well, I think that is probably a question that I could ask you. I know you two are up to something. And I want to be involved. Please. I'm bored. I used to be able to travel and do exciting things, and now I'm just an old busybody.

"Speaking of being a busybody, no one knew either of those two men that were following you around town. However, a friend of mine told me they had both rented one of her apartments that she rents out through Airbnb. I texted the info about her place to you, Sarah. I figured you would know what to do with it from there.

"Don't worry. I obtained this information by just being an old lady catching up with other old ladies."

"Thank you, Grace. I am delighted you took precautions, and yes, I will send this information on to people who know how to use it, but Mira and I know there is more than this on your mind, right?"

"Yes. I wanted you to know that I have listed my home to rent. I can get lots of money renting to tourists, you know. I have placed all my private stuff in storage, and I have packed my suitcases. I have told all my friends—the gossipy ones—so everyone will know that I am heading to California to see some relatives. Now, where do you really want me to go?"

Sarah and Mira looked at each other and burst out laughing. "Seriously, Grace. You are an inspiration," said Mira. "I want to grow up and be just like you."

"Well, if that's true, Mira, maybe we should arrange it so you can hang out more with Grace." Sarah laughed.

"And, Grace, since you seemed to have taken care of every contingency, and already know we were debating about sending you somewhere, you best get going.

"Your first stop is here. We have a guest room, and there are some things you need to know. I'll send a taxi to pick you up."

"Do you think that is wise, dear? Someone could track the taxi and know that I stopped off there."

"Okay, now you're freaking me out," Mira said. "Did you used to be a spy or something?"

"Would I tell you if I had been?" Grace answered.

"No need to worry, Grace, it's not a 'real' taxi," Sarah said.

"And since you called us on the home line, I think you already knew that we have lines tested and our house swept every day. So, bring your wise old lady self here, and let's get going on the adventure. Can you be ready in fifteen minutes?"

"Born ready," answered Grace and hung up.

"Well," Sarah said. "I do believe we have our answer. Let's make some garlic pasta for dinner, and get ready for our guest. We have a lot of planning to do."

Thirty

Ava made it to the first destination without any trouble. The car was parked and partially hidden. Evan would eventually find it, but not before she was long gone. The walk to the highway would take her about an hour because she wanted to stay off the road. Picking her way through the woods on the side of the road would not be easy, but it was necessary.

Less than an hour had passed since she had left home, so she wasn't worried about anyone looking for her yet. Still, she was a little concerned about having to walk across the overpass out in the open.

Ava had chosen to wear what everyone seems to wear so she wouldn't stand out: jeans, T-shirt, and a jacket wrapped around her waist. Her hair was tucked up inside her hat which was pulled low over her forehead. Sunglasses and a backpack completed her outfit. She wanted to look acceptable, but not too good. It was a tricky balance, but she had learned how to walk that tightrope while working the bar circuit.

Once Ava's walking rhythm settled in, she let her thoughts drift back. She had tried to forget all about that time for the past nine years; now she knew she needed to revisit it all to get herself ready to do what she needed to do.

Rick's first kiss primed the pump. Now, looking back, Ava knew that Rick was a master of the slow seduction, and he used it to his advantage. At the time it just seemed romantic. He would wake her up in the middle of the night and dance with her on the bed. He would bring her roses and wildflowers.

He brought her gifts that over time felt more like bribes because once started, Rick didn't stop. He wanted sex all the time. Ava learned that it was easier to go along with it than to try and say no when she didn't feel like it. That soon became constant. She saw too much of the ugly side of his sexual desires, and it was hard to let go of those pictures in her head.

Rick came in three flavors. The seductive Rick came first: flowers, food, dancing together. Next was Rick, the sex addict. Always craving it and assuming that Ava would always be ready for him.

And then there was the absent Rick.

Where he went when they weren't together, Ava never knew. No matter what she asked him about his work, he would brush off the question with a laugh or a distraction. Of course, Ava didn't tell him about her work, either, but then, he had stopped asking. He was getting what he wanted.

It was good for a time, though. Rick had moved Ava into a nicer apartment. He didn't like the ugly one she had been renting. Once Rick was paying the rent, she started saving money, tucking it away where she could get to it, but where no one else could find it.

At that memory, Ava stopped to get her breath and laugh. So, here she was, running again on stashed away money. The first time was running away from home. And then there was Rick. And now there was Evan. Would she ever learn?

The overpass loomed in the distance. She would need all her senses to make it across. It was time to focus on the present.

There would be time later to think about what happened next.

******

Hank had chosen him well. The truck was clean, and so was the driver. Pete had stopped at the Snowshoe, Pennsylvania, exit to get food at the diner and clean himself up. On the way out, he bought one of those things that make vehicles smell good. Hank had told him to be on his best behavior, and he planned to be.

His wife was sick, and they needed the extra money for her treatments. The kids were grown and not making enough money to help. He and his wife were on their own, and they were going down fast.

And then, a week before, he met Hank at a coffee shop. They were both sitting at the counter, getting a quick breakfast, if you could call two eggs, toast, bacon and a muffin a quick breakfast. They had ordered the same thing and laughed about it.

"Better introduce myself," said Hank, "Seeing as how we eat the same breakfast."

"Hank," he said extending his hand.

"Pete," was the answer.

They both laughed again. "Same breakfast, only first names, what else do we have in common?" Pete asked.

"Well," Hank answered, "I drive a truck, It's over there," gesturing to the parking lot where a rusty red Toyota was parked in the shade, "and I work in construction."

"Okay," said Pete. "I drive a big truck, and it's over there," gesturing to a big gleaming truck sitting out in the sun, "I'm a long-haul driver."

"Seriously? I always wanted to do that. Where do your trips take you?"

"Across the country. I take Interstate Eighty all the way from the east to the west. It depends on where my load needs to be picked up and where it needs to go."

"Work been good?" Hank asked.

"It's okay. Used to travel all the time, but now that my ole lady is sick, I have to take fewer trips. Makes life hard now that I need extra money at the same time—I'm needed at home. Been married for forty years, I'm not about to leave her alone now. Made her wait for me to come back from the roads for too many years already. I need to slow down."

"Sorry, man. That's rough."

Neither of them spoke for awhile. Each apparently buried in their thoughts and occupied with eating.

Once the waitress cleared the plates away and poured them each another cup of coffee, Hank spoke again.

"Might have a job for you that would pay some big bucks. You can do it along with your regular load, and still make this extra money."

"I am tempted, Hank, but I don't know you, and there is no way I am going to get in trouble doing something illegal. As I said, I am not doing anything that would harm me or my wife, or anyone for that matter. Been living clean all my life, not going to change now."

"Hey, I understand," Hank said. "Nobody wants to make a pact with the devil for any reason. Trust me, I know. No. This one is safe and clean, and it will be doing someone a big favor. The only issue is that no one can know that you're doing it, including the person you are going to help out. Actually, her especially."

"Her?"

"Yep. My boss has a daughter that has decided to hitchhike across the country. He doesn't want to stop her, probably couldn't anyway. But he wants her to be safe. All you have to do is pick her up, as if it was a random pickup, and drive her safely to Los Angeles."

"That's it?"

"That's it. My boss is a bit paranoid, so without her knowledge, he's placed a tracker in her backpack, so he will know where she is going at all times. He's not going to interfere; he just wants to make sure she is safe. I bet if you have kids, you understand."

Pete sighed. "I do. I would probably do the same thing if I were smart enough. "

"So it's a yes?"

"It is. When will this happen? I have a load that needs to go out as soon as possible. Would that work?

"It's perfect timing," said Hank.

Of course, it is, Hank thought to himself after Pete had headed home.

This plan was even easier than I expected it would be. Pete is perfect for this. He is a good man so Ava wouldn't get any hits of evil or bad things happening from him at all. She might even tell Pete things that I want to know. Because of course, I already wired Pete's truck for sound. Can't be too careful.

A week later, Pete walked out to his truck after eating lunch and waited for Hank's call. Hank had paid him half the money he promised him. He had turned it over to his wife after assuring her that it was money he had saved for just such an emergency. This trip for Hank had to be his last trip for a while. Once she got better, he could go back on the road. Or maybe he'd sell the truck and stay home.

Pete's phone beeped. "It's time," the text said.

The pickup was going to be tricky. They both had to hope that Ava did not get picked up by anyone before he just happened to pass her on the highway.

Pete thought that there was no reason anyone should be walking on the road's shoulder, let alone a young woman. He wanted to help.

He wanted to be the one who got her where she wanted to go, safely. If for some reason, he missed her, Pete would track the vehicle that picked her up and follow it until he could get her in his truck.

When Pete's kids were young, they would travel with him. It had been a long time since he had company on his trips. Traveling with someone was going to be a pleasure.

Passing the overpass he spotted her, jeans, T-shirt, hat, sunglasses, backpack; had to be her. *How many girls could there be dressed like that walking on the highway shoulder? Bet she didn't know it was illegal.*

He slowed down and pulled ahead of her, flashers on. She stared at the truck, so he honked and stuck his arm out of the window and waved at her.

She smiled and started trotting towards the open door. *A lovely smile,* Pete thought.

What a nice man, Ava thought as she hopped up into the truck and stuck out her hand to introduce herself.

"Ava," she said.

"Pete," he responded.

"Where are you heading, Pete?" Ava asked.

"Los Angeles," Pete replied.

Ava's breath caught in her throat. *Could things be looking up?*

"Would you take me there?" She said. "I won't be any trouble at all, and I have some cash I can use to help pay my way."

"No trouble at all," Pete replied. "I could use the company; it's lonely on the road."

Ava smiled again and settled down into her seat. She would rather be home with Evan, but this was turning out to be much nicer, and much easier than she thought it would be.

Thirty-One

Sarah and Mira watched Grace disembark from the taxi.

"It's like having Mary Poppins show up at our door," Sarah said.

"All she needs is an umbrella," answered Mira.

Grace was right. If you didn't know her, she would be invisible: short and stocky, steel-gray hair, glasses that were sometimes perched on the end of her nose, other times dangling on a chain around her neck. Sneakers and a ruffled blouse tucked into a long skirt completed the look.

Now that they both knew Grace a bit better, it seemed more like a costume. It was a good one for a busybody, though.

As Sarah paid the taxi, Mira picked up Grace's battered suitcase.

"This is all you're traveling with?" Mira asked.

"Told you, I am a wanderer. If I were younger, I would just carry a backpack. But, yes. That's it. I'll pick up whatever else I need wherever you're sending me," answered Grace.

"Hope you're hungry, Grace. We've whipped up a nice meal, and we can talk and eat at the same time," Mira said as she deposited Grace's suitcase in the guest room.

It reminded Mira of arriving at Leif and Sarah's home the

year before. Bewildered, scared, and timid. Now, she was part of something larger and more important than just her by herself. Perhaps all those fearful qualities are still present, maybe they will never leave, but they now take a backseat to the rest of her life.

Sarah popped her head in the doorway of the guest room to point out to Grace that she had her own bathroom. She could freshen up and then meet them in the kitchen to have some dinner.

"No need, dear, I'm too hungry. Let's eat and talk," Grace said.

During dinner, Sarah and Mira explained that Ava had gone missing. More accurately, she was running away from something. Without going into details, they said they had some enemies that may be responsible, and if not responsible for Ava's disappearance, they were certainly going to try and cause trouble elsewhere.

Would Grace mind moving to Doveland, Pennsylvania and keeping an eye on the local scene for them?

Grace clapped her hands in excitement. "That sounds lovely! New town, intrigue, save my friends. I'm all for that. When do I leave, and where do I stay?"

"I've made arrangements with a friend of mine. You're going to be introduced as his mother's friend. You're coming to visit him in his new home, to see if you want to live there. He will pick you up at the airport. You two can make up a back story when you get there—just let the rest of us know what it is," Sarah said.

"Mira will go with you to the airport in the morning. She is returning home for a bit, but will also be going to Doveland later. If all goes well, Leif and I will be there in August for Evan and Ava's wedding. That is, if we can find the bride first."

"We will," Mira said. "Think of all the people helping us, like Grace!"

******

Before leaving the next morning, the three of them took their coffees outside so they could watch the sunrise.

"Are you going to tell me more about the person—man—that I am going to be visiting when I get to Doveland?" Grace asked.

"I have been debating this for a while," Sarah responded. If I tell you the whole story, it might not be good for you to know."

Grace started to interrupt, and Sarah held up her hand to stop her. "I know, I know, you are trustworthy, capable, kind, and wise, but for now, would you just trust me that it is best this way, if I only give you the basic facts?"

Grace nodded, and Mira said, "Grace, I have a feeling that even I don't know the whole story at this point. But I trust that Sarah and Leif are doing it this way for a good reason. All the same, Sarah, what the heck is the name of the man whom she is going to stay with, and what does he do?"

Sarah laughed. "Of course, I'm going to tell you his name. He is working as a waiter in a place called the Diner—very original name isn't it—and his name is Andy Weir. I met him a little while ago when he came to visit his sister here in Sandpoint."

Mira looked at Sarah suspiciously. "Are you trying to tell me that it is just a coincidence that you met a man, who is the son of a friend of yours who lives in Sandpoint, and then he ends up in the same town as Ava and Evan. Really?"

Sarah laughed. "For now, yes, that is what I am telling you, not *trying* to tell you."

Grace and Mira exchanged looks.

"Yes, Grace." Mira said, "We're just going to have to go along with this for now. And now, we'd best get ready to go. The taxi will pick us up in just a few minutes."

"Are you sure we should be seen together?" Grace asked.

This time it was Mira and Sarah who exchanged looks and laughed.

"I guess that means that we won't be seen together?" Grace said.

"Yes, that's what it means. But I appreciate that you are always going to be asking these questions. Your perspective on what is happening is invaluable. And it's one reason why I am not telling you all the details. I don't want to influence what you are seeing or saying.

"Before I forget, here is a new burner phone for each of you. My current burner phone number is in there. Plus, I got you each a bug-and-hidden-camera detector. Please use it at least once a day."

"Spy stuff, fantastic!" Grace said, stuffing both into her purse.

"Mira, wait a sec, will you?" Sarah said, pulling her to the side.

"Are you practicing both your remote viewing and your remote viewing blocking every day?"

"Of course I am," she answered with a snap. Noticing Sarah's face said, "I'm sorry, I know you just want everyone to be safe."

Sarah nodded and walked them both out to the taxi, hugged them goodbye, and, as she always did, waved at the trees before going inside and quietly shutting the door.

Now, for some serious work, she thought. And thank you, God, for keeping them safe and for our awareness of your presence.

Thirty-Two

Grant screamed as he slammed his fist on the table. "Goddamn it. How many times do I have to tell you these people are dangerous to us! They know things. They can go anywhere with that blasted remote viewing. And since none of you cretins know how to do it or block it, they could be anywhere. They could be here right now, and none of us would know it!

"They could stop all the so-called illegal activity we have going on around the world. Let me remind you that your business and my business is on the line. We can easily distract the public; but we can't distract them. They can see what we are doing!"

Grant turned his glare towards Hank. "And now, Hank, you tell me that you can't find that girl? How could she have slipped away from you?"

In the basement of Grant's house soundproofed and swept for hidden bugs and cameras twice a day, his board of directors sat around a long rectangular table with Grant at the head.

This was where his inner circle came when they wanted to be private and alone. They called it a poker game. Grant's long-suffering, bowed-down wife would have prepared snacks for them, and then, without having to be reminded, she would leave the house.

Once in a while, Grant gave her enough thought to sometimes wonder what she did when she wasn't home. But he monitored all her money and charge cards, and as long as she kept spending, he figured she was happy.

He had long ago forgotten why he married her. It never occurred to him that she might be feeling the same. Women were to be used, passed over, kept down, and appreciated for keeping house and having sex. Not that he had sex with her anymore. She had gotten old and a bit dumpy. He could always have anyone he wanted. He didn't have to worry that he was old and becoming fat. Power speaks, and that is what he had. He could have anything he wanted, and he wanted a lot.

Right now he wanted to know why Hank was not following orders. He turned his full attention to Hank's face projected on a huge screen on the wall of the basement.

If looks could kill, Hank would be dead. Lucky for Hank, he was too far away to get to at the moment, and he needed him—for now.

"To answer your question, yes, we lost her. She made it the entire way to Los Angeles with the driver. Once she got there she must have found the tracker, or just got lucky, and switched her bag. Yes, there are cameras everywhere, but she is obviously doing a good job of hiding her face.

"So, she has been trained well in not being found. But she is probably not hiding from us, since she doesn't know we are involved. She is hiding from Evan and her friends. She doesn't want to drag them into her problem. Anyway, that's what I gathered from the little bit she shared with Pete as they drove across the county. She was pretty quiet."

What Hank wasn't telling was that he had learned more than that from listening in on Ava's conversation with Pete. It had both disturbed him and made him curious. Hank was beginning to hate Grant almost more than he hated and distrusted everyone else, so he was only going to tell him enough to appease him.

There was something about Ava that was bothering him. Perhaps he had been watching her for too long. It meant he was getting to know her as a person, something he avoided at all cost his whole adult life.

Grant was still screaming. "Find her! She is the key to making this work. You know where she is eventually going to end up. Wait for her there."

"Yes, boss," Hank said. He touched the button on his phone to hang up.

On the side of the room, Suzanne and Jerry looked at each other. They were still lucky that no one in Grant's group could detect them. What they had heard troubled them. They couldn't find Ava, either. As soon as she had stepped into the truck, she had blocked all of them from looking for her remotely.

They were going to have to follow Hank since he knew where she was going. They hoped that she would be safe in the meantime, because she was now officially on her own.

****

Ava stared at herself in the bathroom mirror. She didn't think she looked as tired as she felt. She had not slept well the night before. Pete had dropped her near Hollywood the previous afternoon, and she had spent the rest of the day looking for a place to sleep and to get ready for today.

The trip across country was so much easier than she imagined it was going to be. Pete was kind and helpful. He said she reminded him of his daughter, whom he missed terribly. She slept most of the trip knowing that Pete was looking out for her.

She surprised herself by telling him things about her life. She told him about running away from home when she was sixteen. She told him that she had returned home at eighteen to discover that her mom was sick, and that she died a few years later.

She told him that she was taken in by her mom's friend, and how kind she and her father had been to her.

Pete listened and never judged her. At times she was tempted to tell him the whole story so she could share her burden with someone else. But when she realized that it would be passing her burden onto him, she stopped herself. He never learned the truth or even the names of those she loved the most.

He did make her promise to call him if she ever needed his help. She fingered the card he had given her with his number scribbled on it. Instead of throwing it out, she had kept it. In some small way, it offered hope that she would be able to get herself out of the mess she was in and perhaps call Pete and thank him.

She knew he had gone out of his way to deliver her into Hollywood. Well, not completely, He had to drop her off near a freeway ramp. As he pulled away, she tried to hide her tears by waving madly in his direction.

The first thing she had done was find a place to get a cheap bag and exchange it for her backpack. It wouldn't look so out of place. And cut her hair. A pixie cut, like the one she had in her teens, replaced her long brown hair. She tossed every strand of it in the trash outside of a grocery store.

Now, as she stared into the bathroom mirror in a Denny's where she had treated herself to a good breakfast after spending the night in a park, Ava wondered if she liked the look. She appeared different, and that was the point. Even so, she did her best not ever to look up, knowing there were cameras everywhere.

Ava figured she had a few days to do what she had to do before her friends found where she was and came after her. She needed to be long gone before then.

Tears started again, but she stopped them immediately. If she loved her friends as much as she said she did, she couldn't let them find her and get involved.

Ava finished washing her hands, patted her eyes with a paper towel, and went out to eat her breakfast. As she ate, she reread the letters for the millionth time. Ava had a plan in place. She hoped it would work.

Thirty-Three

The dishes had been cleared away and Ava was left alone with her coffee. It was hard not to think about Evan and his promise to always bring her the first coffee of the day.

For a moment she allowed herself to think of him and her friends. But only for a moment because she knew it would bring down the shields she had up to keep her friends from finding her. Plus, her heart would break even further.

In spite of the shield, she sometimes still had a feeling that someone was watching her. Looking around, she saw nothing. Hidden deep in a booth she was alone, remembering what happened with Rick.

For the first few months, life with Rick was okay. Ava had gotten used to okay, otherwise she would have ended the relationship. But Rick was a master at keeping her dangling on a hook: ignoring her one day, seducing her the next. He paid the rent and brought her gifts, but only when he wanted something. Her time, her body.

In the meantime, she continued to work the clubs. The small pleasure of not being touched and or working for only a few hours for a full day's wage had begun to wear off, but not enough to make her look for another job.

The freedom she had craved was not the freedom she had found. Ava had heard once that when someone got free from something, they needed to make sure that something better was already in place. Otherwise, another form of prison, or lack of freedom, would rush in to take its place. That had surely happened to her.

Ava had never told Rick what kind of work she did. He never asked. Which was weird. But since it meant she didn't have to lie, she didn't stop to think about what that might mean.

However, one day, her car wouldn't start, and she had to have it towed to a garage. She was working in Riverside that night, so taking a taxi was going to be a ridiculous expense.

When Rick offered to take her to work, she agreed, as long as he just dropped her off. She told him she was a waitress at a club and if he were there, it would distract her. He opened the door for her and said he would come back for her a few hours later.

She asked him to wait for her in the parking lot after work instead of coming in, and she headed into the club. She always went on stage wearing her street clothes. She had discovered that because of her youthful looks, no one bought her sultry act. Instead, they liked the surprise of having a "regular" girl take off her clothes.

As Ava waited for her music, she thought about what her agent Joe had told her she needed to do if she wanted to keep working. "No way," she'd said. No way was she stripping to nude, and no way was she getting silicone injections. No way at all.

The music began, and Ava began her routine. One piece of clothing at a time, smiling outside, cold and disgusted inside. As she took off her bra, Ava turned and saw Rick leaning against the bar watching. Only long practice with not being distracted kept her dancing as if nothing had happened.

What does he think? Ava wondered. In a way, she was relieved. *Maybe he will take me away from all this. Maybe he will say how sorry he is that I have to do such a degrading thing and help me find another job.*

After her set was over, she went out the back door as always and found Rick waiting for her beside his car.

"That was fantastic, Ava. I never knew you had it in you," Rick said.

Ava smiled as if that was the response she wanted. Inside, her heart had stopped. What had become of her? How was she ever going to get out of both these situations she had trapped herself within? *Maybe it is time to go home,* thought Ava.

But unknown to her at the time, worse things were coming.

She let Rick keep on thinking that all was well between them, as she planned out what to do next. The problem was, she hadn't been feeling well at all. More than once, Ava had to cancel a noon gig, because of her illness.

Lying in bed one morning, she heard the voice within that she had been ignoring for so long. It told her that she had to quit. There were other jobs.

Once Ava started feeling better, she began looking for those other jobs. Dancing wasn't her only skill. She was good at talking to people. Could she get a job helping people?

Finally, she saw a job listing for someone to assist the owner of a company that helped people get work. It was only a few miles from the apartment.

Ironic, she had thought, *but good. Maybe I can keep some other girl from getting sucked into a situation like this.* Plus, she could ride her bike to work. Her car was on its last legs, and she didn't want to put any more money into it. She was still saving money, still thinking that maybe she could go home, but she was not quite ready to go.

Nine years later, Ava still remembered her last dance at a club. Right before going onstage, the manager had told her that Joe, her agent, had said she would strip.

"I will not," Ava said. "I never said I would."

The manager leered at her, "You have to." He softened somewhat seeing her distress. "Maybe, you could do some kind of scarf dance so people don't know you haven't completely stripped. Go to the store across the street and get some scarves."

What could be more humiliating? Ava thought as she trudged across the hot parking lot to do as he had suggested.

The dance was a blur, probably because her eyes were clouded with tears. Ava had found some long pink flimsy scarves and tied some of them together around her waist, and used others as props while she danced. She never learned what anyone thought of it. She had immediately left the club and gone straight to the Tip Top Agency and told Joe she quit.

He laughed. "No one ever quits this business," he said.

"Watch me," Ava said.

She started her new job the next day, thinking that the worst part of her life was over. It was not even close.

Thirty-Four

Hank watched the new waitress as she filled all their coffee cups and took their breakfast orders. There was something off, but he couldn't figure out what. Just an old lady they had hired to help Andy at the Diner? Still, he was wary. Trying to shake off the feeling, he realized he was always wary. When wasn't he?

Never.

Well, maybe, he hadn't been wary when he played with Abbie. Sometimes she would squeeze him so hard it felt as if her heart had surrounded him. He loved those hugs. He missed those hugs. Sometimes he wondered what had happened to her, but it wasn't something he allowed to stay on his mind. It made him soft. He couldn't be soft. He had to remain a badass, both inside and out.

Still, who is that lady pouring coffee? Maybe her manner reminded him of Abbie. Kind? Shit, he couldn't afford kind, sweet, or generous, and neither could the guys on the job, even though they seemed to be melting around her. He went back to shoveling food into his mouth and missed her coming his way.

Brazenly she put the coffeepot on the table and sat down across from him. "Phew, hard work. But, what a nice place. You're part of that crew over there aren't you? Sorry, I am so impolite—I'm Grace," she said, as she stuck her hand out for him to shake. "And you are?"

For a moment, every one in the diner froze. No one talked to Hank except if he talked first, and never with, always at. Hank stared at her for a moment, and then without fully being able to understand why, he put out his hand and shook hers. "Hank."

A collective sigh went out across the room, and everyone looked at each other in wonder. *What was it about that old lady anyway?*

That's what Hank was thinking too. Completely tongue tied he stared at her, tried to bring back his frosty exterior and failing completely, went back to eating.

"Nice to meet you, Hank. Let me know if you need anything else," Grace said as she got up from the table, but not before pouring more coffee into his cup.

In the corner of the room, Andy smiled. *Sarah sure knows how to pick them,* he thought. If anyone can find out if Hank and his crew had something to do with Ava's departure, it will be Grace.

Keeping his head down, Hank allowed himself to look up enough to see Grace behind the counter, refilling salt shakers as if it was the most important job in the world. *Just a dumb old lady,* he thought. *Nothing to worry about.*

And just for a moment, something passed over him. It felt just like it used to when Abbie hugged him. Startled, he dropped his fork on the floor, left it there, and slammed money down on the table and stomped out the door.

What complete and utter bullshit, he swore to himself. I *have a job to do.* As an afterthought, he turned and opened the door and yelled at the crew still eating. "You're done here. Get to work!"

Hank slammed the door of his truck and sped out of the parking lot spitting gravel everywhere.

Grace cleared Hank's table, smiling at herself, and then turned her smile on his crew. "Anyone know what that was about?" She asked. She wasn't at all surprised when they told her what they thought of their boss.

"Scary dude," one said. "Been even creepier since we took this job in town. Disappears for days on end, but we don't get to do the same thing, or we get fired. Never says a word, and if he does, it isn't anything we want to hear. Always pissed at someone for something."

"Speaking of being pissed, we better get to the job site before he gets madder."

"What's the difference? He went the opposite way."

"The difference is, he has eyes in the back of his head. I wouldn't be surprised if he has cameras and listening devices installed everywhere."

"See ya, Grace," they all said as they headed out to their trucks.

"Now, Grace," Andy said, "that was serious working of the crowd. Where did you learn that kind of thing anyway?"

"Never you mind, young man—yes, young to me—I know what I'm doing. And by the way, you aren't getting anything by me either."

"Don't doubt it for a minute," said Andy.

******

Across the country, Ava sat in her booth as long as she could, reading and rereading the letters. It occurred to her that it was pretty old school for them to send letters instead of a texts or emails. *Why? They didn't want them to be traceable? How did they know that Evan wouldn't have opened the letters?* They had to know who he was, and that he would never read her mail, and that she picked up the mail everyday instead of him.

Yes, that had to be it. There would be no trace of what happened, even if they found her phone. Nothing pointed to the fact that she was in Los Angeles, waiting to meet her blackmailers. She knew where she was going. It was only a few miles away, easy for her to walk. They hadn't told her what they wanted from her, just that they would expose her past to Evan if she didn't meet them.

To seal the deal, they sent a picture. Ava couldn't take her eyes off of it. A whole life screwed up. Not just her life; so many lives ruined. *I could have avoided all this,* she thought, *if only I would have started telling the truth the moment I came home. If only I had told Evan right after we met. Maybe he would have understood. But now, too late.*

The waitress came by to fill her coffee again. Ava waved her away. Her stomach couldn't take anymore. Nothing stayed down. Nerves. Fear. Time to go.

She picked up her bag, left more than enough money on the table for the waitress and headed off to meet what she had decided was her fate. One she deserved.

Thirty-Five

Dark. Black dark. Could there be someplace this dark, Ava thought. Her shoulder hurt where she had landed when she was pushed into the room. The memory of hearing the click of a lock echoed in her head. *Oh, God. Now what? Who was that? What happened?*

Ava struggled to her feet and started feeling her way across the room to find the wall, trying to be careful as she shuffled across the floor. *A wall.* It felt like concrete. She slowly made her way around the room. Finally, her fingers found a light switch. *Maybe I should have left it off,* thought Ava as she looked around.

She was in a small dirty room. Smaller than her bathroom at home. *Home...* She sobbed. This place was the complete opposite of home. No windows, one door, one table, one chair, one bottle of water, and one board stretched across some cinder blocks. Nothing else. No clues as to why she was here.

Except maybe the letters. Ava noticed her bag where it had skittered across the floor when she was pushed into the room. Wincing, she picked it up and looked inside. No burner phone. No letters. No clothes. Nothing. Empty, except for a comb— and the picture. They must have taken it all out when they grabbed her and dragged her to this room.

Ava didn't know who "they" were. Just two figures dressed in black with covered faces. Looking around the room, Ava realized she needed to lie down. She chose the board pretending to be a bed. It seemed less dirty than the floor, and her shoulder was killing her. Using her bag as a pillow, she lay down and looked at the ceiling.

Wow, Ava, you have totally screwed up your life this time. No one knows where you are, you put up your shields against anyone using remote viewing to find you, and it's doubtful you'll be able to lower them now. Even if you could, these concrete walls might stop the Circles from getting through to her.

Ava didn't know how long she lay there, eventually falling asleep and waking up with a rocking headache. The water beckoned. Either it was drugged, or it wasn't, but without water, she wasn't going to make it. Maybe they were just keeping her for a short time. *Hope springs eternal,* she thought.

What seemed like hours later, and feeling a little better, Ava thought back to what she could remember about what had happened. She had walked to the address in the letter. The letter told her that if she went there, she would find information on how to contact them and make arrangements for payment. Instead, it was an empty building. She stood at the door for a long time before entering. *This can't be the place,* she kept thinking.

Someone called out, "Are you looking for me, Ava?"

She yelled back, "Who are you?"

"Come on inside and we'll talk," was the response.

Terror clutched at her. She was torn between wanting to run again and wanting to get this nightmare over. She chose to continue into the building. And that's when it happened. Those two figures grabbed her, dragged her to this room, and pushed her inside.

Now she was even further away from discovering her tormentor than she was before. Alone and lost. For real this time.

She kept the light on, afraid of what might scurry out into the dark. There was a small vent near the ceiling, much too high for her to reach even standing on the table, but since she wasn't struggling to breathe she figured it was letting in enough fresh air for her to survive. And, probably contains a camera too, she thought.

So, keep the light on so she could see, or turn it off so they couldn't. She chose the light. She just wouldn't give them anything to see.

She slept again and dreamed of Evan and of the Stone Circle. Everyone smiling at her, laughing, and hugging. And then the air turned black. The smiling morphed to smirking and disgust. Everyone turned their backs on her and started walking away.

"No," Ava screamed.

How did I get here? She sobbed. And remembered.

******

Ava liked her new job. It was a nine-to-five gig, but she liked the security of it. Located on the top floor of an old house that had been turned into office spaces, it was charming and comfortable. Mrs. Duncan ran the agency. She did it with an efficiency and calmness that pleased Ava after her chaotic bar life. She had even arranged a space for Ava to park and lock her bike, and had put her to work right away answering phones.

After a few days, it was evident that Ava was a skilled communicator, so she started booking appointments for people that called in looking for work. A week or two into the job, she learned how to call companies to see if they were interested in placing one of their job applicants. It felt wonderful. She was doing good things for people. She was working. She was helping people get work. All was fine with her world.

Even Rick was behaving. She hardly saw him anymore, even though she was still living in the apartment that he had rented for her. Ava figured that meant she didn't have much time left to earn enough money to get her own place. When she did see him, and he asked why she wasn't dancing at the clubs anymore, she explained that she wanted to learn how to earn a real living.

He gave her a strange look, but knowing what he wanted, she managed to turn away his sour mood with a quickie on the living room floor. By then, she simply didn't care. She was on her way out; she just didn't want him to know. She didn't want anything to stop her from getting her freedom back.

There was only one thing she couldn't figure out. She still didn't feel well. One day she watched Mrs. Duncan turning her pen over and over in her hand, something she did when she was nervous.

"Ava," she said, "I don't want to be a nosy busybody, but I was wondering if you have checked why you don't feel well."

"I figure I just have some kind of low-grade infection. It will go away," Ava answered.

"You have been working here almost six weeks, Ava, and you still don't feel well. And, you seem constantly tired to me. I'm not complaining about your work; I love having you here, I'm just a bit concerned. Have you taken one of these?" Mrs. Duncan asked as she pulled out a pregnancy test.

Seeing Ava go pale, she continued. "I'm sorry, Ava, I think you might want to take this test. It might be nothing, but at least you'll know."

Back in the dirty room, lying on the board, Ava remembered what happened next. She had stumbled out of the bathroom, holding the pregnancy test. Sobbing, she fell into her boss' arms. In a million years, it had never occurred to her that things could get that bad that fast.

She went home that day and fell asleep, hoping that when she woke up, she had only dreamed that she was pregnant. But, hours later, there were still two blue lines. She was still pregnant.

Thirty-Six

Ava held out for a few more days pretending that nothing had happened. She barely slept at night. When she did sleep, she had nightmares. Once she dreamed she was running through town wearing a yellow dress and Rick was chasing her with a shotgun.

Each morning, she was sicker than she had been the day before. Now that she knew she was pregnant, she attributed some of the sicknesses to that, but the rest was fear and nerves.

Luckily, Rick didn't come around because she had no idea what she would tell him. Well, she did know. She wasn't going to tell him anything. There was no way he was going to be a decent father. He was a terrible boyfriend because he was a terrible person in general. Yes, she had finally figured that out and admitted it.

She was even more grateful for the money she had been saving. But that had been just for her. Now, how could she work with a baby? Where would they live?

Each day, she went to work and didn't say anything at all to Mrs. Duncan, who wisely went along with the pretense that everything was the same as before. Then one afternoon, not able to contain her fears any longer she poured out her story to her.

They had finished the last job placement of the day and were closing the office when Mrs. Duncan stopped Ava and asked her if there was anything she could do.

It was the last straw. Ava had to tell someone. Ava needed help, and she knew it. She told her everything. Well, almost everything. She didn't tell her about the dancing. Over the past few months, Ava had become more and more ashamed of what she had done. But she did tell her that she was only seventeen and that she had run away from home. Ava told her that the man who was the baby's father was not someone she wanted to spend her life with, and in fact, she was terrified of him.

They sat for a long time together on the couch, Ava's head buried in Mrs. Duncan's shoulder.

"I'm so sorry, Mrs. Duncan. I didn't mean to lie to you. I just needed this job."

"Call, me Kathy now, Ava. Ava is your real name, right?"

Ava nodded.

"I know you haven't had much time to think about this, but may I make a suggestion?"

Ava sat up and said, "I'm keeping this baby, Mrs. Duncan, I mean Kathy."

"Knowing you even for this short time, Ava, I knew you would. You have a kind and pure heart. When you ran away, you made one choice that I am hoping you would not make again. Now, you need to make a choice that will be the best for you and your baby."

"I can't go home!"

"Why? I imagine your mom has been praying every day for you to come home. You will have some making up to do, but I think you have grown up since you left. You can do it."

Part of Ava surrendered at that moment. She had wanted to go home for months, but her pride kept her from going. Now she had someone else to take care of, someone who would need more than she could give her, or him.

Nodding, Ava swallowed her pride one more time, "Would you help me?"

"It would be my honor, Ava. Let's make a plan."

****

With Kathy's help, things moved quickly. Kathy went with her to the apartment, in case Rick was there. She helped her get everything she wanted to take. It wasn't much. Ava never had money to furnish the place. She had been living with paper plates and furniture that came with the apartment without even noticing the psychological price she was paying by letting Rick keep her.

Glancing at the bed, she remembered Rick and his desires and barely made it to the bathroom before she threw up everything she had managed to eat that day.

She took her toothbrush, makeup, and the cash she had saved. She left the clothes that Rick had bought, which meant she had only a pair of jeans and a few T-shirts to her name. About the same things she had when she left home. *Well, I have one extra possession now,* she thought as she brushed her fingertips across her still flat belly.

It took her a few days to gather up enough courage to call home, but when she did, she realized that Kathy had been right.

Her mom started crying and said, "Please, please come home."

"Mom..." Ava said. "I have not been a good girl."

"Ava, you are always a good girl. You just made some choices that weren't the best ones. But we all do. Whatever you did, whatever is wrong, we will handle it together."

Crying, Ava put Kathy on the phone. Kathy explained that she would help Ava get everything wrapped up and would make sure she got on the plane safely.

Kathy helped Ava sell her car and close her bank account, adding two weeks additional pay to the balance

A few days later, Kathy walked with Ava as far as she could into the airport and hugged her goodbye. At the last minute she pressed a tiny package into her hand.

"For the baby," Kathy said.

"I will never forget you, Kathy," Ava said, tears filling her eyes.

"I won't ever forget you either, Ava," responded Kathy.

Slinging her backpack over her shoulder, Ava waited until she couldn't see Kathy anymore before walking into the terminal. Her backpack contained all that she had to show for herself after a year of trying to be so grown-up.

Lying on the board in the dirty concrete room, with no one to help her now, Ava realized that closing her heart had not served her. Her mom and Kathy had opened their hearts to her, and this is how she had repaid them for believing in her. She had run away again.

Ava couldn't bring herself to think about Evan, or Suzanne, or the Circles. They had all trusted her, and she had not lived up to that trust. This time, no one could save her. Once again, she had made a terrible choice.

Still she wondered, *who had sent the letters? Where did they get the picture? Why did they bring her here? They had taken the letters but left the picture in her bag. Why? Probably to torture her,* she thought.

Ava dragged herself off the board and she sat at the table. She put the picture in front of her and stared at it for the hundredth time. *Was it really her?*

Thirty-Seven

"Are you telling me that no one can find her?" Evan asked, trying his best to keep himself from screaming.

"Leif, you're the best at searching for people, and even you can't find her?"

The entire Stone Circle had gathered in Evan's living room, but Tom was the only one actually there. Sarah, Leif, Craig, and Mira were all drifting around the room, projecting from their own homes.

Tom put his arm around his friend, and Evan did his best not to push him away. Instead, he got up and walked out of the room. The front door slammed, and they could all hear his truck start up and roar down the driveway.

Tom got up to follow, but Sarah said, "Let him go. He needs to let some of this pent-up fear and anger out. We have other work to do."

"Well, let me ask for Evan again, then. Seriously, no one knows where she is?"

"We know where she was going. We followed her to Los Angeles. But, once she got there, she made sure she wasn't followed by anyone, including us.

"But and here is the good news, we have a pretty good idea

why she left, and who might know what happened once she got there," Craig said.

"Are you going to tell Evan why she left?" Tom asked.

"Once we find Ava and bring her home, *she* will have to tell him," Sarah answered.

"It will be up to the two of them to decide what happens after that. Ava has the courage though, and Evan has the heart, so we believe everything will be okay."

"So, Tom, we need you to keep Evan focused on the details of the wedding."

"I am coming there in a few days, Tom, and I will help you put it all together. We have to continue as if it is going to happen," Mira said.

"But, what if you can't find Ava in time for the wedding, or what if she and Evan don't work it out?" Tom asked.

"Then we will cancel," Sarah said. "But none of us give up that easily, besides, remember we have friends in high places. And good is always stronger than evil, no matter what form it takes, externally or internally."

"Amen to that," Mira and Sarah said at the same time.

A few miles away, Evan realized that he didn't have it in him to drive madly around the countryside. He pulled off the road and dropped his head in his hands and sobbed. In the background, Evan heard the radio playing. It was still on from the last time he and Sarah had gone to the garden center together.

She loved to listen to the oldies station while they drove. Sometimes they would sing along together. They had spent many happy hours listening to songs and picking the ones they liked, but most of all choosing the one that they would dance to at their wedding.

"Please, God," Evan said. "Please tell me that everything will be alright. I promise to do whatever is asked of me to have her back and spend my life with her. I'm listening, just give me a sign."

When "Unchained Melody" started playing, Evan started crying with joy as he sang along with the Righteous Brothers,

"Are you still mine?

I need your love

I need your love

God speed your love to me."

He whispered, "Thank you! Thank you!"

Suddenly it was all clear to him. It was up to him to believe that he would find Ava, and it was up to him to take action to affirm that truth. That he could do.

Evan pulled the truck back onto the road and headed to town. He needed to visit the Diner and talk to Sam about the food for the wedding. And he needed some food for himself, too. He hadn't eaten since Ava left, and starving himself to death was not going to bring Ava back.

He called Tom as he drove.

"Meet me at the Diner," he said "We have some planning to do."

Everyone in Evan's living room smiled and air hugged as they said goodbye. They all agreed that it was a beginning. A happy one at that!

****

Hank had watched Evan slam the door and roar out of the house, tires squealing as he drove way too fast down the driveway, and headed towards town.

Okay, Tom, now you, Hank thought. He had a job to do. This stage wouldn't take too long.

Within fifteen minutes Tom drove his rental towards town, too.

Figuring that even if they were only doing a quick errand, he still had thirty minutes, so Hank made his way to the house. He had parked miles down the road, in the direction away from town, and hidden the truck well, so even if they had gone the other direction, they still wouldn't have seen his.

Hank knew there were cameras everywhere, but he had a new toy that allowed him to freeze the signal so anyone looking would see a picture that had taken place minutes before—another reason he had to hurry.

In case that didn't work, and he showed up on the cameras, he was thoroughly disguised, if you called hunting clothes and a hat and a scarf over his face a disguise. The scarf smelled disgusting and made him want to cough. *Choose something better next time*, he admonished himself.

One of the men who had installed the locks had been easy to bribe with money and threats to his family, so Hank had a key to the door, making it easy to let himself in.

He released the outside camera signal, right before he opened the door while freezing the inside camera's signal. Crossing to the security systems keypad, he used the password the worker had told him. If it didn't work, he had a backup plan. The alarm company would call Evan, but he had already paired his phone with Evan's and could divert the call to his own burner phone. He knew the phrase he needed say to the company.

He didn't need to do that, though. The code worked. *Sometimes all the planning in the world doesn't work, if you forget to change the small things*, he thought.

Small things were what he was doing now. He was taking pictures of the rooms. They needed to know exactly what the inside of the house looked like. It didn't take long; he had been doing this sort of thing since he was a kid. Before leaving the house, he reset the alarm and unfroze the house cameras and froze the ones outside.

For a moment, he allowed himself to think what a beautiful place it was to have a wedding reception. *Too bad it would all have to be destroyed. Along with everyone there.*

He left the way he came, back through the woods. Once safe, he unfroze the cameras. *Yep, pretty, beautiful actually. What a shame.* But, it was his job to do it.

Next, he was off to Los Angeles, to take care of business there. It was all coming together. Grant would be pleased.

Thirty-Eight

Evan was waiting in their favorite booth, eating. "I'll have the same thing," said Tom as Andy came over to see what he wanted.

"I'm happy to see you have your appetite back, Evan."

"Need the strength to get this wedding planned—and to be helpful in looking for Ava, instead of getting in the way with my worry and fear."

Both of them glanced up as Grace filled their coffee cups.

"Yep, I'm new here, before you ask. And yes, there is something weird about me, and no you have never met me, but yes, I do know who you are," said Grace as she slid into the booth beside Tom.

"Come on, move over. I've got things to tell you, young man."

Tom slid over sending a questioning glance at Evan as he did so.

"Cat got your tongue, you two? Okay, I'm Grace. And Sarah sent me," she whispered.

Both Tom and Evan burst out laughing. Grace watched them and then started laughing herself.

Luckily, there was no one else in the diner, except Andy

who took it all in stride. *Weird that*, thought Tom, but then got caught up in the laughter again.

"Well, I have no idea what that was about," Grace said, "But it has been said that no one can be healed who doesn't have a sense of humor, and this situation surely calls for that."

"Hasn't it also been said that no one can be healed who lies to himself?" Tom said.

"Both true," Grace responded. "I know you two can laugh. Is anyone lying to themselves right now?"

Evan dropped his head and stared at the table for a long moment.

"I believe that I have. I tried not to see how upset Ava was becoming. I think I was afraid if I made her tell me what was wrong, it would be because there was something wrong with me. I was afraid for myself that she didn't really love me, so I didn't ask. I was selfish, and a liar to myself. And now she is gone.

"But, here is what I know now. I love Ava no matter what. I will do what it takes to find her, and let her know. And I will tell the truth to myself to the best of my ability, and I plan to get better and better at it.

"I don't know why it's taken me so long to figure this out— that if I want to change things in the world, I have to start with myself.

"Tom, G.O.B. is fantastic. I love being part of it, but I have to ask myself if I am healing myself of false beliefs and prejudices as I'm doing it, or just covering them up."

Grace stood up, pulled Evan out of the booth, and hugged him. Tom joined them. "Group hug!" Tom called out, inviting Andy into the circle. For some reason, it all felt right.

Sam had stepped out from behind the counter as Evan was talking, and all four of them turned to him and opened their arms. Without hesitation, he joined them.

The door of the Diner swung open, admitting some of the men from the construction crew.

"Hey, what are we missing?"

"Join us," the five called out. And they did.

A few slightly awkward slaps on the back later, the construction crew was seated in its usual booth, and Grace had gone off to serve them. Not before she winked at Tom and Evan and whispered that she would see them later.

Evan had asked Sam to hang back a moment so they could review a few details for the wedding.

"I only have a minute," Sam said, as he pulled a chair up to the booth.

"It will only take a minute," Evan said. "I just wanted to make sure everything was ready. Ava's out of town at the moment, so I thought I would check in with you."

"I'll tell you what, Evan, If you'll be home later I will drop the menu off at the house. That will give me a chance to look at your kitchen. I will have to use the oven to keep some items warm, and of course the refrigerator for the cold things."

After making arrangements for later that day, Sam went back to cooking, and Tom turned to Evan. "You are acting out of the premise that intent is reality, aren't you?"

"Yes, and I intend to stick with the fact that good overrides evil, that Ava is safe and will find her way home soon, and that the Stone Circle will be complete once more so that we can go on with our work."

"I'll join you in that, Evan," he said as they clinked their water glasses together.

****

Later that day, more than 2,000 miles away, Hank's plane descended into LAX. He hated flying. But, as in all things he did, he pretended that he didn't mind.

He kept to himself, eyes closed, earphone plugs in, not listening to anything but pretending that he was so that no one would bother him. All through the flight, he reviewed what he knew about what Grant wanted him to do.

The first three parts were already in place.

Scare Ava enough that she would leave Evan and her friends without telling them why. Grant had supplied him with the letters, and Hank had one of his trusted cohorts mail them from Los Angeles so that the postmark would be right.

They were sealed when he got them from Grant, so he had no idea what they contained.

If Ava hadn't been freaked out enough by the letters, he was supposed to ramp up the scare tactics. He had some ideas about grabbing her and whispering the terrible things Grant had told him to say to her, but it had not been necessary.

The second thing he was supposed to do was to make sure she got to Los Angeles safely. That had worked out well. Pete turned out to be the perfect driver. Ava had felt safe with him, and done more talking than Hank had thought she would.

Next, he arranged for her capture and her detention. Again, he intended to scare the crap out of her and break her down, ready for the fourth part of the plan.

Rescue her. That was the next step in the scheme. He would rescue her. Pretend that it was happenstance that put him in the right place at the right time. The next step was to be friendly enough that she would confide in him, and ask him to help her find the girl in the picture.

He already knew where the girl was. But he didn't know who she was.

Better to not find out more. Hank did what Grant paid him to do. Sometimes he hated the job, but did it anyway. Usually, he was detached enough, but this one worried him. Somehow it had become personal, and he hated that feeling. Not knowing why he felt that way made it worse.

Hank didn't know what Grant's plan was for Ava after they found the girl. If it was to get rid of them, he would. But not the violent kind of way that Grant loved. Instead, he would find a gentle way to move them on into the next world.

He might not like it, but he would do it. He always did his job.

Thirty-Nine

They were getting ready to move her. Ava could hear them talking through the air vent. With no sun or stars to guide her, she had no idea how long she had been there. Ava slept most of the time. Partly because she was exhausted, and partly to escape the panic that would rise whenever she let herself notice that she was living in a cage.

Once in a while, someone opened the bottom flap of the door and slid food and water on a tray to her. At first, she didn't want to eat anything, but eventually, hunger won out.

There was a toilet in the corner that actually flushed. Ava was continually thankful for that one small blessing. She conjectured that at one point the area had been part of a warehouse and the toilet was part of an old bathroom.

After what seemed like days of sleeping, Ava felt as if she was strong enough to try and contact the Circles. She tried standing, sitting, lying, meditating, talking to herself, silence, and even a moment of screaming. But nothing seemed to break through the wall that she had intentionally built.

If I get out of here, Ava said to herself, *I will break that wall down within me no matter what it takes.*

When she heard the voices, she had the sense that they

wanted her to hear them. *Okay,* she thought, *I will be prepared. No matter what happens, I will know what to do.*

****

Hank had stopped at a cheap motel and taken a shower, and changed into clothes that made him look more like a semi-successful man, rather than a grunt for hire. He laughed to himself, as if changing clothes was going to change who he had become.

Hank knew that clothes helped people put you into a box they could understand, so, he thought carefully about what he would wear. He intentionally matched what he was wearing to what he had seen Evan wear, hoping that would trigger a feeling of trust in Ava.

He had rented a small white car that looked like every other car on the road. It was nothing like driving his truck. He hated it. He hated being like other people. *Well, a car and some clothes were not going to make me like other people anyway,* he thought.

Ava was being held just outside of downtown near the railroad tracks in one of those old buildings that every city seems to have. He parked the car a few blocks away and walked to the warehouse. First he wanted to see how Ava looked, and then confirm the plans with the men holding her. They had to make the transfer so she would escape right into his arms.

He didn't like the area. He didn't like the men he had hired, but they had come highly recommended for what he needed. They had no idea who he was, or who Ava was; they just liked getting paid. Hank had told them that if they harmed Ava in any way, he would do twice the damage to them. Seeing the look in Hank's eyes, they understood.

They agreed to head back to Mexico and stay there once the

transfer was complete. If they ever came back to the states, well, they were clear what would happen to them.

Hank pulled on gloves as he entered the building. No point in leaving prints. Hank called out. One of the two men came out and led him back to the room where they had been living.

It smelled disgusting. Cigarette smoke and sweat, and God knows what else assaulted him. *I am seriously beginning to hate this life.* He pushed the thought away. He had a job to do.

The area next to Ava's cell held the camera and the air vent. The two men followed Hank to the monitor, but he waved them away. As Hank looked at Ava, that weird feeling he had been experiencing came back again full force. *God, I will be glad when this is over,* thought Hank. *Something is seriously wrong with me. Maybe I need a vacation, as normal people do. Right, as if I could ever be normal.*

He looked again. Ava appeared okay. That's all he needed to know. Hank and the men returned to the room they had been living in, and he gave them the first half of their money and confirmed the arrangements.

"Where are her clothes that she had in the bag?" They pointed to a plastic bag lying in the corner.

"And the letters?"

One of the men handed the letters to Hank, and he ripped them into tiny pieces, put the pieces into an ashtray on the table, and set them on fire with a lighter that was lying beside it.

"Make sure she gets whatever was in the bag before she leaves. Tell her she is going somewhere that she needs to be better dressed. Make it sound like she is going to be sold to someone. Scare her, rough her up enough to make an impression. Make her so afraid she figures the only chance she has is to escape."

"Got it, boss."

"You better. If anything goes wrong, the best thing that will happen to you is that you don't get the rest of the money. If it all goes well, pick it up at the drop point, and get the hell out of town. No celebrating. Nothing. Do you understand?"

Both men nodded. Hank stood up, scraping the chair along the concrete floor as he did so.

"Have one more conversation she can hear. Give her a time frame, so she's ready. I'll be waiting around the corner. Don't screw this up!"

Both men nodded and looked at each other with relief as Hank left the warehouse. They had no intention of screwing it up. They wanted the money, and they wanted to go home to their families—maybe as much as that girl in the other room wanted to go home to hers.

They had an hour to clean up the place, have the conversation, and get out of there. And then they were free. The girl, well, she would only think she was free. Whatever Hank was going to do to her was none of their business.

Forty

The cell door swung open, hitting the opposite wall with a boom, and two men came into the room, screaming at Ava. One had a stick in his hand and banged it against the wall as he came at her.

Ava thought she had prepared, but the screaming and the banging seemed to take every thought out of her head. She backed up farther and farther until she hit the far wall.

One man stuck his face into hers and screamed even louder. All she could see was a pair of brown eyes flashing anger.

"Are you listening?" he screamed.

"Stop screaming, please," she begged, "I promise to listen."

The man with the stick banging on the walls pushed his partner aside and thrust a plastic bag into her hands.

"Where we are going, you will need clean clothes. Top dollar! Put this into your bag and let's go. Behave yourself. We don't want to put a mark on you. We want to keep that pretty white skin all clean and soft, don't we. But we can hurt you where no one will see."

Ava nodded, stuffed the plastic bag into the bag she had brought with her, and stumbled out into the warehouse. There was just enough light so she could see where she was going without bumping into the walls and old equipment lying around.

The two men kept pushing her along, laughing. The one with the stick rapped her on the head when she paused to get her bearings.

Ava shuffled. Not because she had to, but because she wanted them to think she was tired and resigned. She was neither.

As they stepped into the sunshine and the heat radiating off the sidewalk and road, she paused again. One man grabbed her and pushed her up against the building and held himself close up behind her, and twisting her arm up her back.

"Yum," he said. "Some gringo with money is going to get to taste this. Maybe I should start."

Ava relaxed against the wall, and said, "Go ahead. I don't care anymore."

He laughed as he pushed her away and prodded her forward. One man walked behind her, one to her side. A van with an open door was parked a few feet in front of them. Ava knew that if she got into that van, she would never escape.

There was a loud noise like a car backfiring, and as the two men turned to look, Ava pushed the man at her side as hard as he could so he stumbled and fell against a car parked at the curb. She kept on turning and struck the second man with her bag. She had found a stone in her cell and put it at the bottom of the bag. As he stumbled back, Ava ran away from them, and the van with the open door.

Past the warehouse, she turned at the first street possible, right into the arms of a man walking towards her, almost knocking him over.

"Help me," she pleaded.

He took one look at her and pulled her into an open

doorway in the building. They both crouched behind the door barely breathing.

They both heard the men ask, "where did she go?"

"Shit, man, we lost her. He's going to kill us. We better get out of here before he figures it out."

Ava sighed and leaned in to her savior. She was safe, at least for now.

Ava turned to her rescuer. "Thank you. I am forever grateful. But, now I have to be going."

"Are you sure? They could still be out there somewhere. Let me take you to get a cup of coffee, and maybe some food? There is a shop right around the corner. If you feel like talking, you can, if not, no problem."

Ava looked at the man into whose arms she had run. To her, he looked to be in his late fifties, and although his jacket hid his body, when she had leaned into him, she could feel his strength.

"Okay, thank you," she said and put out her hand, I'm Ava."

"Hi, I'm Hank," he said as he took her hand in his, once again having a strange feeling of knowing her. *What is it about this girl? The sooner I'm off this case, the better.*

None of that passed over his face, though. Instead, what he showed Ava was a calm and serene look, one that had been practiced since he was a boy.

Hank took Ava gently by her elbow, aware that fast movements were going to scare her, but also that a gentle touch could disarm her, and that was what he was doing. He was also aware that he had a gift of warmth in his voice. He only used it to get what he wanted, and in this case, he wanted Ava to trust him more and more. There was a lot to be done, and there wasn't a lot of time left.

As promised, the coffee shop was right around the corner. Some of the other warehouses in the area had been turned into trendy lofts, so a cafe on the street was not as incongruous as Ava first thought.

Hank told Ava to order whatever she wanted and pulled out a few twenties to show her that it was okay. He ordered a latte and a decadent-looking piece of cake, and, after a moment's hesitation, Ava ordered the same thing. Hank added a banana to her order and followed her to a small table she had picked out in the back of the room. She didn't think the men would come back, but just in case it was best to stay as invisible as possible.

With the first sip, Ava sighed and said, "This is heaven. Thank you, Hank. Seriously, I have no idea how to repay you for helping me back there."

"Don't think anything of it, Ava. But, what was that about? You don't have to tell me, but I am a good listener if you just want to get it out."

This is true, thought Hank. *I am a great listener. For once, I am not lying.*

A few moments passed, as Ava sipped her coffee and started pulling apart her cake.

"Would you mind if I just clean up a bit in the bathroom? Ava asked, buying herself some thinking time.

"Of course, I should have thought of that. Go ahead; I'll make sure you are safe here."

In the bathroom, Ava washed her hands, and then ran a towel across her face. She had brought her bag into the bathroom with her, so she pulled out her comb and small makeup bag, and repaired herself the best that she could.

I promised that I would break the wall down inside myself if I got out, she thought. *Is this the place to start?*

In the coffee shop, Hank nursed his latte. He didn't like them all that much, but he knew Ava drank them and it was just one more way to try to gain her trust.

If she didn't come out and talk to him, he wasn't sure what he was going to do. Strong-arming her wouldn't work. He was supposed to be her friend. He had lots of practice pretending friendship; after all, look at his pretend friendship with Grant.

But this was different. He hated Grant. And, if he was honest with himself, he liked this girl. That was going to make it easy to fool her, but what was he going to do later, knowing what Grant's plans were for her and her friends. How could they be that big a danger to anyone? So, they could do some "extra" things that regular humans didn't appear to be able to do. And they claimed to work for good only. So what?

It wasn't up to him to figure it out. He had stopped questioning things like that the day he killed his father. That was a long time ago. He couldn't turn back now.

He looked up as Ava came out of the bathroom, and arranged his face to be open and sympathetic, but not pushy. He stood up and pulled her chair out for her, settled back down, and waited.

"Do you want to talk?" he asked.

Ava stared at him for a long time. She had no idea who he was. She had just escaped from being sold off in what she assumed was the sex trade. She had run away from home. Her past had ruined her future.

She sighed.

"It's okay," Hank said softly. "I understand. Who am I for you to trust? Just some middle age guy. I work in construction part-time to get a little money. I am on my own. I have no family and no friends. I used to have a sister, but now, it's just me. So if you don't need my help, that's okay. But, if you do, I am ready to help."

"You used to have a sister?" Ava asked. "What happened to her?"

"It's a long and terrible story," Hank answered. "But, I promise to tell it to you if we get to be friends, or at least I get to help you in some way. Make up for all the times I never helped anyone."

Ava took a long sip of her latte. Hank had ordered it just the way she liked it, with almond milk. She was stalling, she knew, but she needed just one more second to look at her situation. Without someone's help, it was unlikely she would find what she needed. Once she put everything back into order, she could disappear forever. She knew Evan would be better off without her, so the most loving thing she could do was to continue running.

"Okay," Ava said. "I could use your help."

Hank smiled and said, "I'm listening."

Forty-One

"Let me tell you a true story, Evan," Grace said as she slid into the booth beside Tom.

"Can you keep taking time off like this," Tom asked, slightly annoyed that he was asked to slide over once again, and as sweet as Grace appeared to be, who was she anyway?

"I sense unasked questions, Tom," Grace said smiling at him.

Tom's face turned a bright red, so there was no need to tell her that yes, he was wondering about some things.

"Don't worry, I'm not reading your mind, just your body language," she said. "As you get to know me, you'll find out that besides being a busybody, I am quite helpful, and on your side. Besides, Andy gave me the rest of the afternoon off—not busy as you can see," she said waving her hand around to make her point.

Evan reached across and held Grace's hand. "We can use all the help we can get. Will the story help?"

Grace nodded, smiled, and began.

"As a young business-person, I used to get my nails done every week by the same woman. She would do my nails, and tell me about her life. She was a lovely person, and I loved spending time with her each week. We got friendly enough to exchange small birthday presents. One year she gave me a beautiful pair of earrings, which I wore for years, long after I had moved away.

"Anyway, after a few years, Karen, that was her name, started talking about a man she had met. At first, it sounded innocent. But soon she was talking about him more than about her husband, Mike, and her children.

"I know you may find it hard to believe, but mostly I listened. I was young and didn't think it was my place to tell Karen what to do, but I have to tell you, I did worry a bit. The man she was talking about didn't seem like someone she should be friends with, let alone that she was making him so important in her life.

"One day, after about six months of this progression towards the new man, she told me she had left Mike and the kids and moved in with that guy. I think his name was John. He did *not* sound nice at all, but in her head, everything worked out to make him fantastic. Over the next few months, more and more drama happened, and I was getting worried for her safety.

"In my own way, I prayed that she would wake up in time, and return to her family, but honestly I didn't hold out much hope. But I kept going to her because she was my friend, and I wanted her to be able to tell me anything, just in case I could help."

"Wait, wait. Hold up. Are you telling me that Ava ran away with another man? What man? How could that be?" Evan asked barely breathing.

"No, Evan. She didn't. You know she didn't. Pay attention to the bigger concept in the story."

Evan nodded at Grace, Tom nodded at Evan, and Grace smiled at them both.

"Okay, here is what happened next. After months of increasing drama with John, and apparently no awareness of what she had done to her life, she woke up.

"Literally. Karen told me that one morning she woke up, looked around her, and asked herself why she was there. She felt as if she had emerged from a fog. She waited until John left for the day, packed her bags, called Mike, and went home.

"The important part of this is that she woke up. Mike and his family and his church had been praying to know that Karen could, and would, wake up to her true self. When she returned, her husband, children, her family, and friends welcomed her with open arms. There was no retaliation or resistance towards her. They knew that she had been lost only because of a false set of beliefs, and the real Karen knew who she was, and where she belonged."

"So, let's see if I'm wise enough to get the point, Grace," Evan said.

"Ava is lost because of a set of false beliefs. She can wake up to that fact, and we can help her by knowing that about her, or what some people call prayer. And when she comes home, we will welcome her with open arms and with no hanging on to what happened."

"Like the story of the king and his two sons in the Bible," Tom burst in. "When the wayward son returned home, his father rushed to meet him, and prepared a celebration because a lost sheep had been found."

"Exactly," Grace said.

"Well," Evan said with a catch in his throat. "Two things. I know I can stay in the practice of knowing that Ava will wake up and come home."

Grace and Tom waited for Evan to continue.

"And?" Grace said after a long moment had passed.

"And, I hope I am man enough to run and meet her and never hold the pain she is causing me against her."

"Well then," Grace said, "we'll add that prayer to our list, that you wake up to see the magnificent and unselfish man that you are. And that love so fills your heart that there is no room for doubt or self-pity."

"That's what it is, isn't it? Evan asked. "Self-pity that she doesn't love me enough to not put me through this. That's the fight I need to wage. I need to fight against these thoughts. With your help, I will. I promise I will."

"Yes!" Grace shouted, surprisingly loud for a small woman. "Let's have another group hug," she said as she once again pulled Tom and Evan out of the booth to hug them."

Andy and Sam watched with smiles on their lips. Sarah was going to like what they had to report.

****

Grant had kept himself busy while Hank was distracted with Ava—busy doing things that Grant was not sure Hank would do, so he wasn't going to ask him. In fact, he wasn't going to tell him about it.

Of course, Hank had been doing Grant's dirty work for years. After all, Hank owed him his life. He had found Hank on the streets and taken him in, taught him everything he needed to know about blending in, being invisible, while holding people's lives, and sometimes their deaths, in his hands.

Hank owed him. And Grant had been demanding payment for years. But, lately, there was something off about Hank. He was going to have to test him somehow to make sure he was loyal. But not now. Right now, he needed Hank to help Ava find what she was looking for so the plan could continue.

Ava was so easy to manipulate, and in response, so had been her so-called Circle. *What a bunch of bull crap, this better than you stuff.* But, bull crap or not, they could do it. If they wanted to, they could be anywhere at all. Blocking a good remote viewer is hard. And what about "reading" what you were thinking? How dangerous was that?

The thing is, they hadn't yet discovered how powerful they could be. They ran around the world doing what they called good works through that stupid, incipient Good Old Boys club. It was sickening.

Grant had heard that Mira had been asking if it was possible to call a woman, 'dude.' If so, then it could be the Good Old Dudes club G.O.D. Even more sickening. But, it didn't matter what they called themselves, none of them were long for this world.

And since Grant was positive that there was nothing after death, just a big black emptiness, he was happier than he had ever been thinking about how he was going to send them all to that blackness.

For himself, he was planning to have power over everything he could in his remaining years. At seventy-five he still had some great years ahead of him. He would continue to amass his fortune, build his army of destroyers, and unleash them against anyone with any ability to stop him.

For now, he just had to get rid of this one group of people. Since that first Circle had died off on its own, heading into blackness, he didn't have so many people to kill at once. But, that would ruin half the fun. He was planning to take them all out. The Circle, and all their friends. The young, the old, the innocent. All at one time. Boom. It would be glorious.

A spectacle that no one would ever forget.

Forty-Two

Ava looked around the coffee shop and asked Hank if they could go somewhere else—someplace where no one could hear them. Hank pretended not to be knowledgeable about finding a secure place, even though he was usually the one listening in and knew all the tricks.

He let Ava guide him. Eventually, they ended up in a place that Hank had never seen. It was a small room at the bottom of the escalators in the downtown library. Ava said that if no one was using it, they could go there for a while and talk. Sitting at the long table in the room, facing the glass wall they could see everyone going up and down the escalators.

Hank was impressed. It was a relatively safe place, one he might use again, if necessary. He was also impressed with the library, and he let himself express it out loud. It made him more real to Ava. To Hank, it was a relief to be able to share something he always kept hidden: the love of beautiful architecture and design. It was one reason he did construction work. He could sometimes design and build something that pleased him in its beauty and function.

Ava was delighted that Hank appreciated the library. It was one of her special places. The library had been a haven for her the few years she lived in Los Angeles. It seemed as if that was a thousand years ago; so much had happened since then.

Once they were settled, Ava gave Hank a brief history of her life.

He nodded and listened. Once in a while he would ask clarifying questions so Ava would know that he was paying attention. It was hard to do because he seriously didn't want to know anything about her. Inside, he was becoming more and more distressed. Learning about her life would make it harder to get rid of her if that is what Grant asked of him.

When she got to the part where she returned home pregnant, she paused. "This is the tough part," she said. "But it is the part that I have to tell you, because it is why I am in Los Angeles, and why I need your help."

"Take your time, Ava," Hank said. "Otherwise, we might miss something important that could make the difference in whether or not we succeed. And you should know, Ava, I always succeed in what I do."

Something about the way Hank said those words brought a tinge of fear to Ava. But when she looked at him smiling at her in a soft, gentle way, she thought she was overreacting. Still, she needed to keep her options open in case something went wrong. She would have Hank help her, but then she would need to be gone, even if she had to leave secretly.

Taking one long glance at the escalator, she thought how much she had loved it when she used to come to the library. As it made its way up through the building, it always seemed to her as if it was taking people to heaven. *Right,* she thought. *What did I know?*

"Okay. I went home. My mom welcomed me with open arms. She made me tell the whole story of where I had been and what had happened. She said she didn't want any secrets between the two of us. She sometimes cried, but she never got mad or made me feel guilty.

"I see you wondering if that would be true, Hank. But that is how she was. She and I talked quite a bit about what I was going to do. I could tell that in spite of it all she was happy that there would be a baby in the house. I didn't understand why until later. She had been carrying a secret, too. One that she had been keeping to herself for a few years. It was only later that I found out what it was, but at that moment she put all her attention on me and what I needed.

"She would have supported me if I wanted an abortion, but I didn't. I'm not sure why. In some ways, it would have been easier, but it was as if the baby was talking to me—telling me that she had chosen me to be her mother. The baby even told me her name in a dream. She said her name was Hannah.

"That made it even harder for me to make the choice I did."

Hank knew what she had done, but he let Ava continue in her own time. He let her fidget, pull at her hair, stare into space, until finally, he asked, "What did you do?"

"Remember when I told you about Mandy? She was the girl I met in the laundromat. I lived with her for a brief time—she helped me get my first gig in the bar, and then she kicked me out of her house.

"Well, not kicked me out, but helped me move to my own place. We kept in touch a bit for a while. Mandy would call, and we would get together to take a walk on the beach. But she had her own life going. After a while, I realized she was probably working as an escort or something like that, and a sugar daddy or two taking care of her.

"I was grateful that she hadn't asked me to join that life. Of course, it is possible that the life I was leading was worse. But at the time, it didn't feel that way.

"Anyway, before I left town, I walked with her one last time on the beach to say goodbye. I didn't tell her why. I just told her I was going home. She hugged me and wished me well. I thought she was my friend."

"She wasn't?" Hank said.

"Not sure, because she did help me out one more time. Or, I thought she helped me out one more time.

"One day, when I was out grocery shopping for mom and me, she called the house. I should have wondered how she got the number, but I was still pretty innocent. My mom was even more so. Mandy told her she was my friend and asked how I was. Mom said something about the pregnancy going well, and since I hadn't come home yet, they talked for a while. Later, mom told me that she thought Mandy was sweet, and I was lucky to have such a good friend.

"I had to decide if I was keeping the baby or not. I thought I would. My plan was that mom could help me raise her, and we could be a little family of our own.

"That's when mom told me her secret. She said that she had cancer and had been having treatments while I was gone, but there wasn't any hope left. That meant she couldn't be counted on to help raise Hannah."

Ava looked up at Hank and was touched to see that his eyes were filled with tears.

"I'm so sorry, Ava. Do you need to take a break before you tell me the rest?"

Ava nodded, grateful that Hank understood, but she said they needed to plow on. Ava needed to tell Hank the rest of the story as quickly as possible. Time was running out.

Taking a deep breath, holding her trembling hands as still as possible, she gathered her courage and told Hank the rest.

"Well, obviously the choice was now down to me raising a

baby on my own, or adoption. I didn't have any skills; I hadn't even finished my last year of high school. I wanted so much for Hannah. I realized that I wasn't the one who could supply what she needed.

"We didn't know where to turn though. We thought about an adoption agency. But one day, Mandy showed up at our door with an idea. Mom had told her that we were looking for a couple to raise Hannah and Mandy said that she knew the perfect one.

"Mom and I checked out everything Mandy told us. We even scraped together enough money to hire a lawyer to make sure the paperwork was completely legal. Even though we were going outside of the system, we believed we were doing the right thing.

"I didn't want to see Hannah after she was born. I was afraid if I held her I wouldn't be brave enough to let her go. The secret remained with mom, me, and Mandy. I never saw Hannah. Until now."

Ava pulled the picture out that she had carefully tucked in her bra before being pulled out of the cell. No matter what, she couldn't lose that picture and what was written on the back.

She placed the photograph between the two of them and waited. Hank slid the picture towards himself and stared. A little girl about eight years old looked back at him. His heart flopped over. He found himself gripping the table and shaking. He was staring at Abbie.

How had Ava gotten a picture of Abbie? "Where did you get this?" Hank whispered trying to keep the fury out of his voice. Had he been played? Was this never about Ava? Did someone know his secret and had used Ava to trick him?

Ava was focused on him, wide eyed and afraid. "In a letter. It's Hannah. I have to get her back. Please, can you help me?"

Still trying to contain his own upset, Hank said, "How do you know it's your daughter? You never saw her?"

"Look on the back," she said.

Turning the picture over, he read, "Pretty girl, your Hannah! Better come get her before she ends up somewhere you will never find her."

Hank lifted his gaze and looked at Ava, and then at the picture. It couldn't be. It was just a resemblance. He would play this out the way Grant told him to. Then he would find out who was lying. And when he did, God help them.

Forty-Three

Sarah woke with a start. It had been awhile since she had had such a vivid dream. Given what was happening with Ava, she wasn't surprised. She had been worried before she fell asleep. It had been over a week since anyone had managed to find her.

She and Leif had both tried to contact Ava, as had everyone within the Circle. Sarah had hoped that perhaps the answer would come in one of those times she called a "there" experience, when she would be in her body, but be somewhere else at the same time as an observer. But that hadn't happened.

She noticed that since they had met Suzanne and Earl she had fewer of what she called the "here and there" experiences.

It was because the line between the two had blurred. More and more, Sarah was able to be present in everyday life and still be present in the other place where she saw people who lived in what she understood to be another dimension.

The illusion of time had become softer and the awareness of the line of light that stretched throughout life was clearer.

It was the same for Leif. Still, neither of them had been able to find Ava. Until the dream.

Turning over in bed, she realized that Leif had already gotten up and was waiting for her to join him outside on their deck.

Sarah pulled on her warm morning clothes, trying to keep the dream clear in her head so they could talk about it.

They kissed and hugged and settled into their chairs to watch as the stars moved across the sky, and, listen for the first morning bird to sing.

"You met Ava's mother, too?" Sarah asked without speaking.

Leif continued the same way. "Yes, the same dream I believe. Ava is back online so to speak. But her mother has never disconnected from her. I think that's why no one knew where she was; she couldn't spare the energy or time to do anything but never let Ava out of her sight."

"So Ava has a little girl, named Hannah. What lovely news. But, apparently Ava doesn't think Evan will believe it's lovely," Sarah said.

"No, she doesn't appear to, and I believe we should let her tell him in her way. But, of course, we need to get her safely back first."

"Without letting Grant know what we know," said Sarah. "And, for sure, let's continue to keep Abbie's presence secret until she decides to reveal it herself."

"Yes," Leif replied, and then they both lifted their mugs to the woods where a light twinkled in return. There would be more than one Circle helping them.

****

Ava knew that Sarah and Leif had found her, and felt relief. She was still running, but being cut off from her friends was even more painful than she had imagined it would be. Ava had heard once that evil would always try to make you doubt the people who could help you the most. Its goal was always separation.

Perhaps that was what she had done—turned from the people who could help her the most. Maybe she wouldn't run after they found Hannah. Perhaps she would go to Sarah and Leif and ask them to help her decide what to do. But for now, she didn't want to bring anyone into this problem. It was still too dangerous. Whoever Hank was, she was going to have him help her, and then decide what to do about him.

"Ava, let me see if I understand. You got letters threatening your daughter. Someone grabbed you off the street. You ran away from people that care about you. You don't know where your daughter is, and you're afraid for her. Does that about sum it up?" Hank asked.

Ava nodded.

"It doesn't make sense, Ava."

"Maybe because there is more to the story. A wonderful couple adopted Hannah. We knew they lived in Santa Monica, but I didn't want to know more than that. Mandy promised to keep an eye on her, but not to tell me where she was because, I might try to see her. We both knew that would be too painful to me, and not fair to Hannah.

"She did tell my mom, though. Right before my mom died, she gave me a key and told me that if I ever needed to find Hannah to use it. All the papers would be there. At the same time, mom had arranged for me to live with her best friend, Suzanne. Suzanne, well, Suzanne moved on a few years ago. At the same time, I met Evan.

"About a month ago, letters arrived threatening Hannah. They also threatened to tell Evan about my past life, and that I had a child. They said if I didn't come to meet them, they would tell him.

"But, the worst threat of all, they would make sure Hannah was never happy. They gave me an address. I was supposed to go to that to address to get a clue to where she was, and how to pay them to keep them silent. That's where I was kidnapped and locked in a room.

"It seems stupid now. I should have told Evan when I first met him. I should have gone to him when the letters came. But I had kept these secrets for so long, I was afraid. The longer I waited to speak, the worse it got. It was lies upon lies."

"What about your friend Mandy? What happened to her?"

"That's the thing. I think Mandy might be part of this. After Hannah was adopted, she stopped writing. Neither mom nor I could find her. We had given her every cent we could find to carry out the adoption with the agreement that she would be there for Hannah. And then she disappeared. Maybe she was never my friend." Ava sighed.

Ava looked up at Hank pleading with him to understand.

Hank was having his own problems. He was remembering his sister and the last time he saw her, wrapped in a blanket and left in the waiting room of the free clinic. He had been running ever since. He had never tried to find her again, thinking that she was better off without him.

He and Ava were just alike. Both running from the people they loved. Maybe he could make up for leaving Abbie by helping Ava.

"I understand," he said. "Let's go get those papers."

Forty-Four

Ava took off her shoe, and slid the heel back to reveal a key. She handed it to Hank with trembling hands. Every part of her screamed not to trust anyone this much. *What if he simply takes the key and walks out of my life?* Her world tunneled down to watching herself hand over the key to her daughter to a stranger. Had she grown at all, or was she still too naive and stupid?

Hank stared at Ava, admiration growing. A key in the heel of her shoe. *Clever!* Well, now that he had the key, they were ready to move to the next phase. All these months of preparation and they were heading down the path of resolution.

The problem was, he wasn't sure what he wanted the resolution to be anymore. He suspected Grant was doing things behind his back, and if that were the case, there would not be a happy outcome for any of Ava's friends. If it were just Hank, then he wouldn't involve everyone else. His concern was what happened, and how it happened, to Ava and Hannah.

He knew what Grant wanted that outcome to be. Hank just wasn't sure if that was what he wanted.

It took just a second or two for the conflict to pass through him while taking the key from Ava. If Ava noticed, she didn't show that she did. *We're both experts at keeping secrets.*

"A bank deposit key? How do you know it still works? And do you know what bank it goes to?" Hank asked.

"My mom was a planner. She paid twenty years in advance, and yes I know where it is. But, I'm afraid to go. What if those people also know where it is, and they grab me on the way? That's why I need your help, to get into the bank and the box."

"Do you have a plan yourself?" Hank asked, knowing that he had one in case she didn't.

Ava did. A few hours later, a man and his daughter entered the bank together. Hank had changed into a pair of gray slacks and a buttoned up blue shirt, and Ava into a flowered dress and black heels. A long blond wig and heavy makeup completed her look. Ava figured that once they signed for the box, someone might know that they were there, but it would be too late.

She was carrying a huge purse over her shoulder. Inside was a different shirt, glasses, and a hat for Hank, and a change of clothes and a new wig for her. On the way out, she wanted them to appear to be other people.

Hank knew that she didn't have to do that part. After all, he was the one who was watching her. There was no one else. But he admired her ingenuity and planning skills and told her so. Ava blushed and hugged him.

"You clean up nice, Hank, and I will never be able to thank you enough for this," she said.

Hank smiled at her. No one had ever been this nice to him, not since Abbie, anyway. Too bad it couldn't last.

Inside the bank, Ava asked to see her box. The teller led Hank and Ava back into the vault, inserted his key and her key, pulled out the box and set it on the table and then left them there.

Shaking in anticipation, Ava stared at the box.

It seemed incongruent that a plain gray box could contain such life-changing information.

Hank stood to the side, giving Ava privacy. He watched her pull a set of papers from the box, and a stack of letters.

Ava peered into the box at something stuck in the back. Reaching in, she pulled out a stuffed, and very ragged rabbit. "Oh," Ava said. "Mom kept our rabbit."

Hank stared at the rabbit. *No, No, No, this can't be happening.* He yanked the rabbit out of Ava's hand and slumped against the back wall. *No, no,* was all he could think.

"Hank, what's wrong? Are you okay?" Ava asked.

Still holding the rabbit, Hank shook his head, no.

Ava waited. She had waited for years to find out what was in the box. This stranger had showed up for her, and saved her; the least she could do was wait for him to tell her what was wrong.

It was only a minute of silence, but to Hank, it was an eternity. To find out about the rabbit, he would have to step over a huge chasm. On one side he was who he had become. On the other side was who he was before.

What if the answer made him choose. What would he do?

Looking down, he saw that Ava had grabbed his hand and was holding it gently while his other hand clutched the rabbit to his chest. He didn't know that tears were falling. It had never happened before.

There were two straight-back-brown chairs in the corner of the room, and Ava led Hank to one and helped him sit. She pulled the other one over and sat on it with her knees touching his.

"Tell me. What's wrong, Hank? Let me help you, as you are helping me."

Finding his voice, Hank finally asked the question that would change everything. "Where did you get this rabbit?"

Ava smiled at him. "It was my mom's. She let me have it when I was young. It was her most prized possession. I promised to always take care of it, but couldn't find it after she died. Now I see that she put it here knowing that someday I would come get these papers, find Hannah, and give it to her."

Hank asked the next question, the one he was afraid to hear the answer to. "You have never told me your mother's name, Ava. What was it?"

"Did you know her, Hank? Is that what this is all about?" When Hank just continued to stare, Ava told him.

"We called her Abbie, but her name was Abigail. It's Hannah's middle name. Hannah Abigail Evans. I gave her my last name."

For Hank, the world went black for a moment, and then everything changed. It was as if a light that had gone out of him more than fifty years before had come on again.

Both he and Ava felt it at the same time.

"Is there someone here?" Ava asked.

Forty-Five

Hank looked at Ava, at himself clutching the rabbit, at the papers on the counter, at Ava's bag in the corner, and told himself to get up and deal with the rabbit later.

Standing up, he grabbed Ava and told her they had to go. Ava just continued to stare. In the past five minutes, Hank had officially freaked out, and she had felt someone in the room with them. But of course, there wasn't anyone there, and now Hank appeared to be back to himself.

Not true. Not himself. Not the Hank that Ava had met a few hours before. This one was harder. This one was pushing her to get a move on. This one was afraid. Ava knew a cover up for fear when she saw it, but what he was afraid of she didn't know.

What was up with the rabbit anyway? Hank had grabbed the papers, and the rabbit, and stuffed them into the bag, and slammed the box back into its slot.

"What about changing clothes?" Ava said.

"Ava listen to me. It's more important that we get out of here, than spend another second changing clothes. Come on, we are going somewhere safe, and we'll talk there."

Ava stepped back and summoned all her courage. "Give me my bag. I don't know what's going on, but you are scaring me. I can do this on my own."

"Trust me, Ava. You can't," he growled at her. "This is a much bigger problem than you think. I promise. I will tell you more when we get out of here." Looking at Ava, and finally understanding why she felt and looked familiar, Hank softened.

"I know this is a lot to take in, it is for me too, but you are safe now, and I want to keep you that way."

Still not sure, Ava hung back. Hank had her bag slung over his shoulder, and there was no way she was going to overpower him to get it back. She would have to play along with him. She would still use him to get to Hannah, but then keep running. She remembered Pete had given her his card. Perhaps she could contact him, and he would help her go to the next place.

Inside, Ava was planning an escape. On the outside, she was attempting to go forward with Hank. Ava felt a small pressure on her back pushing her towards Hank and the door.

Spinning on her heel, she looked behind her, but once again there was nothing there, and Hank was at the door waiting for her. "Go" was what she heard in her head.

Once she started moving, Ava walked quickly through the doorway and into the bank, where she held tightly onto Hank's arm.

A rush of well-being flooded through her, though there was no reason to feel relieved. The situation had gotten even crazier, and yet there was that feeling. As they passed out of the bank, Ava glanced up at Hank and saw the same look on his face that she thought was on hers.

What is up with him and the rabbit? Did he know my mom? How weird would that be? Ava thought.

Hank kept Ava close to him as they walked—not because he thought she would run. He knew she wouldn't. His insurance policy was that he was the one holding all the information about

Hannah.

No, it was because he was beginning to wonder if he, like Ava, had been set up. Grant must have known who Ava was; he just hadn't told him. He was going to have to admit it to himself, she was his niece. *Abbie's daughter!* His breath caught in his throat as he thought about what that meant. But he couldn't afford that emotion, not now.

There was a reason Grant had kept that information from him when he put him on this job. It was a special kind of cruelty to send a man to a niece and her child to destroy them and possibly everyone in their life. Had Grant been planning this all along? Did he know that Hank had been thinking about leaving and this was his way to stop him, by destroying him in the process?

All these thoughts were running through Hank's head while keeping a hyper-alert vigilance for anyone watching him with Ava. Grant had to know that Hank would eventually figure it out. At some point Ava would have said her mother's name, and Hank would finally notice, or admit, that Ava had some of his sister's features.

What had happened to Abbie? Did she have a good life? Who took care of her? Who was Ava's father—and where was he?

Too many questions to be thinking about as they were hustling down the street. Hank decided that it might not be safe to take Ava back to his motel room. It was possible that Grant had been tracking him there. At the last minute, Hank veered into the Marriott. He asked Ava to wait in the lobby, while he booked two rooms.

Ava took in her surroundings. It was a far cry from the room she had been locked in. The hotel faced Figueroa Avenue, but in the back was a lovely patio. Ava sat in one of the comfy chairs that faced the patio, and a sense of quiet peace settled over her. She could see Hank at the counter. He was no longer the laid back stranger who rescued her. He was tense and uneasy, glancing around him, tapping on the counter as the clerk prepared a room key. She could see that he was checking on her by the reflection in the windows leading out back. With a start, Ava realized he was scared. That meant he hadn't been afraid before. *Why was that?*

Everything had changed when she took out her mom's old rabbit. As Hank walked towards her, something about the way he turned his head seemed so familiar. It reminded her of someone. With a start, she realized it reminded her of her mother, and a few pieces fell into place but left gaping holes where there had once been solid ground.

****

Once they got to Ava's room, all the adrenaline that had kept her going for the past few weeks clicked off and was replaced by a sinking fatigue. She barely made it to the bed before falling asleep mumbling that she just needed a few minutes to take a nap and then they could look at the papers.

Hank covered Ava with a spare blanket he found in the closet and swept the room for cameras and microphones. It would have been hard for anyone to have been in the room before them, since it was a last-minute decision, but he wasn't taking any chances. Once everything was secure, he locked the papers into the room's safe.

There were things he needed to do to clean up behind them, so he left Ava a note saying he would be back with some supplies and not to worry. He would take care of everything. Hank had never been sentimental, but he couldn't help himself when he put the rabbit under the covers with Ava. It had been a long time since he had tucked anyone into bed. Perhaps he was being given a chance to make up for what he had been doing with his life.

Before leaving the room, he changed his clothes using the ones in the bag and headed out the door being sure to hang a "do not disturb" sign on both bedrooms. He intended to sleep in Ava's room, but he didn't want anyone to know that. Hank knew he had to be extremely careful. If he was ever going to screw up, it could not be now. It was no longer just about him.

A few hours later, he quietly returned to the room. He had paid off the two guys by putting the money into the agreed spot. There was no point in picking up any more bad karma by not paying them. He had also bought some grooming items for himself and a few things for Ava. Then he returned the rental car, went to a new agency and rented another car under another name, using cash.

Ava was still sleeping; he wasn't surprised. He pulled out a few pillows from the closet, laid another blanket on the floor, and lay down. Years of training himself to fall asleep fast in any place came in handy. He stilled his mind, relaxed his muscles and drifted off, but not before he swore he heard a small voice say, "Thank you." He peeked up at Ava, but she was still asleep.

His last thought was of Abbie and the life that he had missed with her. He hadn't wanted to drag her down with him, and he didn't want to drag her daughter and grand-daughter down, either. But, perhaps there was a chance to have a small bit of happiness in his life.

A few hours later, Ava woke up to a dark room. The bathroom light was on, and the door was open a crack. *Hank must have done that,* she thought. It's exactly what I do, too. She quietly slipped off the bed and saw Hank sleeping at the foot of it, just in time to not trip over him.

She smiled. Yes, Hank was frightening, but at the same time, he had become her guardian angel, and for that, she was grateful beyond words. On the desk beside the bed, she found a clean T-shirt and jeans. *He must have gotten the sizes from my clothes in the bag,* Ava thought. Picking them up, she found a package of underwear waiting for her.

Ava almost laughed out loud thinking of how embarrassed he must have been shopping for them. Clutching the clothes to her chest, she smiled down at Hank and whispered, "Thank you," and went into the bathroom to shower and change.

Hank had awakened the moment Ava opened her eyes, but had kept himself still and silent as if he was sleeping, he was wide awake when he heard Ava's whisper, "Thank you." It sounded just like the first one.

His eyes flew open. "Abbie?" he said.

Forty-Six

Grant silently fumed.

The innocent-looking weekly meeting of his team in the back room of the local Panera Bread was in session. Grant had brought along one of his new members, Lenny. A guy in his thirties. One of his roundups off the street, like Hank. Except this guy was starting and Hank was ending. If all goes well I will get a good twenty years out of Lenny, Grant thought.

Lenny was practicing his presentation skills today. Grant liked giving his guys a chance to practice. Grant wanted to let other people believe that they were leading. Plus, if he didn't lead the meetings, it gave him the opportunity to watch everyone else. That was one of his greatest skills, watching, He was a master of deceit, and being quiet was necessary some of the time to observe what others were doing.

Of course, this meeting was a sham. The team talked about doing good out in the community. Today, they were planning their annual street carnival. Lots of sticky, sweet food and cheap hot dogs and sausages were sold to raise money for a local charity. They changed the charity they supported every year. Grant wanted everyone to see these men as decent and helpful members of the community.

Because of their public profile helping charities, no one would ever question why they hung around together, or what they were doing in Grant's basement, other than playing poker. Deception. Grant was the king of deception.

Except, Hank was pissing him off.

On the surface, everything was going well. Hank kept checking in. He told him about rescuing Ava and now they were heading off to find Hannah. It didn't make any sense. Hank should have figured out by now that Ava was his niece. He should be furious; he should be running, he should be afraid.

But, Hank didn't appear to be any of those things. Grant wanted Hank to be very distracted when he found out about Ava. But, he didn't indicate that he was distracted. He promised to get Ava home in time for the wedding. Either Hank was smarter or stupider than he thought.

Either way, Hank would get Ava where he needed her to be in time to take care of them all at once. Yes, Grant was the king of distraction, manipulating everyone so that they focused on the wrong place and people, including Hank. Everyone had their attention on finding Ava, getting her home, and having a wedding.

Grant smiled to himself. He loved the movie *Three Weddings and a Funeral.* He was producing a real live movie. He would call it *One Wedding and a Hundred Funerals.*

******

As Ava finished toweling her hair in the bathroom, she heard the room door open, and she froze, relaxing only when she heard Hank's voice and the door close again. An extra toothbrush and a tube of toothpaste lay on the counter. More gratitude for Hank's thoughtfulness came over her as she brushed her teeth. By then, the smell of fresh coffee and food had made its way into the bathroom, and she realized she was famished.

Hank was sitting at the small round table in the corner. He had kept the drapes closed and turned on a few small lights. *Safety first,* Ava thought.

"Hank, thank you so much for all of this. I know we have so much to talk about, but can we eat first? I'm afraid I will lose my appetite if we start talking."

Hank nodded and tucked in to his pancakes. Ava lifted the lid of her plate and found a stack of pancakes for herself, plus eggs and bacon, and what looked like an extra order of bacon. The exact breakfast she and her mom would order when they would go out to breakfast together.

Both of them rushed through their food, partly because they were so hungry, but also because they were anxious. When they were done, Hank cleared the table, keeping the coffee. He put the tray with the dishes into the hall, after first checking through the peephole to make sure that the corridor was empty.

He opened the safe and brought the papers to the table. "Ready?" he asked.

"Yes. But first, can we talk about the rabbit, and who you really are? You kinda look like my mom. Are you related? How come I never met you if you are?"

Hank held up his hand to stop her. "I will answer these questions. At least I will tell you what I know, but first, do you want to find Hannah?"

"I do want to find Hannah. But won't I trust you more if I knew more?" Ava asked.

Trust. There was that word again. It followed her everywhere. She had run away from Evan because she thought he would realize that she couldn't be trusted.

And yet, she demanded trust from everyone else.

"I am trustworthy," Ava whispered to herself.

"Are you?" Hank asked. "Because if I begin to tell you about myself, I need to know that I can trust you. It's not the other way around.

"I always do what I say I'm going to do. Do you? You told me that you ran away from your mom, and then it sounds like you ran away from Hannah, and then from Evan. These are people who loved you. You let them down, not the other way around. You were afraid of being hurt, so you hurt them. Is that being trustworthy?"

Ava sat for what seemed like hours but was only a few seconds before answering Hank. "Yes, I did all those things. I wouldn't open my heart to let people in. I admired people who had that mature love; I think it's called *Pragma*. It binds people together in trust along with love. You are right; I have been lying to myself. It has never been about how other people behaved; it's always been about my reactions and choices.

"But, I am willing. Sitting here with you, you must see how willing I am. I know you didn't just rescue me. I know this has been a setup of some kind. But I still trust you. Please, let me prove that I can be trustworthy, too."

Ava smiled at Hank with tears running down her face. "Please," she said.

"I am not a nice man, Ava. I am a nasty man. I have done terrible things in my life. But you will never have to be afraid of me. There was one person in my life that I have loved. I would have done anything I could to help her and save her. And now, I will do the same thing for you, because, Ava, your mother, Abigail," Hank paused, he couldn't say it out loud, it would become real if he did.

"My mother, Hank? My mother what?"

"Your mother was the one person I loved. Your mother was my sister."

Ava wasn't surprised. She had begun to figure that out, but she waited for a beat to give Hank time to collect himself.

"Making me your niece, and Hannah your great-niece," Ava said calmly, but her hands gave her away as she reached for her coffee.

"I think you'd better tell me how come I don't know you. My mother told me once that she had a brother, but she hadn't seen him since she was eight. She never explained why. When I asked her, she told me that he abandoned her, and when she grew up and tried to find him, she couldn't so she figured he was dead.

"But, here you are, very much alive. I believe you. I see my mom in you. But you broke her heart. What will keep you from breaking mine?"

Hank sighed. He had sealed the pain of leaving Abbie in a locked room inside himself for his whole life. Now it was seeping out beneath the door, and Ava was rattling the doorknob with a key in her hand. But would that pain be worse than what he had been inflicting on himself and others so that he didn't have to think? *I'm just as guilty as Ava,* he thought. *I ran away too.*

"I wanted her to think I was dead. I wanted her to find a life that didn't include the horrible things she saw as a child. I didn't want her to know what I had become. I thought I was making the right decision. Maybe I was, maybe I wasn't. We have both been running, but maybe I can stop now, too.

"I don't think you are going to like me at all when I tell you this story, but that can't matter. You must trust me. There are evil, sick-hearted people out there, and one of them has focused on hurting you. I was sent to be part of that, but instead, I am now your protector. But, to do that, I have to continue to work for that man. Can you trust me enough for that?"

Ava nodded. "Go ahead, tell me the worst of it."

Hank felt a weight begin to lift from his heart as he told the story of his dead mother, his horribly abusive father, and the last night of his life. Hank explained why he hit and killed his father and burned the house down. Hank relived breaking into the free clinic with Abigail wrapped in her favorite blanket and carrying her favorite stuffed rabbit. Hank told about watching her sleep, wishing he could stay, but knowing that he couldn't.

He told her how he had hidden outside the free clinic until he saw the man Eric come in and find her. Eric had once helped Hank when he had been hurt and stumbled into the clinic, so he knew that Eric would take good care of Abigail.

He told Ava how he had watched Eric put Abigail in his car, watched how loving he was to her, and watched Eric drive away with his sister. Hardening his heart, he turned away and became a runaway on the streets.

Hank's story continued with how he learned to steal food and cash from stores to survive, and how one day he was almost caught by the police when a man in his twenties, dressed in nice clothes, rescued him. The man was Grant. Grant kept him fed on the streets until the day Hank trusted him enough to come inside. Grant changed his name from Tim Samson to Hank Blaze.

"That's why mom couldn't find you?"

"She was right. Tim Samson died. Hank Blaze was born. Grant encouraged my evil ways. He just wanted me to do things in his way. I learned that men dressed in nice clothes could be even more dangerous than the ones you think are criminals because of the way they dress or the color of their skin. Grant was, and is, one of the truly dangerous ones. He understands the system and uses it to do whatever he wants, to whomever he wants, and when he wants.

"The trouble is, he hates your kind. The kind of people that believe that good is all powerful, that are learning how to do weird-ass things like telepathy and remote viewing, Your kind that slows down enough to think instead of being too busy to see. Your kind is hard to fool. Your Circle, whatever you call it, is what Grant sees as the most dangerous kind of people out there. And he intends to eliminate you before you pass your knowledge, and your gifts, on to others.

"So, let's stop talking, and go find Hannah, because it is possible that he knows where she is, and although I have been checking in as I should, he won't stay fooled for long.

"Are you ready now to look at these papers and get started?"

Ava didn't move. Could she believe him? Was all of what Hank said true? Or was it just another lie in the pack of lies that people told. He was her uncle. Good once, bad for a long time, but perhaps good was hidden beneath the surface, waiting to rise again.

With a flash of insight, she realized Hank had been sent to her. It was part of the line of light again.

Without speaking, she stood up, walked behind Hank, and put her arms around his neck. He was hot and sweaty, not having had a chance to clean up as she did, but his smell was familiar. He was family. He was her uncle. Hank froze, and then placed his hands on her arms holding them close to his chest. She was his niece. Abigail had come back to him again within Ava. Hank knew what he had to do, and he always did what he had to do.

This time, they both heard it, "Thank you.'

"Mom?"

"Abigail?"

Forty-Seven

Finally, the papers they had taken from the bank were placed on the table. There was a letter addressed to Ava. She laid it aside, afraid her emotions would derail her from doing what she needed to do next. Perhaps she would have Hank read it first in case it contained information they needed to know.

For the moment both of them were focused on the papers in front of them. Two of the documents were birth certificates: Ava's and Hannah's.

Hank struggled not to get caught up in the emotions of seeing them. Two people—his family—born without him knowing about it. Hannah Abigail Evans, no father listed, and her mother, Ava Timothea Evans.

"Oh man," Hank said sinking into his chair. "Timothea. She didn't forget me."

"She always told me that if I were a boy, she would have named me Timothy, but got too emotional to explain why when I asked. See, we are related, you and me."

"I have something to show you," Hank said as he unclasped his watch. As he laid it flat on the table, Ava could see a little pocket sewed into the watch band. When Hank squeezed the band, it opened to reveal a small pouch which Hank pulled out and handed to Ava.

"Open it," he said.

Carefully, Ava opened it and with a puzzled expression pulled out a tiny lock of hair.

"Your mother's."

"Oh," whispered Ava, "It's the same color hair as Hannah's in her picture."

"Yes," Hank answered as he tucked the hair, the color of gold, back into the pouch and watchband. "I suppose if we ever need to prove we are all related we can do a DNA test."

Ava put her hand on his wrist. "No need to prove it to me, Hank. Or should I call you Tim?"

"Let's keep it Hank for now. It's safer that way, and I think I'm much more Hank than Tim. For now, the important thing is to find Hannah's adoptive parents. It says here that they are Linda and John Minks."

Ava frowned, wrinkling her forehead. That name sounded familiar to her, but she couldn't place it.

Research was the next order of business. Hank and Ava needed to find out more about the Minks family. What was their latest address? They also hoped to find social media profiles for Linda and John. Ava secretly hoped they would show pictures of Hannah.

Hank explained that the safest way to look was using the hotel's computers. He had plenty of practice disguising himself online.

They agreed to pack everything up, just in case they needed to leave immediately, but would keep both hotel rooms for another night. Hank went next door to the other room, and messed up the bed and left towels on the floor, so it looked as if he had stayed there that night.

The two of them scanned the room one last time to make

sure they hadn't left anything. Two people used to running away were now running towards something. Ava was doing her best to keep her panic under control. What if they were too late? What if she couldn't find Hannah? Their search didn't reveal anything on social media. That scared Ava. Why wouldn't there be anything there? If everything had been okay with the adoption, wouldn't they have been proud parents?

The adoption papers held more information. They listed Linda as a stay-at-home mom, and John as an English teacher at Santa Monica College. Hank thought they should try there first before running a deeper search which might trigger something someone could catch.

The plan was for Ava to go to the admissions office and ask for the office hours for John Minks. As a former student, she wanted to thank him for her teaching her how to become a writer. Hank would play the role of her dad, proud of his daughter, and he would wait outside in the quad for her. It wasn't going to be a hard sell; they did look like father and daughter, which pleased them both.

Finding parking was a nightmare, so Hank dropped off Ava while he searched for parking. They agreed to meet in front of the school's administration building after Ava got the information they needed. With her all-important bag over her shoulder, standard jeans, and tee, Ava did look like a student, or perhaps alum.

If they asked for her name, Hank had searched the year books of the college from the past few years and found a student who looked like Ava. They were prepared to use her name. It was risky since someone might know that student, but it was a chance they were ready to take.

What they weren't prepared for happened when Ava asked for John Minks' office hours. She learned that there was no teacher named John Minks, and there had never been.

Ava's heart beat harder. No Linda and John Minks? Minks? Where had she heard that name before?

And then she remembered. Mandy. Mandy Minks.

When she first met her, Ava had thought Minks was a stage name and promptly forgot it. Her heart was now racing. This has been about Mandy all along? She tricked me. I believed her when she said she was my friend.

Dazed, she walked out of the school as that all too familiar internal voice got louder and louder, berating her for being so stupid.

As soon as she got outside the building, Ava started hyperventilating and weaving back and forth. Hank, always alert, saw her coming. He wrapped his arms around her, led her to a bench, and pushed her head down between her knees. "Breathe," he said, rubbing her back.

"What happened?" Hank asked.

"Mandy happened. John and Linda Minks do not exist. I can't believe I was so stupid as to think that Mandy was my friend and trying to help me."

Hank grunted. "Yeah, I know that feeling. But, I see what I have to do next."

Hank led Ava to the campus library and found a table far away from everyone else. He took the letter out of his pack and handed it to Ava.

"First this," he said.

"I know. Still running," Ava answered as she picked up the envelope and stared at her mother's handwriting on the envelope.

"What if it tells me something I don't want to know?" Ava asked.

"Good god, Ava, you're in the middle of everything you

didn't want to know. Grow up!" Hank whispered as loudly as he could in her ear. He was getting angry. Really angry.

"I am sick of secrets. I am tired to the bone over lies and running and being scared. If you can't deal with this, then perhaps you don't deserve to have a child, and I need to get back to my own life."

Ava responded with a fiery glance in his direction and tore open the envelope, glanced at the contents said and burst into tears.

Hank took the letter, read it, and ended up with tears in his eyes. It was a love letter to Ava and Hannah from Abigail. Beautiful, but nothing that would help them find Hannah.

It was time for him to call Grant. *That's what Grant expects,* he realized. He expected Hank to find out that Hannah was his niece. And then Grant expected Hank to call and be mad about the deception. And once that happened, he would tell him where Hannah was being kept, or living, or whatever he had done.

But first, Grant wanted him to grovel. Well, grovel he would. He could be as deceptive as Grant. Whatever Grant's next play was he was going to have to outsmart him.

"Hank," Ava said wiping her eyes on the edge of her T-shirt. "What about Eric?"

"Eric?"

"Yes, Eric. I called him grandfather. I knew he wasn't. Mom told me that he adopted her, but she called him dad, so I called him grandfather."

"Okay, what about him? Where is he now? How come you haven't mentioned him before? I thought he must have died or something."

Ava glanced at Hank to see if he was being callous. He wasn't. Just logical. It was her fault she hadn't mentioned him before, not his for not knowing.

"When mom got sick, Eric was devastated. It was his idea that I go live with mom's friend Suzanne.

"After adopting mom he had continued to work at a medical clinic. Not the one you took her to, because they had moved. But helping is in Eric's blood. So, after Mom grew up and moved out, he started volunteering to be an aide to groups like Doctors Without Borders.

"When mom died, he got more and more involved, so I hardly ever saw him. Running, I suppose. I understood though, and he kept in touch through postcards letting me know where he was and what he was doing.

"When Evan and I started planning our wedding, we sent his invitation to the last address we had for him. Right before I left I got an answer back from him saying he would come and that he had moved back to California. He gave me his address. Maybe *he* knows something about Hannah."

"Well, that would have been helpful to know before now, Ava."

Seeing Ava's dejected face, Hank softened.

"Okay, we'll go see him. But first, I have to call Grant and tell him I can't find Hannah and that I know who you are. He likes being in control, and I have to let him think that he is still running my life."

"Isn't that dangerous?"

"Yes. But if I don't do what Grant is expecting, it will be even more dangerous. Where is Eric?"

"Carlsbad, south of here. We can get there in a few hours, depending on the traffic."

Hank grabbed his burner phone and turned it on. "First the phone call."

Forty-Eight

Grant laughed. Cackled actually. At least that is what it sounded like to Hank. He probably meant it as a warm fatherly type-laugh. One that went along with his words, "Hank. Been waiting for you to call. How can I be of help to you?"

Hank almost heard the word "son" after his question. He was sure Grant wanted him to think that it was implied.

Hank pumped up his voice to the level that Grant might expect since he was never going to believe too much emotion from Hank. He told him about discovering that Ava was his niece and how unbelievable it all was.

And then, cautiously, the way he would do it if he still believed in Grant, Hank asked him if he knew all along.

Apology filling his voice, Grant said that he had, how he had just wanted to give Hank some fun at finding out, thought it would be a great surprise, and all that.

Hank still heard the evil laughter behind it all, even though it was silent. Maybe if he had been listening more carefully to Grant, he would have heard it all along. But Hank pretended that he still didn't notice the evil in Grant's voice. Grant might think he was the world's best deceiver, but then he didn't really know Hank, did he?

"How far along are you in getting to Hannah?" Grant asked.

Hank explained about not being able to find the Minks family and Ava had just told him about Eric.

"Well, there you go, Hank. That's the next step. I promise Hannah is close. Once you find her, get everyone to Pennsylvania in time for the wedding. It's gonna be a good one."

"After I get her there, what happens next, boss?" Hank asked.

"Say 'yes' to Ava when she invites you to the wedding. I need you to get into the house to set some of the explosives. Doing this job is your big payoff. After this, you'll be able to live wherever you want to live. Your debt to me will have been paid."

"Will do," Hank said. "I'll be happy to get rid of this whiny woman, and I'm sure her kid will be just as bad. Probably more so. I never wanted to be tied down to a family. I'll be glad when this is over."

"Me, too, boy. Me, too."

Hank stayed on the line one second longer. He knew Grant wouldn't be able to help himself. Grant's laugh was still audible as he hung up.

As if I'd believe him, thought Hank. *He is going to have me set those explosives and then make sure that I am still there when they go off. Not going to happen.*

Grant wanted Hank to hear him. Grant knew Hank didn't believe him. He didn't want him to. Yes, Hank would be setting some explosives, but then so would someone else. Hank could sabotage the first explosion, but not the second.

If Grant could still skip, he would have.

He loved this game. He loved being the smartest person. He loved getting rid of anyone standing in his way. He didn't care who they were. *It's especially fun to give Hank the pleasure of finding his family and then taking it away.*

At the last minute, Hank would know he had failed. And then he, too, would join the blackness.

****

Ava watched Hank come back into the library. His face told her nothing, which, she was beginning to know, told her everything.

He grabbed the bag and started walking out without her. She watched him. *Is he leaving? What's happening?* A few steps away from the doorway, he turned around and stared at her, pointed out the door, and kept on walking.

Ava stood up, pushed both chairs back under the table, and casually strolled out of the library.

Hank was waiting. He grabbed her arm and pulled her around the side of the building.

"Are you kidding me? You are sulking?"

She shot back, "Are *you* kidding me? You're taking this out on me?"

Neither said anything as they stood a few feet from each other trying to out-stare the other one. Finally, Ava blinked. "Now what?"

Still holding anger back with every cell in his body, Hank said, "We are going to see Eric."

The first hour driving south was tense. The traffic was terrible, as always. They would go fifty miles an hour for a few minutes, then up to sixty-five for another few miles, which always signaled that there would be brake lights up ahead. Then they would crawl forward at twenty or thirty miles an hour for fifteen minutes or so, and start the process again.

It was the perfect backdrop for not talking. Finally, as they passed Irvine, traffic eased up enough to let them go a little faster. At that point, Ava asked if he could pull off the freeway and find a bathroom.

Plus, she was hungry. Low blood sugar was not helping her mood, and probably wasn't helping his either. "Get me some carbs, fat, and salt," she said. "And some caffeine wouldn't hurt, either."

Secretly, Hank was glad. He needed the same thing but, wasn't about to admit it. While driving out of LA, through the horrendous traffic, Hank was able to let most of the anger dissolve. He owed Ava an apology. He wasn't angry at her, and he couldn't even be angry at Grant. Grant was an evil snake and always had been. He was mad at himself. He had chosen the lifestyle. He had stayed when he could have left.

"Right there." Ava pointed. A McDonald's sign beckoned right off the freeway. "They have great french fries. Mom would always get them for me when I was a kid," she said.

"You are still a kid," Hank said.

Ava smiled. Hank was talking again.

Hank handed Ava a wad of money after she came out of the bathroom and told her what to order for him, while he used the bathroom.

Standing in line for food, Ava smiled again. He had stood guard while she was in the bathroom. He was protecting her. She would protect him, too.

Five minutes later, they both had slowed their eating down enough to just pick at their french fries. Ava thought she would give Hank a break, so told him that she understood why he was so mad.

Perhaps they could be angry together and use it to accomplish what they needed to accomplish, rather than taking it out on each other.

Hank nodded agreement and said, "Here's the good news, Ava. Grant has been playing me all along. He still won't tell me where Hannah is. He thinks it will be fun for me to have to look. But, since what he wants is for you to find her, and then go back and get married, obviously she is somewhere safe."

Ava jumped up out of her chair, clapped her hands, and almost yelled as she said, "Let's go get her!"

"Not so fast," Hank said, pulling her back down. "That's the good news, but we still have to follow his cockamamie plan to find her."

He didn't want to tell her about the explosives. There was no need to worry her. He would take care of Grant and Grant's plans himself.

Forty Nine

"I hate not having my smart-phone, Hank," Ava said. "How did people ever find anything before GPS?"

"Maps. You've heard of them." Hank said. He was carefully watching the exit signs off the freeway. Miss one and he would have to go to the next and travel back. They had stopped at a 7-Eleven to ask for directions. Ava had remembered that there was one right beside the flower fields. They weren't blooming at the moment, but Hank thought when they did it would be a sight to see.

By chance, someone knew which exit to take to get to Eric's street. From there, they were on their own. It seemed as if the person was waiting for them to come in to them give the directions. *There I go again,* he thought, *imagining things.*

They followed the directions given to them by the man at the 7-Eleven. They wove through a maze of winding streets until they came to the address that Ava had for her grandfather.

As they pulled up, a man stepped out of the front door onto the tiny porch.

Ava jumped out of the car and ran full speed into his arms. "Grandfather, I have missed you so much!"

"And I you, child," he said. "This must be Hank, sorry, Tim.

I've heard so much about you. Come in, come in. Time for some tea or perhaps you prefer coffee?"

Eric gently guided them into his home and settled them on the couch, since both of them seemed incapable of deciding what to do next.

"You know who this is? Have you been expecting us? How can that possibly be?" Ava asked.

Hank stood up, angry at being pushed around and fooled once again. "So, you know Grant, don't you? You work with him?" Hank asked, poking Eric in the shoulder and pushing him backward.

Eric reached up and gently put his hand on Hank's cheek. "It's okay, Hank. Sit, I'll tell you everything I know. But we don't have a lot of time so can we get started?"

Ava reached up and took Hank's hand and pulled him back to the couch. Reluctantly he let her, hoping against hope that Eric was not working with Grant.

Watching Hank's internal struggle, Eric smiled at him and began. "Yes, I've heard of Grant. But, no I am not working with him. I knew you were coming because Abbie told me."

"My mom told you? She died. She can't tell you anything."

"But you know that she could, don't you? You have felt her beside you all along. Both of you have. She has even thanked you once or twice.

"Yes, she did die from cancer. But, she chose to stay behind to make sure that you would find Hannah one day.

"I have always known she was there. She told me before she died that she would remain until all was well with you.

"And you, Hank. She found you and watched over you, too. You have never left her heart. And now she is grateful that you are taking care of Ava for her, and me."

Hank's bravado had faded, and he looked at Eric with

gratitude. "I saw you take Abigail in your car that day. I left her there because you had been so kind to me when I was hurt. I thought Abigail would be safe with you. At least I did one thing right in this world."

"You did many more things right than you think, Hank, and we both trust that you will do many more good things in the future. For now, though, Hannah is our priority," Eric said.

A car door slammed outside. Ava turned to look out the window, and then jumped up and ran outside. She stopped herself in time. The child running towards the house didn't even know her so how could she run into her arms?

But that is exactly what happened. Hannah ran directly at Ava and jumped up into her arms. Hannah hugged Ava as tightly as she could. Stunned, Ava wrapped her arms around her whispering, "Hannah, Hannah."

Ava turned to take Hannah into the house, but Hannah said, "What about Auntie Mandy?"

Only then did Ava look back at the car and the woman standing by it. *Mandy?*

Ava placed Hannah on the ground and ushered her into the house, before she could walk towards the car and her past.

"Should I be happy to see you, Mandy? Why do you have Hannah? Are you part of this craziness that's been going on?"

Mandy didn't say a word.

Eric called down to both of them. "Get into the house, you two. Now."

Mandy still didn't move. Ava slid her arm around Mandy's elbow. "You heard him. Let's get inside, now."

At the door, Eric handed Ava a phone. "Call Evan. Put him out of his misery. Use my bedroom," he said pointing down the hall. "I'll entertain the troops. All your questions will be answered. Now get moving."

Ava found the bedroom. A twin bed sat in the middle of a room just barely big enough to hold it. But, it was neat and clean. Nothing was out of place.

Looking around, with a pang in her heart, Ava realized that there wasn't much to be out of place. A small chest of drawers held a single picture of her mom and her when she was a child. The bed was covered with an old blue chenille bedspread, so thin that the blue was almost white.

Ava held the phone in front of her. What could she say? What would Evan say?

As she sat there, she realized that the presence she had always felt with her was still there, but now she knew what it was, who it was. It was her mother. How could she have not known that? What was the promise she had made? That she would open her heart?

It didn't matter what Evan said. It mattered that she loved him. She just needed him to know that.

He picked up on the first ring. "Evan," Ava said, and then burst into tears. "I'm sorry, Evan. I love you."

Back in their house, Evan fell into the nearest chair upon hearing Ava's voice. "It's Ava," he screamed so loud that Tom and Mira sitting on the back deck heard him.

Dropping everything, they ran to the living room to find Evan crying and laughing at the same time.

"It's Ava," Evan said again holding the phone towards them. "Ava" Tom and Mira yelled! "Come home!"

In Eric's house, Ava laughed so hard she slipped off the bed onto the floor. "Evan, I want to come home, but I have to tell you a few things first."

"No, you don't, Ava. Whatever made you run away doesn't matter. I don't care. We'll work it out. You'll explain. I'll understand. Just come home."

Ava glanced out the door and thought about who was sitting in Eric's living room.

"But I need to bring a few people with me," she said.

"Bring as many people as you want to, Ava. Just come home."

Fifty

Ava found them all sitting around Eric's tiny table. A feast of fruit and muffins were sitting in the center, and everyone had a drink in front of them.

In the corner, a tall fan was moving the air around, doing its best to keep the room cool against the late July heat. Even though Ava had never been in this house before, it still smelled and felt familiar. Eric had made it a home, as he always did.

One of the five mismatched chairs sat empty. It was the one beside Hannah. When she saw Ava, she patted the seat and said, "Mommy, sit here beside me."

Ava sat as if it wasn't the weirdest thing in the world to be sitting at a table with the four of them. Old family, new family, and Mandy.

She took a sip of coffee that she found in front of her. It was made the way she liked it. Was she the only one confused by this? Everyone was eating and smiling as if this was normal.

Finally, not able to stand it another second, she asked, "So who is going to explain this to me?" Hugging Hannah close to her, she continued, "As forever grateful I am that Hannah knows me, how does she know me?"

"Oh, that's easy, Mommy. Auntie Mandy showed me

pictures and talked to me about you every day. She promised that one day you would come and get me. And you did! And you look even more beautiful than your pictures!"

Ava wondered if she would ever stop crying. With Hannah's sticky arms around her neck, even with tears running down her face, she felt at peace for the first time in her life. Smoothing down Hannah's hair, so like her own when she was little, she kissed Hannah on the cheek and then turned back to the table.

"Mandy, how did you end up with Hannah? Eric, how did you know they were coming? The same way you knew Hank, and I were coming, or did you know where they were the whole time?"

Hank spoke for the first time since Mandy arrived, "Hannah, why don't you show me around your great-grandfather's house, and maybe we can take a walk around the neighborhood and see what's happening out there."

"Yes, so fun," Hannah said and then looked back and forth between Ava and Mandy.

Mandy said, "Yes, Hannah, now you ask your mom if that's okay."

Ava nodded, and the two of them went off holding hands. Hank looked behind him at Ava. It was evident he was going to want a full report when he got back.

"Okay, which one of you is going to tell what is going on."

Mandy looked at Eric and spoke. "Eric only knows a piece of it, so I might as well tell you the story.

"I know you must be furious with me, and it's possible you will be even angrier when I explain what happened, because it was a setup from the beginning."

Ava started to speak, but Mandy held up her hand. "No, let me tell you the whole thing. Otherwise, I won't be able to get it told. Afterwards you can ask all the questions that you want to."

Eric reached across the table and touched Ava's hand. Ava nodded and said, "Okay."

"Actually, not a setup from the very beginning. It was a chance meeting at the Laundromat. Of course, Eric has clued me in to the fact that no meetings are by chance, but at the time, it felt that way.

"You were so young and beautiful and clueless, and you had no idea what I did for a living. At first, I thought I had found you like a lost puppy, but then discovered that I had found a friend.

"What you could not have known was that I had gotten myself into deep trouble. As you probably figured out, I was working as an escort. Like you, I had run away when I was sixteen, but unlike you, I got caught up in the wrong crowd. I liked it. I wanted the attention. I needed what I believed to be love.

"But then I started using the money to gamble. Poker. I enjoyed playing poker with the guys. All the attention and adrenaline I could want, combined to be my drug of choice. But I was terrible at it and more interested in the atmosphere than learning the game, so I kept losing and owing money.

"I see you are starting to figure some things out, Ava. No, at first I had no intention of using you to help me. I liked you. You were so innocent and naive, and friendly, and open. You were everything that I had lost.

"I was afraid of pulling you in, which is why I sent you off to live by yourself. I tried to stay out of your life. Really, I did. But things got worse and worse, and I was told to start finding "friends" for a few guys of the big boss. One of those guys was the man you knew as Rick Sanders."

Mandy paused to take a sip of water.

Ava was less surprised than she thought she would be. Part of her had figured some of this out. Meeting Rick had seemed just a bit too strange. He had always seemed like a wolf after its prey. Too bad she hadn't paid more attention to how she felt.

But as Mandy said, she was young and naive. For the first time, Ava looked closely at Mandy and realized that Mandy had lost much of her stunning beauty. She was still pretty, but now she was way too thin and her once-beautiful auburn hair was stringy. Dark circles sat under her eyes. For a minute Ava felt sorry for her. For a minute.

Mandy continued, "Okay, so Rick met you. He got what he wanted. But he started getting bored and I had to find him more girls. It seemed as if I would never get the debt paid. I realized much too late that I was right. I would never get it paid.

"When Rick started getting bored, I think you were happy that he was beginning to leave you alone. I thought you were out of the woods and I breathed a sigh of relief when he told me he was moving on.

"But he kept an eye on you. He didn't like not knowing what happened to 'his girls.'

"He watched you go to work with Kathy Duncan. Once or twice he followed you in his car as you rode your bike to work. He hated that you were choosing to walk away from him—people don't do that with men like Rick. So he bided his time.

"I knew he was watching you. I should have warned you. But it was part of my paying off my debt to not say anything."

For a moment, Ava was stunned into speechlessness. He had been watching her all that time. Then it occurred to her, "Wait, does that mean he knew I was pregnant?"

"That's what it means, and of course he knew it was his because he had been watching you and there was no one else but him."

Ava looked at Eric. "Did you know any of this?"

"Honey," Eric said, "you know I didn't. Mandy came to me just a week ago and told me the story. There's more though, so let's hear the whole thing because until you do, you won't understand what Mandy has done for you in the end."

Ava turned back to Mandy and said, "I feel like I should be furious with you, but at the same time, you've brought my daughter back to me, so go ahead, tell me the rest. It couldn't get much worse."

"Yes, it could," Mandy replied.

Fifty-One

"Did she say more than that, Evan?" Mira asked, bouncing in her chair.

It was quite uncharacteristic of her, bouncing, but she was too excited to think about the image she was creating.

Tom looked at his twin sister bouncing up and down and decided that it was a good idea. But, instead of bouncing he chose to jump.

Evan watched his two friends who had stuck by him in the worst time of his life and decided that bouncing was the exact correct response. He jumped out of his chair, linked arms with Tom, and starting jumping up and down, soon to be joined by Mira.

Laughing, they jumped all over the living room until exhausted and the three of them tumbled into the couch together, arms and legs all askew.

Finally, after catching his breath, Evan said, "Well, she said..." But that was as far as he got before the words throat caught in his throat and tears poured down his cheeks.

Mira brought him a glass of water, and they all waited as patiently as possible until he could speak again.

"Well, she said," he continued, "that she was coming home

and bringing a few people. Not much more. I didn't even ask her where she was, or what people. I just wanted her to come home."

"I can tell you a bit more," Leif said as he slowly came into view in the room.

"Leif! You know? What more? How do you know?"

Leif waited patiently until the three of them settled down a bit and then spoke.

"Sarah and I have been able to see bits and pieces of what has happened since Ava was rescued."

Seeing the expressions on their faces, he said, "Stop. I promise you will hear the whole story. Just don't interrupt, we have other work to do. Suffice it to say, that she was rescued by her uncle."

"Okay, what? Her uncle? I didn't know she had an uncle," Evan said.

"Well, neither did she. Nor did he. It's a long, drawn out story, which also involves the people that are trying to stop you all any way that they can, including killing every one of us. So the details of how this happened are less important at the moment than the details of how to stop them and keep all of us safe.

"There is much more to this story, but Ava deserves the chance to tell you herself, Evan. What you do need to know, is that she is coming home to get married, if you will have her.

"Knowing you as I do, shocked as you may be once you see who she brings home, you will want to marry her even more. Your hearts have been joined throughout lifetimes. You know this, so nothing can stop you from being joined in this one.

"Sarah sent me to tell you this much so that you will get moving on the wedding plans. Grace, Sam, and Andy are part of the preparations. You can trust them. Craig and I have another part that we will tell you about later.

"In the meantime, wedding plans need to be finalized. It's in only fourteen days. So get moving."

"Wait, Leif!" Evan shouted as Leif started fading away. Are you still going to marry us?"

"It has always been my pleasure, Evan. We will be here in plenty of time. And, as always, pay attention."

****

Grant laughed. As if paying attention would get them anywhere. The undetectable microphones that Hank had planted in Evan's house before he left were working just fine.

In fact, everything was going according to plan. Ava would bring everyone home with her. The three amigos at the Diner would be present, and every member of that damn Circle would be at the wedding and reception—a happy gathering, just for him.

Rick Sanders had done him a big favor. Grant hadn't known it would turn out this way. Rick was just a minion in his forces from around the world. He had been one of many little tiny evil men driven by their lust and greed.

They did what they were told, and with the rest of their time, they could do what they wanted to do. Lustful men were easy to manipulate. Their animal passions overrode clear thinking. That's what happened to Rick. He got too greedy. He wanted more, and more, and more. But to get what he wanted, Rick tried to steal from Grant.

Can you imagine? Steal from him? How stupid could he get? But all those tiny men like Rick were stupid and easily gotten rid of, which is what Grant had done. How he did it, didn't matter much. He used another lust-minded evil man. He gave him free rein to do what he liked best: hurt people. That man didn't know who Grant was, or who ordered the hit; he just liked the money and the pain he caused.

Grant always made sure that no one knew anyone up the chain. He had made a mistake with Rick. He had let him know his name. Something he would never do again, except for the ones who worked closely with him. And those men didn't know him either. Even his gray-haired-balding-old-man crew who believed they knew him and were friends, didn't know him at all.

No one did. And that's the way he liked it.

What pleased Grant the most was how the universe, as those stupid people called it, fell into place to give him what he wanted the most, even before he knew he wanted it.

He could never have planned that Rick would have a kid, and that the kid would lead him back to the people he hated the most. The Circles The do-gooders of the world royally pissed him off, and that Circle with all its additional "powers" were even worse.

However, if he told the truth to himself, they scared him. And nothing that scared him could be allowed to exist.

The wedding was only two weeks away, and all his plans were falling into place. It would be over soon.

Grant laughed to himself. Controlled chaos and destruction were what he loved the most. *What fun.*

Fifty-Two

In Eric's kitchen, the fan was working overtime. It cooled off the air a little, but didn't come close to keeping down the heat of anger and upset that threatened to explode inside of Ava.

She was trying to be cool and calm, but it wasn't working. All her training about pausing and then being grateful in order to diffuse an internal situation was not helping.

And then Mandy had to go and say it could be worse.

Worse for whom? All of us? Or her? Yes, that was the question to ask.

"Worse for whom? Mandy" she asked brusquely, trying and failing to be kind about it.

"Worse for everyone. But, you'll see if you let me continue the story. But, may I remind you, there is a happy ending here for you and Hannah."

"And me too," chimed in Eric.

"You're right," Ava said with a touch more kindness in her voice. She grabbed the glass of water that Eric had gotten for her, drained half of it in one gulp, and said, "Go on."

"We are back to Rick. He found out you were pregnant and then demanded that I get in touch with you. I wanted to for myself, and so I was happy to accept his request. However, with

Rick, there was always a catch, and it didn't take long before he told me what he wanted."

Mandy gulped, stared at the table, and finally whispered, "He wanted the baby."

Ava slammed her hands on the table and stood up so quickly that the chair she was sitting on fell backwards with a bang. "What? No, tell me you didn't do what I think you did. No, please tell me."

Mandy sat quietly with nothing to say, pain radiating from her.

Within seconds, Ava's anger dissolved, swallowed by sorrow. Ava allowed herself to be pulled back to her chair by Eric and Mandy. Each of them held her hand until her trembling eased.

"I am sorry, Ava," Mandy said. "But that is what happened. His wife, yes, he was married, wanted a baby, but she couldn't have a child herself. So, he forced me to give Hannah to her. He said it was his anyway.

"I know this sounds terrible, but you wanted the child to have a home, and he and his wife promised me that they would cherish her.

"I did keep my promise to you. I watched over Hannah the best that I could. But I was too ashamed to stay in touch with you and your mother."

Ava took a long practiced pause before answering. "Okay. I see. Or, I accept that you did what you needed to do and that you kept an eye on Hannah. But, I was sent threatening letters telling me I had to find her, or else. And then you turn up with her as if everything is okay."

"I can speak to that," Hank said from the doorway. "At least the part about the threatening letters, and I'm betting that the rest of it fits in too.

"Don't worry, Hannah is safe in the other room. We had a

nice long walk, and she told me she wanted to read and take a snooze. Her words."

"Thank you, Hank," Ava said. "Is the threat part of Grant's plan to distract us?"

That prompted questions from both Eric and Mandy. After Ava and Hank gave a quick explanation, Mandy was not satisfied that Hank would be able to fool Grant and keep them safe at the wedding.

"He is a mean son of a bitch," she said. "And you're wondering how I know. I know, because Rick worked for him. And I only know that because I overheard their conversation one day, and Rick said his name.

"When I asked Rick about it, he brushed it off, but he seemed very cautious after that. And just a few months later, he died, I mean was killed. The police said it was gang-related, but I'm not sure."

"Rick is dead? How long ago did he die? And then what happened to Hannah?"

"This is the part I am getting to, Ava. He died about two years ago. Hannah remembers him as a nice man. His wife, though was not nice at all. I saw Hannah often because they had me as a permanent, call-me-anytime, babysitter.

"I took as much advantage as possible. Once I knew Hannah could keep a secret, I started telling her things. She was old enough to know. But also because Hannah was so unhappy with her "mother" who ignored her from the beginning. After Rick died, the only attention she gave Hannah was to be cruel. I promised Hannah that one day, I would bring her to her birth mother.

"No, I didn't know how. I just knew I would do it. I couldn't live with myself anymore."

"That's why Hannah calls you Auntie because you were

always there for her?"

Mandy nodded, head down, hiding tears.

Ava stood up. This time she wasn't angry. This time she was filled with gratitude for Mandy who had been a guardian angel for her daughter. She pulled Mandy to her feet and hugged her. "Thank you," she whispered.

Ava could feel the tension start to ease out of Mandy's body, and she realized what a sacrifice Mandy had made, and how courageous she was. Mandy was not someone who ran away. Ava could learn from her.

"Okay, one last piece of this puzzle. Or, one last piece that worries me. What about Rick's wife? Isn't she going to come after you?"

"Oh, here's the part you are going to love. I can be quite a real trickster, and in this case, it was for the good.

"You must have seen the adoption papers. There is no 'Linda and John Minks' as I bet you found out. I told them they had to make up fake names so you wouldn't know. What I didn't tell them was that meant the papers were not legal. Once I told Rick's wife she hadn't actually adopted Hannah, she practically threw us both out of the house and made us promise to never come back. She was happy to be rid of Hannah. That was a year ago, Hannah has been with me ever since.

"And now, she is returned to you. She has never been adopted away. You have always been her mother."

"And you will always be her Auntie Mandy," Ava said as she hugged her. "And you will always be my friend."

Fifty-Three

Grace was huddled with Andy, talking about something, when Evan, Tom, and Mira walked through the door of the Diner.

As soon as she saw the three of them, Grace squealed, causing Andy to put his hands over his ears.

Evan stopped mid-stride, so abruptly Tom and Mira almost bumped into him.

"You know? How could you know?"

Andy looked at Grace who nodded and gestured to a booth big enough to hold them all. Sam, seeing what was going on, came out of the kitchen and turned the sign on the door to say "closed," and then pulled the shades so that no one could see inside.

"What the heck is going on?" Evan said. "Who are you people anyway?"

Grace said, "I'll start. I'm just what I look like I am. An old busybody. I used to have a job that required me to know everything I could about everyone I met or researched. It required me to keep secrets.

"You might not all realize this, but I'm the person who told Sarah and Leif how to find Earl and Suzanne.

"Ava had entrusted me with the information. Then Sarah and Mira entrusted me with more when Mira visited Sarah in Sandpoint. They told me about your Circle."

Tom and Evan looked at Mira. "You kept that secret from us?" Tom said.

"Well. Sorta. Grace wanted it to be that way, so we didn't give her away by mistake."

Tom glared at Mira and then smiled. "Okay. I get it." He turned to Grace and he asked her to continue.

"The fact that you are a Circle is no surprise to me. I know about Circles. If you keep your eyes open, you see them everywhere. I belong to one, too. Everyone has one. Most people haven't noticed it, but once they do, the magic of belonging begins.

"And then those Circles converge, and overlap, and expand, and continue on and on, long after what appears as our bodies disappear.

"You know what the teacher Robert Monroe said about humans don't you?

"No? Well, he said, 'Don't get addicted to being "human." This is only temporary.'"

Andy broke in. "Grace, have you forgotten to answer the question?"

"Oh, yeah. Sarah told me. No, I can't see them as you can, and I don't get those words in my head like some of you do. She did it the old fashioned way. She called me and told me to tell Andy and Sam.

"They already knew, though. Andy, perhaps you should talk now."

"Stop!'" Mira said. "Please, can we get some food with this conversation? I'm so hungry I could eat anything. You don't have to make anything new, Sam. How about those yummy muffins you make—and coffee."

Everyone agreed that a little food was necessary, although Tom thought it was also useful for getting some time in for thinking, which, knowing his sister, was her intention all along.

He knew he was lucky. Part of his Circle arrived in the form of a family member. He knew it didn't often happen that way As he thought about Circles, he watched Andy help Sam get the food. It was the first time he actually stopped to look at him. And now that he knew Sarah knew Sam and Andy, it was time to pay attention. Looking closely, Tom realized that take away the beard, lose a little weight, —he had seen Andy before.

At that moment, Andy turned to him and smiled. "Recognize me, do you? Good, I was going to tell you all now anyway, but, trust me, I can't wait to shave this beard off and lose this weight."

Evan stared at the two of them. "What do you mean? How does Tom know you?"

"I don't know him, I just recognize him. I caught a glimpse of him when we were at Earl's last year. Mira, you're the one you should really know who he is, since he was your doctor."

"What? Gillian? Crap. What the heck are you doing here? I thought you went with your Circle into the woods?

"Wait, now I'm flummoxed. Who are you exactly?" Evan asked.

Sam and Andy brought a plate of muffins to the table. Andy had piled on some of Mira's favorite croissants too.

"Mira, I'm not surprised you didn't recognize me. Besides the physical changes, when you got sick, you only saw me a few times, and your mind was focused on getting better, not looking at me.

"And, yes, Tom, you and Sarah saw me briefly at Earl's last year.

"Evan, I'm Suzanne's brother and Earl and Ariel's son. Yes, part of the Forest Circle. I thought I had completed my work here and was ready to go with them. I closed up my practice, and moved back home so that I could leave with my family to do our work—as Sarah calls it— in another "there." But, Suzanne asked me to stay behind, at least until you all were more settled. She was worried about Ava—for good reason as we all know now."

"That's why Sarah sent me to Andy, otherwise known as Gillian," said Grace. "He told me the rest of the story once I got here."

"What about Sam?" Evan asked pointing to him, with a bit more anger in his voice than he meant there to be.

"Who is he, and why not tell us who you were. Why all the pretend 'we don't know' you stuff?"

"I think that's fairly obvious," Andy said. "If you knew who we were, you would have acted differently. We didn't want the people going after you to know that you had protection, and we were aware of the danger.

"And as for Sam, besides being a fantastic cook, and an old friend from college, he works with the FBI.

All this Circle stuff is new to him. I'm speaking for him here, of course, but I think he still thinks it is kinda weird, and isn't sure about it."

Sam laughed. "Come on. It is weird, and it's true, I'm not sure about it. But, what I do know is that one of the men we have been watching for years, Grant Hinkley, seems extraordinarily interested in your group—Circle—whatever you call it.

"We are hoping to find a way to catch him at something that we can pin on him. We think he's planning something for your wedding, and he was behind Ava running away."

"This is ridiculous, and frightening, and it pisses me off," Mira said.

"It's all that and more," said Andy, "But when Ava comes home, we will have a few more details. But, no matter what, remember that all we are doing right now is planning your wedding, Evan."

Evan had been chewing his lip as Andy and Sam told their story.

"I don't like this at all. Maybe Ava and I should cancel the big wedding and elope. Take away the chance to do any harm to anyone."

"I would have probably said the same thing, Evan," Andy said, "but if we don't stop Grant now, you two will be running forever, and both our Circles will never be safe. In fact, no Circle will ever be, because it is the power of that community and the expansion of spiritual understanding and the freedom it brings that Grant, and men like him, hate.

"That construction crew that's in town? Some of those men are our guys. We are all over. We are watching over you. Some of them are Grant's crew. But we know which ones and are observing them constantly.

"Another advantage we have is that Grant believes that when you die there is nothing, which means he doesn't know what he thinks he knows.

"It will be dangerous, but there are many people here to protect you. Give Ava a chance to tell you what happened, and let Sam and his men do their job."

Evan stood up along with Mira and Tom. He felt shaken to his core, but steadfast in the faith of the strength of his friends, and those who were there to help him.

"Thank you," he said as he hugged both Sam and Andy. Sam held back for a minute and then gave in.

As they were leaving, Mira glanced behind her and winked at Sam. "You just might be surprised at what you'll find here, Sam. Be prepared to change."

Sam watched her go, knowing that it had already begun to happen. At first, it had only been a job to do. It had turned into something much more.

Outside, Grant watched the Diner. No one knew he was in town. The job was too important to leave to someone else. He had dyed his hair, grown a beard, and used his skills to add theater putty to his nose and forehead. With a fake driver's license, he was a guy looking to buy a farm here in beautiful Pennsylvania.

It looked like they were planning Evan's wedding, but Grant wasn't taking anything for granted. He had backup plans upon backup plans. He would blow up that wedding and no one, absolutely no one, would be able to stop him.

Even Hank would not recognize him, and it was Hank that Grant was particularly interested in watching. The decision to include Hank in the explosion had been made. He couldn't be trusted anymore.

Time to groom the new guy, Lenny. Or at least test him. This wedding would do both. Grant laughed as the three friends piled into the car. Safe for now. But not for long.

Fifty-Four

Tom and Mira wanted to go to the airport, too, but Evan insisted that someone stay and watch over the house. They both understood that before coming home, Evan also wanted time to be with Ava.

Evan had asked that they make sure the extra bedrooms were ready in the bunkhouse. They still didn't know who they were for, but suspected that one of them might be for Ava's grandfather—not that they knew anything about him, but Ava had a picture of him in her office.

They had plenty of help. Evan's housekeeper had come over and brought a few friends. Everything was getting thoroughly scrubbed in anticipation of the valued guests, and the wedding reception.

Gardeners were outside doing the last-minute preparation for the grounds. By the time Ava returned home, everything would be sparkling.

They couldn't wait.

Neither could Evan. He had hired a limousine and driver, one that Sam recommended. In fact, Evan suspected that the driver worked for Sam.

Evan knew he would be too nervous to drive, besides, he wanted time to meet the people Ava brought with her, and hold her close to him without distraction.

He had purchased Ava's favorite flowers, Calabasas lilies and put a few in a vase that made the car smell heavenly. The Pittsburgh airport was more than an hour away, so he had plenty of time to collect his thoughts.

Soon, Evan found that he had too many thoughts, so he pushed them aside and gazed out the window. Summer had peaked, and early fall flowers were beginning to appear. The calendar said it would be summer for another six weeks, but he knew that seasons started at least a month before announced on the calendar.

A slight fog hung between the soft slopes of the mountain ranges, with different shades of violets and greens reflected in the slanting sunlight. Each season was beautiful in a unique way. Soon the mountains would be ablaze with color, and later, white with snow.

What would my parents think of all this? Evan wondered. A great sense of sadness at not having them at his wedding rose up inside him. He believed he had put that all aside, knowing as he did now, that they were not gone, but living a new life, probably together, but elsewhere.

The love he felt for them, and they for him, would never die. That love tied them through dimensions and time. That is how he felt about Ava, too. Such a deep standing love. The love that Greeks called *Pragma*.

Until he met Ava, he didn't understand that kind of love.

Then, reflecting on what he had learned, he smiled to himself. Of course he understood that kind of love. He and Ava had experienced it in many lifetimes together. Not always in the same form, but it was the same love. He had just forgotten until seeing her again at Earl's house the year before reminded him.

What was it Sarah said to him? "Love transcends time and space." That was it.

"Sir, we're almost here," the driver said through the intercom.

"Thank you," Evan replied as he sat up straight and closed his eyes, imagining Ava in a bubble filled with love.

The limo pulled up outside the waiting zone. With no Ava in sight, Evan got out of the car. The driver said that if he had to, he would just keep circling until he came back out. Evan gave him a thumbs up and headed into the baggage area.

Because he had electronically sent money to Ava, and Ava had purchased the tickets, he still didn't know who he was looking for to be with her. She told him they were flying Southwest.

Southwest had its baggage collection just inside the door on the right. The conveyor belt was running, a good sign, but the crowd was so thick he couldn't see Ava.

And then he heard his name coming from the direction of the windows. She stood there, looking more beautiful than he could ever imagine. The crowd parted. Perhaps they knew what was coming. He ran towards her, and she towards him. *Just like a movie scene*, he thought as he pulled her close.

For a long, long moment, they clung to each other, and then backed up to arm's length, looked to make sure it was real, and then hugged her again. "You look beautiful, Ava," Evan said as he breathed her in.

Ava laughed. For a brief moment when she called his name, she was terrified that he would not accept her, that he didn't really love her, that he would be too angry to welcome her home.

But it lasted only as long as it took for him to reach her. Once he wrapped her in his arms, she knew all would be well.

Keeping one arm around him, she pointed him towards the window, where two men and a child stood.

Ava didn't say anything. Evan saw the little girl who looked just like his Ava, and his heart stopped. "Yours?" he breathed.

"Ours, if you will have us."

"She is beautiful, just like her mother," he said as he walked towards the little girl.

He put out his hand and said, "Evan."

Hannah responded in kind, "Hannah," she said.

Evan knelt down beside her and whispered, barely able to speak, "Hannah, I am delighted to meet you. I love your mom, so may I love you, too?"

Hannah laughed, and flew into him, knocking him onto his butt on the airport floor. "Yes," she said, wrapping herself around him.

Unbeknownst to Evan the moment he started running, everyone waiting for their baggage started watching, and with Hannah's words the crowd started applauding. Evan couldn't do anything but bury his head on Hannah's shoulders and cry with happiness.

As Hank watched Evan meet Hannah, he slowly began to slip back into the crowd. But Ava grabbed his arm and pulled him back to the wall.

"Where are you going?"

"You know I can't stay and hang out with you guys. I have to continue to work for Grant. But, I promise, Ava, I will be watching over you."

Ava watched Hank's back as he disappeared, and wondered when and if she would ever see him again. She had invited him to the wedding, and he said he would try to be there, but Ava wasn't sure that would happen.

Returning to Evan, Ava saw that he had introduced himself to Eric, and while still holding Hannah's hand, was helping him take the luggage off the carousel.

Ava pointed out two more suitcases coming through the chute, and Evan went off to get them. She had brought all of Hannah's clothes and toys with her. This was Hannah's new home.

"Didn't I see someone else with Hannah?" He asked when he returned. "Who was it—and where did he go?"

"He's my uncle. He can't stay with us. I'll tell you more about him later, but there is still someone else for you to meet. Perhaps Hannah will introduce you to her?"

Ava pointed to the window where a woman was standing alone. Holding onto Evan's hand Hannah led him towards Mandy.

"This is my Auntie Mandy. She's with us, too."

Evan took in Mandy. *Is she tired, or not well?* Evan wondered as he extended his hand. Mandy shook his saying, "I'm not her real Aunt, but I love that she calls me that. But then, I guess Eric is not her real great-grandfather, either."

"Sometimes we get to pick new families. Welcome to ours," Evan said.

"If you are half as wonderful as Ava told me, I am honored to be included. I plan to be a valuable member in whatever capacity I can," Mandy answered.

Hannah grabbed both their hands and brought them back to where Ava and Eric were waiting beside a pile of baggage.

"Let's go," Evan said, smiling at each one of them in turn. "It's time to go home."

Fifty-Five

As soon as Hank returned to Doveland, he called Grant. After explaining that Ava and her family were safely home, he asked Grant what he wanted him to do next. He wasn't surprised when he was told to return to Ava's house as an uncle and get to know the family. That would make it easy to plant the explosive devices that Grant had ordered from the dark web, and had left in the safe house for Hank to pick up.

He was to use his knowledge of Evan and Ava's house, bunkhouse, and grounds to hide them in the places he had already discovered. Hank told him that Ava had already invited him to the wedding and that would put him in danger.

Grant assured him that they would be detonated remotely using a cell signal, and Hank would have plenty of time to get away.

Hank agreed, as if he trusted Grant, and faked being eager to get the job done because he wanted to get out of Doveland. It reminded him too much of his former life. His dad being buried just a town away freaked him out. *That much is true,* Hank thought. *Always pack lies with truth.*

Grant said he understood and reminded him that this would be the last job Hank would have to do.

They both hung up. Hank was pleased. He would plant the explosives as directed because he knew Grant would know if he didn't. But he also knew he was going to stop Grant from detonating them and that he would need help to do it. He already had someone in mind. He knew the cook in the Diner had been with the FBI for years. Hank had kept watch over the FBI agents assigned to stop Grant. That had been part of his job, and he was good at it.

Samuel Long. That's what he called himself. Having watched him for years, Hank discovered that Sam was one of those rare birds. Honest. He made mistakes, but he always made them while trying to do the right thing. And once he realized he made a mistake, he said so, corrected himself, and fixed what was wrong.

This time, he couldn't let Sam make a mistake. Too many lives were at stake—and most astonishingly—ones that he had come to cherish. The trick was to talk to Sam without being seen. Hank knew that Grant's eyes were everywhere. He would have to be at his most secret and devious self to make sure all would go well.

Grant too was pleased. He knew that Hank was planning to stop him. In spite of Hank's training at hiding his feelings, something had changed in him the minute he met Ava. Grant had known Hank since he was an angry and defiant boy—but he was no longer angry in the same way. That made him very dangerous to Grant. Grant wanted Hank to try and stop him. He wanted Hank, and the people he asked to help him, to have all their attention on the explosives in the house. Misdirection was his favorite trick. It worked every time.

The explosives weren't fake, that would be easy to discover. Besides, if Grant was wrong, and Hank didn't try to stop him, he could still detonate them for an extra fun effect.

****

Evan was content with Ava sitting beside him on the swing hanging from the beams on the back deck. Both of them were silent, looking at the rolling mountains, listening to the sounds of summer. Cicadas were at their peak, so loud that sometimes they could interrupt a conversation. This time, though, they were background music to a beautiful day. Leaves in some of the trees were beginning to turn red. The height of fall was still a few months away, but the signs were there that it was coming.

There are always signs something is coming, or things are changing, thought Evan.

Neither of them spoke. There was no need. Ava and Evan were home together at last. Ava had yet to tell her story, because she wanted to tell everyone at once. She said that it needed to all be brought out into the open so she could be free. They would wait until after dinner that night.

When they got back from the airport, they all had lunch together, and then the three travelers had headed to their separate rooms to nap and have some quiet time.

Hannah loved her new room. Girlie things would have to be added to it, and Ava had promised Hannah they would attend to that soon. Mandy and Eric occupied the other two extra bedrooms in the house. Tom and Mira had moved into rooms in the bunkhouse once they knew Ava was bringing people home with her.

Tom and Mira were headed into town saying that they had an appointment. They didn't say with whom, and Ava and Evan were too taken with the reality of each other's presence to ask.

Tom and Mira were planning a surprise. They had decided that it would be better if they were closer to Ava and Evan, besides they had fallen in love with the area, so they'd set up a meeting with a Realtor to look at a few places. The plan was to buy two properties, hopefully adjoining each other. Without saying anything to each other, Tom and Mira had realized that perhaps it was time to live separate lives. But neither wanted to be far apart, as they had already missed too much of a life together.

Tom suspected that Mira had her eye on Sam, and he had definitely caught Sam looking at Mira with a sheepish smile on his face more often than necessary. And he had to admit to himself that something about Mandy, as sad and sick as she appeared at the moment, had moved him. They were each open to the possibility of finding someone to spend their life with— someone who understood what that life entailed.

Most of all, they wanted to surprise Ava and Evan. It was going to be a wedding present to them. One that would make them available for them whenever they needed help, or perhaps just a baby sitter.

Back at the house, Evan and Ava rocked back and forth in the swing. Evan reflected on the moment he had first seen Ava in this lifetime. Glancing down at Ava whose head was now resting on his shoulder, he noticed that she had fallen asleep. And then he heard the words, "Thank you."

Looking up, he saw a woman standing in front of him. Having been around the Circle and the strange things they did, he wasn't surprised that he could see right through her to the fields beyond. Evan didn't have to guess who it was. He recognized Ava's mom from the picture Ava had shown him. Besides, they looked so much alike it would be hard to miss.

"Have you been here before?" he asked.

"Yes, I have always been near Ava, and Hank, too, once I found him after I died. I chose not to move on until I knew they were both safe. But I also decided not to be seen, even by the Circle, because not everyone in these other realms are good people. It seemed prudent to stay hidden. However, I will have to leave soon. I want to go. It's time, and my husband waits for me. That means that I will not be here to watch over them, so I wanted you to know that I trust that you will, Evan."

"I will. And so will our friends. I promise," Evan said. "Will you be able to stay for the wedding? It's only a little over a week away."

"I am going to try—I would love to be there. And you know that there is still an extreme danger. Please stay alert. Hank will help you. You have to trust him. He has done some terrible things because he was lost. Now that he has Ava and Hannah, he will protect them and the ones they love too—even if it looks as if he isn't. He has to continue to act evil.

"Will you trust him?" she asked Evan.

Neither Evan or Abbie had spoken any of these words out loud. No need. They flowed between them like a silver thread. Each word like a note of music in life's symphony. So Evan did not have to reply. Instead, he opened his heart entirely to Abbie and let her see how deep his love was for Ava and all of her family. For a brief light-filled moment, they touched hearts and were as one.

They smiled at each other. It was a promise.

"Hank's here," Abbie said as she faded away. At the same time, Evan's phone beeped and showed him a picture of a beat-up old truck coming up the driveway. Mixed emotions flooded in. He would trust Hank, but he also knew that things could go wrong. Hank symbolized what could and what had happened, that was dangerous and evil.

Still, there was much work to be done, and Hank was the

key to getting it done safely. Evan slowly lifted Ava's head off his lap and laid her gently on the swing. Then went to meet Hank.

Eric was on the way to the front door at the same time. They looked at each other, and agreed without speaking, that they were united. Ava came first.

Before Hank rang the doorbell, Evan opened it and stood face to face with him.

"I changed my mind," Hank said.

Fifty-Six

Hank was invited back that evening, which made for a full and noisy dinner table as everyone shared stories and got to know each other. Taking advantage of the still warm evenings, they ate outside on the deck.

After the meal, and after Hannah was safely tucked into her bed in her new room, and every person had gone in to say good night to her, Ava was ready to tell her story.

Sarah, Leif, and Craig were also present, even though some of the group couldn't see them.

Ava started off by thanking them all for taking Hannah into their hearts so quickly. Then she began to tell the story that they had all been waiting to hear. She started with running away from home. She asked Mandy to help her fill in the details, and, as the story unfolded everyone could see that the telling was helping both Ava and Mandy let go of some of their feelings of guilt.

Ava had expected to get at least some disapproval for doing her semi-stripping, but instead, they were interested in the women who felt that was the only way to make a living. Instead of more negativity when she spoke about her decision with Hannah, she heard murmurs of sympathy.

The only disapproval voiced to Ava was when Evan and the Circle said they were sad and disappointed that Ava hadn't come to them in the first place. Ava promised to keep on practicing letting go, and asking for help. At the end of the story, Ava went to Mandy and hugged her as hard as she could. Healing had begun.

Hank turned to Eric and thanked him for taking care of his sister. He asked if one of these evenings he would tell them all about Abbie growing up, and if Ava could talk about Abbie as her mother. With tears in their eyes, they could only nod at Hank.

By 9:00, darkness had fallen. The twinkle lights around the deck had come on, and the fireflies sparkled in the fields and woods. Frogs and crickets had begun their nighttime singing, and the night-blooming jasmine that Ava and Evan had planted opened up on the trellis. It was a perfect evening. Ava marveled how everything that had felt so hopeless before was filled once again with hope.

Everyone drifted off to bed. Only Hank and Eric were left sitting on the deck watching the moon rise. Ava had asked Hank to stay at the house, and he had agreed. It made it easier to plant the devices that Grant had left for him. It also made it easier for Hank to steel himself for what he needed to do, and he needed to do it quickly.

Eric interrupted his thinking. "Can I help you with the problem, Hank? I remember you as a young and brave, but terrified, boy. I know that you have many stories you could tell, but I also know the love you feel for your family now that you have found them again. No one is going to expect this old man to be doing anything dangerous, and yet, I have lived through many dangerous situations."

Hank paused, taking in Eric. *Was he in his eighties now?*

His hair and close-cropped beard were gray. He wore Keds and Dockers and a nice shirt. Would Grant suspect that Hank and Eric were planning something? Perhaps, but he had to give it a try as long as Eric understood the risk.

As if he had heard him thinking, Eric said, "I do understand what I'm getting myself into here. But Ava and Hannah are my family too."

Hank nodded and the two of them pulled their chairs closer to the small fire that Evan had made before heading to bed. Someone watching might have thought that they were just enjoying the evening. The fact that plans were being made was well hidden. Unless you had a suspicious mind, then perhaps you would wonder and make plans of your own.

****

Breakfast the next morning was a chatty affair. Everyone's breakfast needs were different, and Ava and Mira did their best to figure out how to meet them. After struggling to get everything done, they both agreed that help was needed and decided to ask Grace to come in and help manage meals.

Besides, she would make an excellent liaison between the group of people in the house and the co-conspirators at the Diner.

It was a week before a wedding, and plans had to be completed. The most important item on the agenda was Ava's dress. The plan was that Mira would take Ava into town for the final fitting. Then everyone would meet at the Diner to finalize the menu for the reception. Sam had agreed to have samples.

After that, a stop at the bakery to confirm the cake, and then to the post office to mail two last-minute wedding invitations. Ava wanted Pete and his wife to come. She hoped he wasn't riding around the country and would get the letter in time. His kindness had sustained her during the trip west, and she didn't want to lose him from her life.

The second invitation was for Kathy Duncan. After telling her story, and how Kathy had helped her, Tom had done some research and found an address for her. Ava included a special note inside, just in case Kathy had forgotten her. She also added a picture of Hannah, knowing Kathy would love to see what happened to the baby she helped save.

Eric agreed to stay at the house and look after Hannah. She had been promised a shopping trip for the next day to personalize her room.

Tom and Evan said they had plans of their own, and left right after breakfast. Ava knew that Evan probably was making sure his suit was ready, but he only winked at her when she asked where he was going.

Hank went to work. The work overseeing the construction of a home across town. While he was in Los Angeles, he had left the foreman in charge, telling him he had a family emergency. At the time, he didn't know how true that would become.

Hank liked working in construction. *Perhaps,* he thought, *I can make this into my real job and not a cover-up.* He also suspected that Sam had planted people on the crew, which meant that so did Grant. How to figure out which was which would be a trick. Not one that he had found yet. *Was anyone what they seemed?* he wondered.

And then he thought of the group of people he had left back at the house and decided that yes, there were. If they were hiding anything, it was the extent of their kindness. He hoped that would protect them, and if it didn't, he would.

Fifty-Seven

The week flew by. Everyone was busy with wedding preparations. There was an air of joy and happiness that permeated everyone in the house and spread out into the town. By now, the people of Doveland had come to know the new people that had moved into the farm down the road and were glad to have them.

Evan sent the limousine back to the Pittsburgh airport, this time to pick up Sarah and Leif, and Craig and his wife, Jo Anne. Both couples stopped at the farm to ooh and ahh over it, and exchange hugs, but had opted to stay in town at the local bed and breakfast.

Hannah's room had been furnished exactly how she wanted it to be. No one was expecting that she would choose a forest fairy theme, but they weren't surprised. Although no one had talked it over with her yet, they suspected she had been visiting the Forest Circle, even if at the moment it was only in her dreams.

Mandy and Mira's bridesmaid dresses had been fitted and were hanging in their rooms. Each was designed specifically for them, but with varying shades of mauve which Ava had chosen as the color of the wedding. At first, Mandy had refused to be a bridesmaid, saying that she didn't deserve it, but both Mira and Ava had shown her the other side of the story. Without her, they may have never found Hannah.

The garden was ready, and the local florist was pleased as punch that they had ordered flowers directly from him rather than through the internet.

Behind the scenes, Hank had been busy, too. He had done as Grant asked, and proved it to him by taking photos of where he had placed the small explosives. They were small but powerful, and would demolish every bit of the house and the bunkhouse. Although the picture of silence and calm on the outside, inside he was terrified that the plans to stop Grant would fall through.

Eric had been instrumental in getting information to Sam, and back to Hank. Plans for a raid were already in place to take out Grant's headquarters in Ohio before he could detonate the devices. The timing was tricky. If he suspected anything, he would simply step up the time.

Hank was sure that Grant had something else up his sleeve. Although he didn't know what Grant had planned, he knew it would be devastating if it happened.

However, no one knew where Grant was, and even if they found him, it couldn't be Hank that stopped him. Hank was expected at the wedding and reception, and if he wasn't there, Grant would be suspicious. Sam kept assuring him that everything was in place to assure everyone's safety, but Hank wasn't so sure.

Every moment in the house for Hank was agony. He and Eric had decided not to tell anyone what was happening. They were afraid that someone would give it away without knowing that they did. Everyone understood that they had to eliminate every part of Grant's network, or no Circles would be safe, but the waiting and not knowing was almost unbearable for Hank.

Ava and Evan had selected a small local church for the ceremony. Built of stone, with arched stained-glass windows that ran down each side, it felt peaceful and safe. Simple wooden pews spoke of years of services, of people kneeling, praying, and worshiping.

At the Friday evening rehearsal, everyone in the wedding party was dressed in casual clothes, laughing, and chatting together. Ava thought it was the most beautiful thing she had ever seen.

Craig and Tom were the ushers. Eric was to walk her down the aisle. Mandy and Mira would follow her, and Hannah would be her flower-girl. Leif and Evan would be waiting for her at the front of the church and Sarah would hold her hand while she prepared, and then would sit at the front of the church, as a surrogate mother.

The rehearsal was a mess. Everyone forgot where they were supposed to be and then cracked up laughing. Someone said that a chaotic rehearsal would foretell a peaceful wedding. Ava was surprised to realize she didn't care. The whole thing could be a mess, and all she cared about was the final words that would be spoken by Leif to her and Evan.

After rehearsal, they went to the Diner for the rehearsal dinner. Not fancy at all, but the perfect venue for good food, and lots of talking that began with "remember when?" Sam had put together a buffet, so he, Grace, and Andy could join them.

As Ava looked around the table, she felt a wave of gratitude rise up inside of her. *Could anyone be more blessed?* She paused for a long moment, taking an internal picture of what love looked like to her. She never wanted to forget it.

During the dinner, Ava noticed that the men had some quieter discussions, and Hank appeared extremely nervous, but she was too happy to be worried. Everything would be okay.

****

Grant was pleased that his presence had gone unnoticed. For the past few weeks, he had been holed up in a small motel a few miles out of town. His excuse for being there was he was researching the area to find a place for his family to live away from the city.

Of course, he didn't have a family. What a pain in the ass that would be. He never considered his wife, family. She was just a prop. Grant never went with a Realtor to look at any properties. But it gave him a great excuse for driving out every day to do his business.

He was proud of the fact that even the small team he was working with in town didn't know who he was. They thought he was another one of them, and the big boss was back in Ohio running the show. *Ha,* he thought, *Lenny as the big boss. That would be the day.* Well, maybe it would, but only after he was dead and that wasn't going to happen anytime soon.

He was a little worried about Lenny. He was young and impetuous, and completely without any sense of morality. That part didn't worry Grant. How could it? He was the same. However, Lenny might do something stupid; he had more training to do with him before he trusted Lenny completely.

Grant drove by the Diner one more time. Yes, they were all still in there laughing it up. *Not for long though.* The drones were in place for the wedding reception. Nothing could stop them now. Between the drones, and Lenny handling the explosions from Ohio, that laughing group of idiots didn't have a chance.

The wedding would take place, everyone would come back to the house, and that would be the end. He would be free of the Circle, and if there were more like them out there, he would go after them, too. One by one, if necessary. Power was what he craved; power and money. Nothing was going to take that away from him. Nothing.

Fifty - Eight

Instead of going back to the house after the rehearsal dinner, Ava went to the Bed And Breakfast Inn with Sarah. It seemed like both a practical and traditional thing to do. Ava had never been there before, and was delighted to find that the conversion to a bed-and-breakfast was charming. Every room was simple but comfortable. Each room had its own heating and cooling unit, a plus in Pennsylvania where it can get very hot and very cold. Quilts hung on the wall, along with prints of what Doveland and the surrounding area looked like a hundred years ago.

Large chairs and deep couches beckoned to guests in the sitting room, and that is where Sarah and Ava went after the rehearsal dinner. *It is time for a mother-daughter talk,* thought Ava, and since hers wasn't there, and Suzanne was elsewhere, it would be Sarah.

After making a pot of tea, and grabbing a few biscotti they had found waiting for them in the kitchen, they settled down into the two chairs facing each other, with a small coffee table between them where they placed tea and cookies.

"Would you like to talk, Ava?" Sarah asked. "Or would you prefer companionable silence?"

Ava placed a cookie on her saucer and laid both on the table. Folding her legs up under her, she leaned forward. "Talk."

Sarah waited while Ava gathered her thoughts. "I know you are aware of my whole back-story by now. I told some of it, but I know you and Leif were watching, and know even more of the details, so I don't need to tell you that part. What I'm most worried about is my ability to love.

"What if I do something stupid again? What if I close off, and don't let Evan into my heart as fully as I desire to? I still feel a wall, and I want it to dissolve and go away. It is, but so slowly I'm afraid it will always be there. Plus, how good a mother will I be? I already abandoned my child once. What if I do it again by mistake?"

"Ava, honey, just the fact that you *are* worried means all will be well. Of course you will make mistakes, and of course your heart is not as open as it will be ten years from now. Think how lovely that will be, each year being even more aware of the love you have for Evan and he for you. It's that mature love that lasts. Yes, you will both have moments, but when you choose to keep moving forward together, the next stage will be even better than the last.

"You and Evan will be more than fine. You have Hannah now, and perhaps your family will grow from there. But one thing you have that you must never forget is the awareness of the bigger picture. Remember that this is all temporary. Some say it is an illusion, but still, it is temporary. What lasts is love. It shows up everywhere. It slides along that line of light that we often discuss. It is always powerful. Like water. It's persistent. It's always present, and you know how to step into it. That is all you need to know."

Ava sat still, digesting what Sarah had said, and then stood up, and hugged her, whispering, "Thank you."

Sarah returned the hug, and then, holding her at arm's length, looked into her eyes and silently promised her that all would be well.

Sarah could see Suzanne and Abbie smiling at her from the corner of the room. Proof once again that love transcends time and space. *Ava will be delighted that they are here for her wedding,* Sarah thought.

"Phew, that's enough lecture for tonight. It's a big day tomorrow. Let's get our beauty sleep," Sarah said.

After one last hug, Sarah watched Ava make her way to her room, and then turned to Suzanne and Abbie and asked them if it was true that all was well. "It is," they both said, and then were gone.

****

A bachelor party was vetoed by Evan after Ava ran away. He didn't need a last-minute celebration of his freedom if she came back. He was as free with her as he was by himself. In fact, freer. She upheld him and sustained him as he did what was necessary in his life to do.

Once Ava returned, he was even more certain that he didn't want a party to celebrate freedom. Their love was the center of his life, but it didn't encase him within a false boundary.

So the boys, under Tom's leadership as best man, decided there would be a party to celebrate that their friend had found the love that was both security and freedom. Leif had brought Evan a small present. A print of the word *Pragma* and its definition. It was, after all, what he and Sarah had, and now so did Evan and Ava. A mature, deep, long-standing love.

After the rehearsal dinner, Hannah, Mira, and Mandy went to bed. Craig, Andy, Leif, and Sam came over to the house and helped Evan, Hank, and Tom celebrate love with beer, chips, and salsa. They told stories and jokes and in general made each of them laugh out loud so hard Craig said he had to stop because the beer was coming out his nose.

Finally, it was time for bed. Sam had not been drinking, so he was the designated driver. As he walked into the driveway in front of the house to get the car, he took out a throwaway phone and placed a call. "Are you in place?" Sam asked. When the answer came back as a "yes," he took out another phone, and made another call, and asked the same question.

Satisfied, he put both phones back in his pocket and continued his walk to the car, where he found Mira standing by the car door. She came up to him and put both hands on his shoulders. "I am trusting you, Sam," she said and walked away.

As he watched her walk away, Sam felt his heart twist. *What if I am not doing enough?* Sam thought. Strangely, he thought for a moment that Leif had come out of the house, because he thought he heard, "You are doing just fine, son." But when he turned to look, there was no one there.

Fifty-Nine

On the day of the wedding, the sun rose with a red hue into a blue sky filled with white billowing clouds, tinged with a golden glow. *Perfect,* Ava thought as she looked out the window of her room at the Inn. She was ecstatic that today would be the start of a new life. She would be Ava Anders. And with the new name would come a new and fresh beginning.

From downstairs she heard Sarah and Leif laughing and wondered how lucky she was that they were here for her. Well, they were here for love. Weddings are about sharing love. *Nelson Mandela's quote, "For love comes more naturally to the human heart than its opposite" is so true,* she thought. *I am not fighting what is natural to my heart any longer.*

Ava ran her fingers through her short hair, slipped on a robe, and headed downstairs to begin the best day of her life.

Craig and Jo Ann were already dressed and sipping coffee with Leif and Sarah. They all got up and hugged her and she, without thinking, hugged them back just as hard. *How easy,* thought Ava. Just stop resisting the hugs! They all laughed at her startled face, and Sarah said, "Yes, it is easy, and it gets easier."

"Sometimes I forget that you can hear what people are thinking," Ava said.

"Not always. And we intentionally shut it off most of the time. Today, though, we are listening."

Ava thought she caught a hint of something other than happiness when Sarah said that, but let it go. If she needed to know, Sarah would tell her.

At the house, Evan was up preparing coffee and breakfast for everyone. Grace was there to help, having come over even earlier to get a start on all the preparations. He had been too excited to sleep much, and couldn't wait to begin the day he had been thinking about since the moment he saw Ava at Earl's house.

Yes, he had waited months before asking Ava to marry him, but the moment he saw her he knew that she was going to be his wife. When Hannah came to the table asking if she could have Cheerios, his heart opened even wider. And now, not only did he get Ava, but he also got a kid. As soon as possible he was going to adopt her officially. He had already phoned a lawyer to get the papers started. It was the best day of his life, and it would only get better.

Mira and Mandy were up because they had hair appointments in town. Ava would meet them there. It was part of the whole wedding experience, and they couldn't stop giggling about how much fun the wedding was going to be. Over the past few days, Mandy had lost much of her pallor, and Mira thought she was getting more beautiful every time she looked at her.

Andy and Sam had been up for hours. There was more work to be done to get everything ready. They had made a call to Sarah to check on last-minute details and were given the okay signal to go forward with plans they had made.

Grace had engaged some of the women in town to help her with decorations and was meeting them at the church after she was finished helping Evan with breakfast.

Hank was also up and about—not out of excitement, but out of fear. He was terrified that they had not planned well enough. Everyone else was planning a beautiful wedding, and he was trying to stop it from being a bloodbath. He didn't think he had ever been this frightened before in his life.

Sam too, was frightened. He left Andy in charge of food and began making all the necessary calls. Cameras were checked to ensure that they were working. Time and again he had been told that everyone was in place in Ohio, but he still checked again. He hoped and prayed they had planned well enough to stop Grant.

Grant was sitting on his bed in his motel room, making sure of all the details on his end were completed by Lenny in Ohio, and Grant's small team in Doveland. Everyone assured him that they had things under control. His heart expanded in joy, knowing that by the evening of this day, there would be nothing left of that group of friends. He might even stay around for the funerals. *Wouldn't that be a kick...* Grant thought.

****

Evan stood at the front of the church and waited for his life to begin.

Dressed in a tuxedo and looking as if he was born to wear it, he was sure that his heart was beating so hard the small mauve carnation tucked into the lapel would bounce off at any moment.

Leif stood at his side, breathing out quiet patience, and Evan did his best to take in every bit of calm Leif sent his way. Dressed in a cream-colored suit, with black glasses perched on the end of his nose, he was ready to read the vows that Evan and Ava had written for each other.

Tom and Craig were also dressed in tuxedos, although neither of them looked as happy in theirs as Evan did in his. They stood by his side as if they were sentinels guarding a prince.

Hank had declined to be a groomsman. Instead, he sat beside Sarah in the front row. Sarah patted his arm and whispered something in his ear which seemed to ease the tight expression on his face.

The whole G.O.B. team had shown up, along with various girlfriends, partners, and wives. Every one of them smiled at Evan, trying to project encouragement and reveal how happy they were for him.

A local harpist played in the corner of the church. The children's choir gathered behind the wedding party. Evan and Ava wanted singing instead of organ music as the backdrop for their marriage.

As the children sang the first note of "Glory to God on High," Hannah stepped into the aisle holding a basket filled with mauve rose pedals. As she walked down the aisle, she spread them on the carpet before her. Her dress had been made by a seamstress in town to match Mira's and Mandy's, and her face beamed with happiness.

To Evan, it felt as if a hundred years went by before Ava stepped into the aisle to walk towards him. She had delicately balanced her hand on Eric's arm who looked like he would burst with pride.

Ava wore a white off-the-shoulder full-length dress with tiny pearls sewed into the bodice. They sparkled as she walked down the aisle, but they could not match the sparkle in her eyes.

She carried a sheaf of calabasas lilies, and Mandy and Mira held bouquets with multiple shades of mauve carnations.

Evan was positive that he had never seen anything so beautiful in his life, even though he was looking at it through a sheen of tears in his eyes.

The choir finished singing as Evan and Ava faced each other, clasped hands, and turned to Leif. No one moved except to dab at their eyes as Leif read the words that would join Evan and Ava in this lifetime. A collective sigh of happiness escaped all their lips as Evan and Ava turned to face them as husband and wife.

Evan and Ava took in the church that held all the people that they loved. Even Pete and his wife were there. Pete was looking as happy as if he was the proud father. In the corner, Ava saw Kathy Duncan, who smiled and blew her a kiss. *It seems that everyone loves a happily-ever-after story,* Ava thought, a*nd I have one.*

At that moment, the whole world seemed to stop breathing, as Ava saw her mother standing in the back of the church with Suzanne and the rest of the Forest Circle.

As they passed Sarah, Ava bent down to kiss her on the cheek, and Sarah whispered that Abbie would be at the reception, too, which eased Ava's mind because she wanted to have time to talk to her.

Outside, the crowd threw flower petals and clapped and clapped as the newlyweds stood on the church steps.

Everyone had been asked to leave their cars at the church, and a line of white limousines waited to take them to the reception. The wedding party stayed behind to take some pictures and would be along in a bit.

The long-awaited wedding had taken place, and now it was time to celebrate.

Sixty

Grant watched the limos pull away. Everything was going according to plan. He would wait until the wedding party had made their way to the reception and then all hell would break loose. The drones would release the gas, and Lenny would set off the explosives. No one would know he had been there. He had already checked out of the motel, and his bags were in his car.

He couldn't wait to feel the joy of destruction. He would send the signal to start the plan and then wait for the explosion a few miles out of town. Once he saw it, he would start driving in the opposite direction to New York, where he planned to take a plane to Costa Rica and enjoy a few weeks of well-deserved vacation. Perhaps he would come back for the funerals and feed on the misery.

If Grant had any humanity left in him, he might have enjoyed watching the wedding party posing for pictures. Nothing could be quite as beautiful as two people who have committed themselves to the partnership of love, and who are surrounded by others who wish them well.

But he didn't. Which is also why he was not aware of Suzanne and the Forest Circle who were also present and watching—not only the picture taking, but also him.

He did notice that Hank was no longer with the wedding party, but he didn't care. Grant figured that either he had already started running, or was at least wise enough to stay away from the blast. If he turned out to be loyal, well then, he would welcome him back. If not, Grant was sure Lenny would be happy to replace him.

****

At the reception, everything was ready. Andy, Sam, and Grace had outdone every expectation. A local band was playing music from the sixties and seventies. It was loud enough to dance to, soft enough to hold conversations.

Hank surveyed the scene, hyper-alert to the movements of everyone in the room. He wasn't sure if he had ever cared this much about anything. The only thing in his life that had been important before was his sister, Abbie, and now she was dead. But Hannah had stolen his heart, and he promised himself that no matter what, nothing would harm her.

However, if all went well, he would still not be able to lead a normal life. He had paid a price to ensure their safety, but it was one he was willing to pay.

Someone yelled, "They're here!" and everyone turned to welcome the wedding party.

Hank looked at Sam, who had come to his side holding a cell phone in his hand. "Go ahead and tell him," he said into the phone and held it out for Hank to take.

Hank listened as the voice explained that all cell service in Grant's small town in Ohio was down. Some kind of tech glitch, the person said with a laugh in his voice. While the cell service was down, the raid had taken place. No one was hurt, but all of Grant's operatives in the room were in FBI custody.

A small ray of hope opened in Hank's heart as he watched Ava and Evan pick up Hannah to dance with her.

"And the other one?" He asked. "We also disrupted and brought down all of Grant's drones. We had sharpshooters at the house just in case we weren't able to take control, but we did."

Hank was silent. The voice on the other end had one last thing to say. "I know you're worried, but we had him in our sights the whole time. We captured him fifteen minutes ago as he waited outside of town for everything to happen."

Hank was so choked up he could only say, "Thank you," as he handed the phone back to Sam.

"Stay for the party, Hank. We'll decide what to do with you afterwards. But, you deserve this."

Hank nodded his thanks. "Did they get everyone?"

"We think so. The only person that wasn't there was that young guy, Lenny."

Hank looked around the room; it was beautiful even though it was the high school auditorium. Filled with plants, flowers, balloons, and more sparkles than he had ever seen, it was breathtaking. It had been Sam's idea to move the reception, just in case.

Hank was grateful to Sam and his team, but now that he knew Lenny was still out there, he knew what he needed to do next.

Well next, after enjoying this party, he thought.

As the lights dimmed, he turned to watch the wedding dance. Evan and Ava had practiced a beautiful dance together to their song, Roberta Flack's "The First Time Ever I Saw Your Face." *A perfect choice,* Hank thought.

Everyone clapped as they walked off the floor, and Mira handed Ava a beautiful silk jacket to put on over her dress. She turned and waved to the crowd, and everyone sighed with joy.

And then the lights came up, Abba's song "Dancing Queen" came on, and Ava started strutting across the floor. She laughingly peeled off her jacket and threw it into the crowd.

Everyone laughed. They knew what she was saying. You know my history, and you love me anyway. It was a challenge, and they took it. The wedding party poured onto the floor to dance with Ava, throwing jackets and sweaters into the air as they celebrated love and freedom.

Hank laughed for the first time in years as a huge flow of gold sparkles spilled out of the rafters and onto the dancers below. It would be weeks before everyone got all the sparkles out of their clothes and hair.

To Sarah, it was a perfect symbol of how love flows and stays.

In the midst of it all, Ava slipped out of the crowd and made her way to the side of the auditorium where she had seen her mom waiting for her.

"I have to go now, Ava."

"I know, mom," Ava said. "Thank you for being here for me all this time. I am sorry for any grief that I caused you."

"Oh, Ava," Abbie said. "You were just growing up."

As they stood together, Hank joined them.

"I can see you, Abbie," he said. "How can that be?"

"You are willing now, Hank. Thank you for taking such good care of me as a little girl, and for being here for Ava and Hannah now. You are a good man, Hank."

Hank and Ava held hands and watched Abbie fade away. She blew them one last kiss.

Then the two of them turned together to see a crowd of people dancing together in a gold haze. Celebrating love.

Ava wondered, *What could be better than that.*

Hank answered, "Nothing."

Epilogue

Two months later, Ava made her way to the small cemetery in the next town. Hank had sent her the directions to Concourse and asked her to come by herself. He had something to show her.

It was a cold October day, but she didn't mind. She was just happy to be able to see Hank again. Many things had changed since the wedding. Tom and Mira had surprised them with the perfect wedding gift. They were moving to Pennsylvania to be near them.

Hannah had started school and was settling into her new home life. The adoption was progressing well, and Hannah loved Evan as if he was her real father. To Ava, he was.

Mandy had gone back to Los Angeles, but she and Tom seemed to be exchanging a lot of text messages. Sam was still in touch because Lenny had not yet been found. Ava suspected that there was more than that going on. Mira seemed always to be present when Sam was around.

Sarah and Leif had returned to Sandpoint, but there were weekly Circle meetings, which also included Craig who was hinting about spending time in Pennsylvania with them.

It was only Hank that had been missing.

As she stepped out of the car, she saw him waiting for her. He had changed. He was lighter in spirit and weight. *Maybe they went together.*

Hank put his arm around her and guided her to his dad's grave. I need to show you this, Ava," he said.

"I killed him in anger, protecting your mom, and then I punished myself for a long time. I almost turned myself into him because of it."

"I don't think that's possible, Hank. You just hid your kind heart from everyone, including yourself. Are you able to come home yet?"

"Not yet. But I'm always around, even if you don't see me. Sam found a place for me, and I just might be able to make up for some of those evil things I did."

As he walked her back to her car, he asked. "Boy or girl?"

Ava laughed. "See, you *do* have the gift," she said as she started the engine.

As she drove away, he waved, and thought, *perhaps I do.*

Author's Note

All characters in this book are fictional. Some are composites of people I have known. Some are completely made up.

However, like all authors, there is part of me in every story. In this case, it's Ava.

Del and I were visiting our friends, Linda and Dorothea. We don't get to see them very much, but when we do, it's always inspiring. Talk flies around the table while we eat, have coffee, sit in their living room, go to coffee shops, and take walks. They are fantastic listeners!

During one visit I shared a story about my life in the seventies. It was one I have only told once or twice before. For years, I kept it a secret because I was worried what people would think, but later, it just wasn't important anymore. But for some reason, it came up to tell, and, when I finished, Linda said, "You should write about this."

I think she probably meant that I should tell the true story of it, but instead, it triggered the inspiration for this next book in the *Karass* series, this book, *Pragma*.

So when you read about Ava and her experience dancing in a club, that is partially mine. And yes, I drove a green car just like the one I described, and even lived in a garage for a time.

But no, there wasn't a Rick then, although much later I did date someone who did make me wonder why I was dating a wolf.

So some of the stories around the dancing were made up, as is the whole book. However, fiction is always flavored with real-life stories told a new way. It's one of the ways I learn about life.

Hopefully, my stories help you learn more about life, too.

I hope that you are enjoying this *Karass* saga. The next one in the series is called *Jatismar*. It's the Hindu word for someone who remembers his or her past life. It was fun to imagine what that would be like. Would it be wonderful or awful?

Read *Jatismar*, and let me know what you think! Find it on Amazon and many of your other favorite places to buy books.

And if you have a second, please review *Pragma*. Books go out in the world and authors never know where they go. It's like sending your kids off to school and never seeing them again. Reviews help in so many ways! I thank you in advance!

Would you like a ***free*** copy of the *Pragma* print mentioned in the book. All you have to do to get the PDF version of it is send an email to pragmabook@gmail.com. You'll immediately get an email with the link to download the print.

I would love it if you followed me to keep up to date with what I'm writing. You can do that on Amazon from my author's page. Amazon will let you know when the next book comes out.

Or come sign up for my email at https://becalewis.com, and you'll hear from me a bit more often.

Connect with me online:
Twitter: http://twitter.com/becalewis
Facebook: https://www.facebook.com/becalewiswriter
Pinterest: https://www.pinterest.com/theshift/
Instagram: http://instagram.com/becalewis
LinkedIn: https://linkedin.com/in/becalewis

ACKNOWLEDGMENTS

I could never write a book without the help of my friends and my book community. Thank you Jet Tucker, Jamie Lewis, Kathleen Piper, and Barbara Budan for taking the time to do the final reader proof. You can't imagine how much I appreciate it. A huge thank you to Laura Moliter for the last look editing.

Thank you to the fabulous Elizabeth Mackey for the fantastic book covers for the *Karass* series.

Thank you to every other member of my street team who helps me make so many decisions that help the book be the best book possible, Cheryl Kirk, Diane Solomon, Shawna Hixton, Corinne Pierce, Linn Moffett, Tiffany Loosvelt, Merri McElderry, Fay Christie, Joanna Pieters, Barbara Best, Diane Cormier, Rosemary Serafin, Nicole Petzolt

And always thank you to my beloved husband, Del, for being my daily sounding board, for putting up with all my questions, and for being the love of my life.

OTHER BOOKS BY BECA

The KARASS Series - Fiction
Karass
Pragma
Jatismar
 - Keep watching for more!

The Shift Series - Nonfiction
Living in Grace: The Shift to Spiritual Perception
The Daily Shift: Daily Lessons From Love To Money
The Four Essential Questions: Choosing Spiritually Healthy
Habits
The 28 Day Shift To Wealth: A Daily Prosperity Plan
The Intent Course: Say Yes To What Moves You

Perception Parables: - Fiction - very short stories
Love's Silent Sweet Secret: An Adult Fable About Love
Golden Chains And Silver Cords: An Adult Fable About
Letting Go

Advice: - Nonfiction
A Woman's ABC's of Life: Lessons in Love, Life and Career
from Those Who Learned The Hard Way

ABOUT BECA LEWIS

Beca writes books that she hopes will change people's perceptions of themselves and the world, and open possibilities of things and ideas that are waiting to be seen and experienced.

At sixteen, Beca founded her own dance studio. Later, she received a Master's Degree in Dance in Choreography from UCLA and founded Harbinger Dance Theatre, a multimedia dance company while continuing to run her dance school.

After graduating—to better support her three children—Beca switched to the sales field, where she worked as an employee and independent contractor to many industries; excelling in each while perfecting and teaching her Shift® system, and writing books.

She joined the financial industry in 1983 and became an Associate Vice President of Investments at a major stock brokerage firm, and was a licensed Certified Financial Planner for more than twenty years.

This diversity, along with a variety of life challenges, helped fuel the desire to share what she's learned by writing and talking with the hopes that it will make a difference in other people's lives.

Beca grew up in State College, PA, with the dream of becoming a dancer and then a writer. She carried that dream forward as she fulfilled a childhood wish by moving to Southern California.

After living there for more than 30 years, she met her husband Delbert Lee Piper Sr., at a retreat in Virginia.

They traveled around the country for a year or so and lived in a few different places before returning to live near his family in a small town in Northeast Ohio.

When not working and teaching together, they love to visit and play with their combined family of eight children and five grandchildren, read, study, yoga, taiji, feed birds, work in their garden, and design things. Actually, designing things is what Beca loves to do. Del enjoys the end result.

84795541R00165

Made in the USA
Lexington, KY
26 March 2018